DARKER DAYS

A COLLECTION OF DARK FICTION

KENNETH W. CAIN

Let the world know:
#IGotMyCLPBook!

Crystal Lake Publishing
www.CrystalLakePub.com

WELCOME TO ANOTHER CRYSTAL LAKE PUBLISHING CREATION.

Thank you for supporting independent publishing and small presses. You rock, and hopefully you'll quickly realize why we've become one of the world's leading publishers of Dark and Speculative Fiction. We have some of the world's best fans for a reason, and hopefully we'll be able to add you to that list really soon. Be sure to sign up for our newsletter to receive two free eBooks, as well as info on new releases, special offers, and so much more. To follow us behind the scenes while supporting independent publishing and our authors, be sure to follow us on Patreon.

Welcome to Crystal Lake Publishing—Tales from the Darkest Depths.

COPYRIGHT ACKNOWLEDGEMENTS:

"A Ring for His Own" first appeared in Post Mortem Press' *Jamais Vu – Journal of Strange Among the Familiar* Issue 3

"Heirloom" first appeared in the Dark House Press anthology *Exigencies*

"Passing Time" first appeared in the Rocking Horse Publishing anthology *Spirits of St. Louis: Missouri Ghost Stories*

"Her Living Corals" first appeared in the Firbolg Publishing anthology *Enter at Your Own Risk: The Beginning is the End*

"By The Crescent Moon" first appeared in the Charon Coin Press anthology *State of Horror: North Carolina*

"The Hunted" first appeared in the Post Mortem Press anthology *44 Lies by 22 Authors*

"Mantid" first appeared in the Perpetual Motion Machine Publishing anthology *Truth or Dare?*

"Adaptable" first appeared in the Post Mortem Press anthology *44 Lies by 22 Authors*

OTHER TITLES BY KENNETH W. CAIN

ADULT FICTION:
Alien Born (The Infinite Cycle)
United States of the Dead
These Old Tales: A Collection of Dark Fiction
Fresh Cut Tales: A Collection of Dark Fiction
Embers: A Collection of Dark Fiction
Lifeblood
Jade
The Adventures of Alexin

NON-FICTION:
Writers on Writing

Middle Grade fiction:
From The Deep Will Rise (Book 1 in the series)

EARLY READER:
How Marbles Roll
Hardy the Allergic Cat & Willy the Wrong Way Woodpecker
RE: Animated: Three Apocalyptic Tales for Kids
When Vampires Eat Fast Food & Cooking with Monsters
3 Fun Tales About Monsters
Math Is For Mummies: Addition & Subtraction
Frankie's Alphabet: an A to Z alphabet picture book
The Big Book of Monsters & Friends activity book

Tales from the Darkest Depths

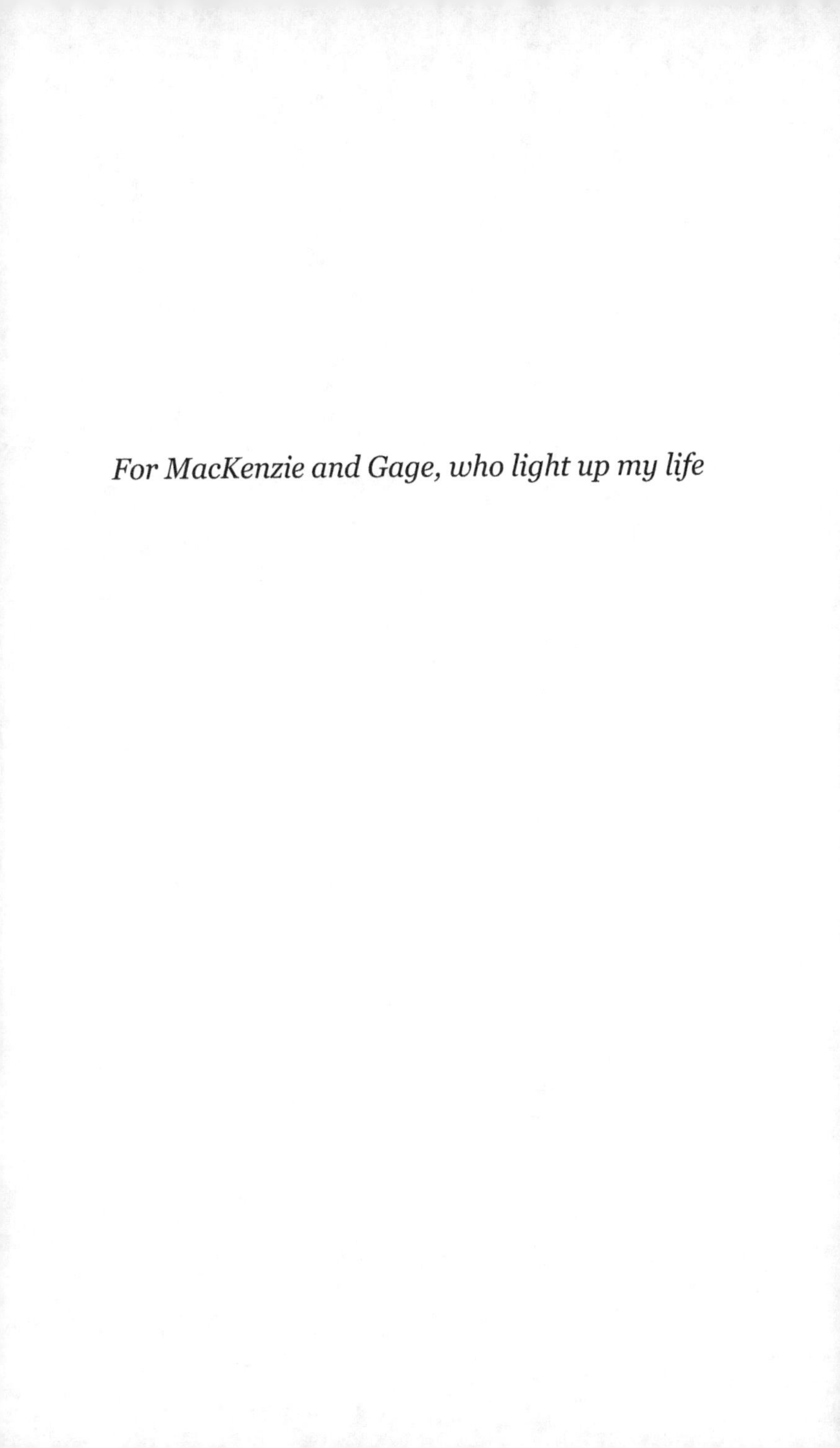

For MacKenzie and Gage, who light up my life

TABLE OF CONTENTS

A RING FOR HIS OWN

MARSHAL BEN DONEGAL burst through the batwing doors, heart pounding, and observed the chaos outside. Half the residents of Oakwood had taken to the streets, all of them admiring each other's jewelry. Hideous creatures of saggy white flesh walked among them, taking notice of his sudden appearance.

How did I lose control of the town?

When the stranger strolled into town, no one paid him any mind. Traveling salesmen often peddled their wares in Oakwood, as it was a regular stop for any stagecoach heading out west. Ben doubted this one would be hawking anything more than some sort of snake oil. This alone might have been the reason nobody informed Ben of his arrival.

The fact the man had come on foot, carrying nothing more than a suitcase, should have at least raised an eyebrow. Most salesmen came by way of carriage, but not this one. Somehow Ben had neglected to notice that, too, but upon seeing the man he meant to rectify the matter as soon as possible.

In his defense, Ben had been daydreaming about Sarah at the time. She had captured his soul, and he often wondered if his visits pleased her as much as they did him. He prayed she didn't see him as just another client because he wanted to be more than that to her. She had given him little indication otherwise. As a result of her indifference, his heart ached for her even now.

She does love me.

A frown creased his forehead. Doubt nagged him, as did the townsfolk's opinion of his frequent visits to her. In their eyes, any woman of *that* profession was doing the work of the devil. He wished he had been more successful at keeping his visits a secret.

After leaving the window of his jailhouse for the airy porch, he observed the salesman from a distance. The stranger had set up shop lickety-split and stood behind a table outside Jake Myer's saloon. Ben bit off a plug of tobacco and sauntered across the dusty street. His spurs clanged against the wooden boards of the saloon's porch. He poked his hat back with his knuckle and sized up the stranger.

"Where'd you get that cart, Mister?" he said.

The man wore a black top hat that tilted to one side when he regarded Ben with a fake-like grin. Ben had never seen clothes like these before, the man's attire appearing fancy, yet odd. The salesman's nose looked three sizes too big for his beady eyes.

"Why I brought it in with me . . . um Mister . . . ?" the salesman said.

Ben arched his back and stretched. He eased his hands into his front pockets, allowing his overcoat to spill open and reveal his badge. Nothing more needed to be said.

"Oh, I see, Marshal. I'm quite sorry. Let me

introduce myself. My name is Dustin Haverford. I've come a great distance to sell my jewelry. I assure you, there is nothing more than respectable business practices to be found here, sir."

When Ben just stood there staring at him, Haverford's expression soured. "As I've yet to sell a single trinket, I don't believe I've wronged anyone. Or have I?" He hummed. "Have I offended you in some way?"

Ben narrowed his vision on Haverford. After a quick glance at the man's wares, he thought them hideous. These trinkets were nothing more than painted, misshapen tin with bits of glass bonded to them for decoration. He couldn't fathom what type of person would be interested in purchasing this junk.

"Not yet," Ben said, "but next time you stroll into town, make sure to check in with me first. Got it?"

Haverford nodded and offered a brief look of remorse.

Ben returned his gaze to the jewelry. None of it appealed to him, but he had to admit, he might have been a little too quick to judge the merchandise. "What exactly do we have here?"

Haverford's eyes twinkled, perhaps considering Ben a potential buyer. "Only the most exquisite jewelry available to man." His hands waved over the table, presenting each section. "Here I have some rings and cufflinks. There are earrings for the ladies over here and extravagant necklaces here. Each piece of jewelry is constructed of the finest metals and most precious jewels."

Most of the jewelry disgusted Ben. The likeness of an unfamiliar strange animal had been set into each charm. He had never seen any creature with such a bulbous head, two tiny chipped-glass eyes, and eight snake-like legs.

So much for precious jewels. If that ain't glass . . .

He turned and spit. Tobacco juice struck the throat of a nearby spittoon with a ring. "Don't bother. I ain't interested."

Haverford beamed. "Of course, Marshal. I just thought you might have . . . a lady friend."

Ben flinched, wondering if someone had clued the salesman in on his personal life. Visions of Sarah in a frilly dress danced through his mind. She had the palest skin, so soft it hurt not to touch her. Whenever she pressed her naked breasts against him, he swore he could feel her heart throbbing.

"Oh, I see there is," Haverford said. A coy smile returned to his smug face.

"No, I—"

The man was smart like a fox. He had trapped Ben with his words. Coaxed him to take another look at the jewelry. When Ben did, something didn't feel right. The visions of Sarah were replaced by thoughts of these trinkets. He fancied how a ring might look on his finger. Somehow his hand had crept down to his gun.

What the—

The sheen on the jewelry looked different to him now. He wanted to let his eyes explore each piece again, to trace every edge and admire their beauty.

Maybe I should get her a necklace.

With this seed planted, the thought gnawed away at him like a vulture did a decaying corpse.

Ben rubbed his temple. "What manner of trickery is this?"

The man extended both hands and offered Ben a peek up each sleeve. "No tricks here, I assure you."

Ben felt himself sway in place, almost on the verge of passing out.

He's enchanted me.

Ben studied the man. The lines on Haverford's face indicated how often the man grinned, which seemed quite a lot. Ben loathed men who smiled so much. In his experience, it often meant they were up to no good.

A shimmer caught his eye, and he glanced at the jewelry again. What he had thought had been silver now looked golden yellow. The chipped-glass inlay no longer looked like cheap glass, either. The way the sunlight danced across the brilliant jewels made it difficult to pull his gaze away.

"What do you think, Marshal?"

He ignored the man, mesmerized by the jewelry and the magnificent eyes of the strange creature. Once more, he considered purchasing a piece for himself.

A ring perhaps.

Shaking his head, he glared at Haverford. There were things he would like to ask this man, but he couldn't keep his eyes from drifting back to the jewelry. He barely noticed the trickle of drool running down his chin but wiped it away when he did.

Go ahead. Get something for Sarah.

He revisited the necklace.

That one.

His lips moved to describe the trinket, but all he could manage was, "The necklace."

Haverford retrieved the exact necklace he had wanted and draped it over his forearm. "This one, sir?"

Ben gazed at it. The sensation of drowning

shrouded him, and he relished the feeling. He couldn't stop thinking about *his* necklace.

Sarah's necklace.

"How much?"

Haverford's grin widened, his mouth so full of bright white teeth. "Two bits."

Ben reached deep into his pocket and withdrew the money.

Haverford's face wrinkled with curiosity as he accepted the coins with an open palm. "Perhaps I can entice you to purchase something for yourself?"

Ben traced the path of Haverford's long fingers, watched as they waved over the jewelry. The motion made him woozy. Each piece captivated his senses. They were as beautiful as—

No, they don't even compare to her.

Every necklace looked so delicate, each ring so intricate. Desperation filled him, and although he wanted a ring, he realized any piece would suffice.

Sarah would likely prefer a ring.

The thought forced his eyes away. "No, just the necklace." He wavered and added, "For now. Can you bag it, please?"

This request seemed to annoy Haverford. "Okay, then." He slipped the necklace into a blue velvet bag and cinched it shut. "One necklace for the kind Marshal's best girl."

Ben's wooziness subsided once the necklace disappeared into the bag. Haverford extended his purchase, and Ben seized it with greedy hands.

Haverford tipped his hat. "Until next time, Marshal."

Ben nodded his approval.

"Well then, good day to you, sir." Haverford bowed. The man had such a phony smile.

Of course, it's bogus. The bastard's job is to convince people to buy things they don't need.

There was truth in that, but something else about the man felt awry. Ben considered sneaking one last peek at the jewelry but pushed through the batwing doors of the saloon instead. His fingers gripped the bag as he inhaled the expected odors. Whiskey, tobacco, sweat, dirt, and women struck him all at once.

Although no one acknowledged his arrival, he suspected they saw him and knew why he had come. The preacher had them out doing God's work every day now. They kept an eye on Ben to see how often he visited his whore.

Damn that holy man.

Ben sat at the bar and placed the fine bag on the counter beside him. Leaning to his side, he spat his wad of tobacco into another spittoon.

Jake regarded the bag with a quick nod. "What you got there, Ben?"

Ben eyed the bag, but couldn't rightly recall. He contemplated this and thought about taking a peek inside. Then it came to him, though he no longer remembered the salesman's name.

Hank . . . Handsel . . . Haverton . . .

Finally, Ben shook his head. "Never mind that. Hit me with a drink, will ya?"

Jake fetched a bottle of whiskey from under the bar and filled a snifter. Ben once considered Jake a friend. The near-blind man had been the barkeep at the Oakwood Saloon for as long as Ben could remember. In recent days, Jake had developed a rather sharp eye when it came to Ben and Sarah. He had relayed their trysts to the preacher on more than one occasion. Jealousy or not, the gossip had eaten away at their friendship faster than a beaver took to a tree.

He tossed the whiskey back and slammed the glass down.

One for luck. Two for good measure.

After tapping his finger on the rim, he rolled a few coins onto the bar.

Jake refilled the glass.

Ben spun, seeing how closely Jake watched him. To avoid gritting his teeth, Ben sipped the whiskey, hoping that wouldn't let Jake get a good read on him. Rumors spread faster than a brush fire on a hot day in a town like this. And Jake often played a part in such chatter. Sooner or later, the whole town would be protesting the Marshal and his hooker girlfriend, but Ben didn't much care for their judgments anyway.

This afternoon saw all the usual patrons in attendance: Sally Alderton, Tom Dervin, Delroy Thomas, and even Harold Mays. Four out-of-towners played cards with Delroy. Sally sang a disjointed tune as Tom pounded away at the piano. Three cowpokes sat by their lonesome in the far corner of the saloon. A few others talked at the outermost tables.

When Sarah entered the room, everything brightened. Golden locks spilled over her exposed shoulders as she approached Ben. Her eyes invited him in, irises as blue as a cloudless sky. They sparkled like brilliant stars.

Or the jewels of a certain necklace.

Shaken from his reverie, Ben seized the bag.

But do I want to give it to her?

His fingers methodically rubbed the fabric of the bag.

Maybe I should keep it for myself.

He considered this.

I bought it for her.

He frowned, unsure why he should be so worried about the necklace.

It's her necklace now.

The mere suggestion of this frustrated him.

Bag in hand, time slowed as he crossed to her. Several eyes tracked his progress. He stole glimpses at those people like a thief at night. They all looked away when he did, except for Jake. That bastard feared nothing about Ben's gaze.

Damn them and their disapproving eyes.

She led him upstairs and hesitated outside her room. A warm inviting glow drew him to the open door like a bug to a lantern. Sweet perfumed aromas made him lightheaded with love. He entered, and she followed, pulling the door shut.

She smiled. "I couldn't wait to see you again."

He hoped she meant it. Without looking, he placed the bag on her nightstand and sat on the bed. His throat felt dry and raspy. He swallowed hard. "Me, too."

The glow of a candle lit the edge of her silhouette as she turned her back to him. She slid off her dress, standing only in her undergarments. His heart pounded like the beat of a wild stampede. When she turned around, her magnificent breasts mesmerized him to the point where he stumbled as he removed his own clothes.

There, in the soft glow of candles, they made love.

Afterward, he napped with her in his arms and dreamed of a bag with a special necklace hidden inside.

* — ■ — *

A loud crash woke him, and he sat up on the edge of the bed.

She roused at the same time, her eyes still sleepy. "What's wrong?"

"I heard a noise." He stood and slid on his pants. After he pulled his shirt over his shoulders, he watched her as he strapped on his guns. "I better check it out, just in case."

Her eyes were elsewhere. "What's this?"

When he saw the bag, his eyes traced each stitch, trying to remember why he had brought it along. He recollected the contents, and his thoughts betrayed him.

Don't tell her.

Grinding his teeth together, he told her through pressed lips. "I bought you something."

She beamed with anticipation. He knew she had seen her fair share of gifts from other gentlemen callers. These presents had shown up in her room more than he liked.

None of them can hold a candle to my gift.

He grabbed the bag and couldn't help but run his fingers along the seams. The royal blue bag felt so soft between his fingers. He liked what was inside even more.

"Aren't you going to give it to me?"

For a brief, sickened moment, he wanted to strangle her. He shook the painful thought away and held out the bag.

Still, she had to pry it from his clutches, letting out a frustrated giggle as she did. With it in her hands, he felt dejected, but watched with admiration as she opened the bag.

Her smile faded as she pulled out the necklace with two fingers. Face flushed, she looked up at him, then to the jewelry, and back to him. Her nose scrunched as if the jewelry emanated some offensive odor.

The necklace did smell—like hot apple pie resting on an open windowsill.

"What is it?" she said.

He couldn't believe she could be so ignorant. "It's a necklace."

Her gaze questioned him. "Well, of course it is, silly, but—" An instant glimmer appeared in her eyes and several seconds passed without her saying another word. "It's delightful."

He shared in her excitement. For him, though, this emotion had changed, becoming something unexpected. Envy.

"Would you put it on for me?" She handed him the necklace, more willing to part with it than he. After flipping her hair to one side, she lifted it with her fingers.

The fine metal dangled from his fingertips, and he wanted to wear the necklace for all to see. Before he could stop himself again, he eased the necklace around her neck.

If I do this, I won't get it back.

Her neck looked so soft, her blonde hair so beautiful in this dim lighting. She smelled wonderful. He longed to kiss her. Then his eyes returned to the necklace, and he considered how easy it would be to snap her neck. He fought the urge.

She sounded hurt and bothered. "Can you just put it on me?"

Does she sense my jealousy?

Her eyes flashed over her shoulder. She tapped an impatient foot on the floor from where she sat on the edge of the bed. "Hurry, please."

He clasped the necklace, and her hair trickled onto his wrists. She breathed an air of satisfaction as his hands slid away.

When she turned, her eyes beamed. The necklace glowed on her bosom. It surprised him how much appeal the necklace held even now. Her chest heaved, and her expression was blissful. He had seen this look before, while caught in the throes of lovemaking. Now her passion came courtesy of the necklace.

The tiny, ruby eyes on the trinket blinked to life. Any envy he had felt lessened.

Oh, Christ.

The chain thickened, each link twisting and turning into a living rope, and forming separate extensions. The brilliant gold color altered to something that reminded him of wet clay. Dozens of small saucer-like growths appeared along the underside of each limb. Sucking sounds filled the silence as these limbs writhed about her neck.

He went to help her, but the head of this creature rose and bellowed a deep growl. When he moved away, the creature's eyes trailed him. Then it spoke. Not aloud, but in his head.

Stay away, it said.

Her breathing labored, as passionate as when they made love. And her eyes darkened, too. He couldn't help but slink away.

One tentacle pushed into her ear. A horrifying wet crack indicated the limb had gained access. Even after this, her smile never faltered. She gasped with orgasmic splendor as the appendage forced itself into her skull.

Two other tentacles squeezed up her nostrils. Green bubbles of snot dripped from her nose. A third explored her mouth, choking her as it pushed down her throat. She gagged, bile leaking from the corners of her gaping mouth. All the while, she wriggled in ecstasy.

His hand pawed at his hip and drew his gun, to which the creature hissed. For some reason Ben couldn't bring himself to pull the trigger.

To his disbelief, the creature melted into her flesh like lard in a frying pan. Her eyes turned to him, lips drawn back in a crazed snarl. She convulsed, her eyeballs bulging out of their sockets. The color drained from her already pale skin, turning white as fine porcelain. Her flesh withered, the essence of her life consumed by this creature from the inside out.

When she stood, he got a full view of how emaciated her frame had become. It looked as though her insides had been sucked out, leaving behind a pasty skeleton-looking woman. He couldn't bear to witness this horrific scene, yet he was unable to withdraw his eyes.

She spat out her teeth, a few at a time accompanied by blood and saliva. They rattled on the wood floor. Her lips parted enough for him to see two rows of small, pointed teeth.

His stomach released. Vomit exploded from his mouth and drizzled down his chin.

He scrambled for the door, fumbling with his free hand. Rushing out, he yanked the door shut behind him. Then he ran to the banister where he observed the spectacle below.

Jake gazed at a cowpoke's ring with admiration. Ben could see the gleam in his eyes even from this distance. The card game had ended with only a single competitor without a piece of jewelry. That man couldn't keep from gazing at the other men's trinkets.

A few patrons had started to transform, and no one appeared to give a damn. They were all too enamored by the peculiar jewelry.

Two of the creatures spotted Ben, bared their fangs, and ran at him. He scrambled down the stairway, gun hoisted, hoping to beat them to the exit. But they were fast. He fired a shot at the closest one. The resulting gunfire could have leveled a small bison. Unfortunately, it did nothing to stop the creature.

They continued their assault.

One got close enough to reach out for him. It hissed, and despite his previous result, he unloaded two shots into its chest. The creature reeled back as each slug pierced its wrinkled flesh. Still, it persisted.

He plummeted down the last half of the stairs and crashed into the other creature. Slammed it into the wall, where it staggered back three steps but didn't fall.

He burst out through the batwing doors, disoriented by the sun. His heart felt as though it might burst. Insanity had infested Oakwood.

"Wonderful, isn't it, Marshal?"

Ben looked at the man who had called himself Haverford. Then again, he no longer looked like a man at all. Beneath the tall hat, Ben identified the man's green-colored flesh, wrinkled like a raisin. And his fingers—

Each digit looked like the ass-end of a snake, writhing about and coiling upon one another. Ben realized he still had his gun in his hand and lifted it, wanting nothing more than to kill the guy. But the gun felt so heavy now. Even worse, after everything he had seen, all the atrocities, this evil man's trinkets still tugged at his soul.

He glanced up at the town and saw the damage. It was too far gone. Behind him, the doors opened wide, likely one of the creatures exiting the saloon.

How could I let this happen?

His eyes turned back to the jewelry. Lying there among the trinkets, he spotted the most beautiful ring. It had such an unusual inlay, the image of some unknown creature—perhaps from the sea. He couldn't take his eyes off that ring, especially now that Sarah was gone.

All he wanted was a ring for his own.

HEIRLOOM

THE SLEEK LEATHER dizzied him. His eyes traced each and every contour. Overwhelmed, he sat up and shook his head, but gained little relief.

What's my name?

His concern dissipated upon returning his gaze to the striking object. He had never seen one quite like it. Despite the lightheadedness, he yearned to touch it. Upon further examination, he felt scrutinized by the item's solitary eye.

What a remarkable creation.

With that, he recalled his name.

With some effort, Thaddeus rose from all fours to his knees. He scanned the grassy knoll. No one else was around.

He brushed a light covering of pollen off the camera. When he did, a tingle surged through his fingertips.

Strange.

He glanced around again, feeling almost criminal.

It couldn't have been here long. So, why didn't the person who lost the camera return for it?

He surmised a possible truth.

Maybe it wasn't lost.

People didn't go misplacing possessions on purpose, either, especially when those belongings proved so delightful.

He had used cameras before, quite a bit in his profession. Enough so they had become second nature to him. He had never been so enthralled with any of them until now.

The camera appeared to date as far back as the early twentieth century. Though, the housing, worn and aged, wasn't as boxy as those he had seen in pictures.

Again, he explored his surroundings. From this vantage point in the tall grass, he could see little more than bushes and trees that dotted the landscape. The road barely visible, he spotted his Cutlass still running with the door ajar.

Why'd I do that?

The distance from his car to this place in the grass shocked him. It was a miracle he had even seen the camera.

He remembered severe boredom striking him as he approached the New Hope Baptist Church. He had spotted the graveyard adjacent to the lot, where Thad had buried his mother several years earlier. He always held his breath until he passed the fence that surrounded the cemetery, a silly childhood superstition he hadn't been able to shake. Had he not been counting the rows of pine trees, he might have passed the old Miller place.

It had been abandoned for years, Trevor Miller having lost his job, then his family, and everything else once he had gone bankrupt. The bank had foreclosed and boarded up the property when Miller failed to sell.

People still came here now and then, mostly when they didn't want to get caught doing something they shouldn't. That had been the reason for Thad's visit. He hadn't expected to see the glimmer and find himself so mesmerized by this camera. Seeing it here now, it must have been a one in a million sighting. He couldn't fathom how he had spotted it on such a lush grassy field.

Smiling, he glanced back and seized the camera. Its weight surprised him, as though the camera wanted to be left alone. Another thing he hadn't expected.

I can't just leave it here.

Turning the camera, he spotted a slight crack in its lens. It would be useless for taking pictures, but it would make a wonderful showpiece.

He opened the back panel. A layer of dust covered the guts, along with a few cobwebs.

The mirror's broken, too.

Thad blew hard into the housing. Dust stirred and tickled his nose, making him sneeze. Itchy nose and all, he couldn't stop staring into the camera.

What a great place to hide something.

But what?

Thad closed the lid and held it tight against his chest. That dazed sensation returned when he stood. Still, he hurried to his car, as if thieving this antique. He threw himself into the seat and gently placed the camera on the passenger seat before closing the door.

There we go, nice and pretty. My new camera with its special secret compartment.

He longed to put some trinket inside.

After a moment's hesitation, he threw the car into drive and headed back to his office. The drive back to the city proved tedious. He had made the trip many times, always for business. This time, though, his mind swirled with thoughts of the camera all the way back to the office.

At least he had gotten the pictures of Harry Derbin having sex with his mistress. That would pay the bills for another month, maybe longer.

Money had a way of making problems go away. Then again, it also had a propensity for creating new ones. Last month's setback came courtesy of the scotch he had special ordered.

Was worth the dough.

He poured himself a tall snifter and drank while he browsed the photos.

She'll pay extra for these last few.

He spread them across his desk and then propped his feet onto the desk before separating three photos from the rest. These were as good as the filthiest pornos. Considering that, Thad thumbed to the last one. This picture revealed much of the young woman. He lingered on her curves, becoming slightly aroused.

She's something else.

This provoked thoughts of the sleek antique camera he had discovered in the middle of nowhere. He crossed to his shelves and stared at the camera. After a moment, he picked it up, considering what to put inside.

Why not this photo?

In went the picture. He slammed the door shut and hugged the camera tight to his chest. Exhaling deeply, he returned the antique to its place on his bookshelf.

That looks perfect.

A knock at his door startled him. Thad gathered up

the photos and shoved them back into the envelope. He seeded the best two at the very end, knowing they could be used as bargaining chips.

Jane's fuzzy silhouette looked splendid through the frosted glass of his door. With his name written backwards across her face, he felt somewhat perverted.

"Come in," he said.

Jane opened the door and stepped inside. Her skirt spun and twisted when she turned to yank the door shut behind her.

"Hello, Mr. Claremont. How are you?"

He lit a cigarette, took a drag, and puffed out the smoke. "I'm good. You?"

Her fingers fidgeted. "Did you—" She stammered. "Were you able to get what I asked for?"

This was all part of the game. He took a long drag and let the smoke out slowly. Convinced she would break if he took his time, he did just that.

He went to speak, then stopped, took another drag and breathed a smoggy cloud. "Of course, I did."

She squirmed, anxious now. Eager buyers always paid well. It had worked in the past and would now as long as he remained patient. Especially with a disgruntled wife who would soon secure photos that confirmed her husband's long-suspected adultery.

Did she deserve it? Hell no. But he had stopped trying to appease his conscience long ago.

Jane had no interest in divorce. For her, there were better ways of dealing with an unfaithful husband. She had the kind of money that could ruin a man. Thad kept that knowledge in his back pocket for just this occasion.

"Can I see them?" she said.

Thad tossed the envelope across the desk.

She nearly ripped the envelope fishing them out. She grabbed all the photos and fanned them like a deck of cards. Picture after picture, she gazed at the youthful Miss Harlow.

He had been unable to erase those images from his thoughts. How her spill of blonde hair hung down to her waist. The curve of her neck as it angled to her bare shoulders. Those cute dimples in the small of her back. Pictures of them hugging and kissing. And of course, there were the X-rated pictures he had pretty much memorized down to the smallest detail.

Jane stopped at the last two and gasped. One of these featured the girl on her knees with her head in his lap. The other, she was on all fours with him behind her. These were his favorites. Jane's already flushed face deepened to a fiery red, glancing momentarily at her own breasts as if comparing.

"These . . . these are exactly what I asked for . . . " she said in a solemn voice.

Thad beamed. "I aim to please."

Hurt-filled eyes searched him. "Do you?"

He had expected this as well. She would try to play his weaknesses against him, perhaps as a means of lowering the price. She didn't need to, and he wouldn't allow it. But that didn't mean he wouldn't take her up on the offer. Afterward, he would hit her up for a bonus. Maybe even try to make her feel guilty for stooping so low.

She'll pay. They always do.

Jane set the photos aside and threw off her long coat. He had always thought her a fine-looking woman. What a shame that a man should cheat on a woman like her.

She unbuttoned her shirt, revealing a hint of the red bra beneath. Slid off her skirt, and her lacy red panties captured his attention. Something astonishing followed.

A flash brightened the room, blinding Thad.

Did that come from the old camera?

That would be impossible. The damned thing didn't even have a flash, he was certain.

Ignoring his temporary blindness, he discovered her soft, warm flesh. He took her into his arms, and she stepped closer, kissing his neck. He ran his hands down her sides and cupped her butt.

I don't remember her being so curvy.

He had thought her a thicker build of woman, but now she appeared voluptuous. Caught in the throes of passion, he tried to see her through the white glow hindering his vision. She was all that mattered, her sensuous touch on him. He liked the way she tasted when her soft lips parted, and her tongue breached his mouth. It moved to engage his tongue in an erotic dance. Her hands were on his back, easing off his jacket. She hurried to unbutton his shirt. A single hand slid inside, rubbing his chest and working its way down.

With the white haze clearing, he opened his eyes and the red strap of her bra filled his vision. His hands worked fast, feeling their way around to undo the hook. It came away easy, and he stepped back to let it fall. Only then did he notice.

Bare-chested and clothed only in lace panties, young Daisy Harlow looked astounded. He couldn't blame her. She should be surprised any man would pull away from her like that. Yet, despite his own shock, he couldn't stop from stealing peeks up and down her firm body. Seeing this, she smiled.

This can't be.

He staggered back, and her lips formed a pout. She bit down on one side of her bottom lip and pursued him.

Thad backed away again and soon found himself against the wall. She was at him, hands rubbing and touching him everywhere. How could he resist? Why would he want to? He shook his head but couldn't keep his thoughts from her body and seductive ways.

Now, looking curious, she held him at a distance. "What's wrong? Don't you want me?"

"It's not that." He held up his palms, hoping she would ease up some. "It's just that . . . "

How could he word this without hurting Jane? Hell, he might even be going mad, so he didn't want to just come out and say it. He would be doing her an injustice if he did. Once he started, though, he couldn't stop himself.

"You look like Daisy Harlow," he said. "I mean *just* like Daisy Harlow."

Daisy's smile waned to a frown, but her tone remained playful. "Well, of course I do, silly. Were you expecting someone else?"

"I . . . " He felt wrinkles forming on his forehead. "I don't understand."

"What are you talking about, Harry?"

Eyes widening, he asked, "What did you call me?"

His voice sounded panicked. Then again, it didn't sound like his voice at all. Not only that, but this wasn't his office.

Shaken, he fell back. It surprised him when he landed on something soft.

She was on him, still rubbing, and he couldn't help but surrender to these pleasures. Kissing him hard on the lips, she worked at his jeans. She pulled them off and straddled him, and she gasped when he entered her.

Thad forgot himself. Where he was or what might have happened. He surrendered fully to the passion. Nothing else mattered. Not even the door bursting open. He had been too caught up in their lovemaking to care. Not even the loud crash of a gun shook him out of his desires.

Her blonde hair was tinged red, but only on the right side. Her face, still angled up, lolled down to him. One side remained intact. The other side no longer looked anything like the beauty he had fantasized about. Where her eye should be was a gaping hole.

She collapsed onto his chest, while he was still inside her, blood-soaked hair flayed across his face. He pawed at his eyes and pushed her aside only to see a broad-chested man standing near the door.

Thad jumped to his feet and ran. A loud crack from a gun made him jump, but he wasn't about to stop for anything. The second gunshot struck him. A hot sting tore at his thigh, halting his progress. He regarded the bullet wound and stumbled, unwilling to give up so easy. Hopping on one foot, he continued his escape, heading for the back door, unsure he would make it if he kept losing so much blood.

He heard the click of a gun chamber. A loud explosion followed, and everything went blurry. It didn't clear, either. Instead, everything turned red and gray.

His gaze fell on the door. Part of the wooden door

transformed to glass for a split second and then back to wood again. He couldn't comprehend what he saw or make out the words he heard. It sounded like something about revenge, but he couldn't discern whose words they had been.

He blinked, and for a moment, he returned to his real self. Then he lost that part of himself forever. He tried to open his eyes, but they wouldn't respond. And with that, he yielded to this sensation; let it wash over him, choosing to sleep.

The rest felt good. Never-ending. All encompassing.

✦ ──■── ✦

Harry woke in a haze, not feeling like himself. With some effort, he stood, but the room spun out of control.

Where am I? Better yet, who am I?

He thought long and hard, but only one name came to him. "Thaddeus Claremont?"

That sounded right.

He tried to focus on something, anything, and noticed the aged camera. Staggering to it, his legs struggled to carry him there.

He leaned against the shelving and took the camera. Thad held it tight against his chest. Something about it felt so wrong. Another part of him liked it very much and wanted to keep holding the camera. Whether it worked or not, he thought it would make for one heck of a keepsake.

Then he saw the door in its side and he pried it open. More than anything, he longed to put something inside. Anything. Maybe a picture.

RUST COLORED RAIN

ANNABELLE WASHED HER rage away with a hot shower. That always revitalized her, made her feel whole again.

But you're not whole.

The thought angered her, and she smashed her palms against the tiles. She pressed her fingers into the grout and dragged her nails down the lines as if to excavate them. Rust colored water dripped down and circled the drain before it swirled out of existence.

This isn't real.

Telling herself this often brought back a sense of tranquility, even if it wasn't true.

She submerged herself in the moment once more, the warmth of the shower reminding her of spring. Closing her eyes, she recalled the smell of flowers poking up through the softening ground, blossoming for the first time after a long winter.

I wish I could renew in that way.

Maybe then she wouldn't feel so incomplete. She had never been good at being alone, at exhibiting that inner confidence. So she had always relied on others, on . . .

Him. She cringed. *Damn it.*

She lifted herself over the remnants of colored water in the bottom of the shower and onto the floor mat. There, she gently patted herself dry because it all still hurt too much. Then, she saw herself in the mirror.

Her fogged reflection stared back at her. Offered a glimpse of the woman she had been before the accident.

So beautiful.

They had been happy, too. Many of their friends often referred to them as the perfect couple.

What happened to those days?

A drift of cool air crept beneath the door. It stole the moment away when the haze on the mirror shrank until all that remained was her true self.

How could anyone love that?

She ran a finger down the side of her face. Traced every bump, every indentation, and every bruise, always mindful of how tender the wounds were, but she wanted to explore them nonetheless. One of her eyes, the left in her reflection, was now false. She marveled at how easy it was to tell the difference. The slight discoloration of the iris, the way it never moved where it should. How it defied her.

Metal had met bone, creating the wound that covered most of her left shoulder. The skin there, now a riddled mass of scar tissue, hurt most of the time. Electric pulses of pain shot through her arm whenever she put the slightest strain on the muscles.

If it were just these wounds, maybe she could have moved on. Perhaps she could have even forgiven him. But that wasn't half the damage she had endured.

All thanks to him.

She hobbled closer to the mirror, removing her lower half from the frame before the fog receded far enough for her to see. She breathed easier, still not fully willing to accept that reality.

His discomfort had been obvious. How different it was when he looked at her now. He never really looked at her anymore. His unease angered her most of all.

What right did he have to treat her with such disregard?

Has he ever considered how being looked at in that way made me feel? She clenched her fists. *What a bastard.*

An urge to scream this nearly overwhelmed her. She considered doing just that, but with him being in the next room, she held her tongue.

Like it should matter.

After a brief hesitation, she said, "You're an asshole, Tom!"

Through the closed door, she listened and heard nothing but a grunt.

She returned her gaze to the mirror.

Did you expect more?

No, she hadn't. It did make her feel somewhat better, though. And she had needed that.

She opened her lotion and applied it generously. It probably wouldn't help. Besides, the worst scars were on the inside. Those would never heal. Still, she applied the lotion in methodic circles, letting her thoughts drift back to the night of the accident.

They had been running late, but wouldn't have been if he hadn't wanted to watch the end of the football game. She hated being late, and so she ran around doing things for him; tasks he should have taken care of himself. That's what led to her needing to put her makeup on in the car.

With the passenger visor down, she took care in applying her eyeliner. She hadn't seen much other than her eye in that tiny mirror. Therefore, she had been oblivious to his driving. If she had noticed, she would have asked him to stop gawking at her. If he had paid more attention to his driving, he might have seen the deer in time.

Only, none of that happened.

Jolted out of her memory, she left a smudge of cream on her skin and placed the container on the counter before wiping it away with her finger. She brushed the cream under the eye she had been applying eyeliner to that night, and stared deep into the fake orb, cold as any piece of glass. Worse yet, she could still feel the pain, the sheer agony of her eyeball being pierced.

Transported back in time again, glass had shattered around her. The tires screeched when he panicked and jerked the wheel hard right. She had heard the car slam into the deer. Felt the shudder of metal as it bent around her. Blood splattered everywhere.

He veered off the road and down the embankment. Her visor bounced up and down as the car bounded over slight swells. When the visor flipped up, she saw everything in that moment: the tree, the moon, the stars in the sky, Tom.

If only I'd lowered the applicator.

The car had soared through the air, filling her vision with the half moon. Glass and metal exploded outward, caught in the moon's glow, beautiful yet anything but. They closed in on the tree, and she remained frozen in time, the applicator still at her face. The only part of her still functioning had been her voice, and she had screamed until the car returned to the earth, her voice sounding distant. The impact jerked her forward, her seatbelt constricting around her body like an anaconda. A stray branch shot through the shattered window. Dozens of small limbs whipped across her chest.

The car rammed the tree, and she felt the pain in her eye. It hadn't registered with her yet, though, what caused the injury. Not right away. When it did, she heard herself screaming so loud it didn't seem real.

They were trapped in that car for what felt like hours, him passed out against the airbag, and her awake and alert the entire time. She'd had plenty of time for reflection with her leg pinned between the dashboard and her seat. A single branch had gutted her, blood seeping out around the bark. Her shoulder had been mangled, but through it all, she still hadn't felt any pain. She had felt the brisk cold, which seemed to intensify enough to make her shiver. That was when she saw it.

The apparition stepped out from behind the tree, a mottled form creeping toward her with the caution of any wild animal. It saw her, examined her with oblique eyes. She saw herself reflected in its gaze when the creature shuffled closer. Her situation had felt grim, yet she remained unafraid.

The creature came within arm's reach. Up until that moment, it hadn't looked so different from any other human being. Then she saw just how inhuman it really was.

She tried to speak. "Wa . . . To . . . braaaaa."

Her words had been unrecognizable even to herself. But the creature seemed to understand just fine what she had been trying to convey. That it should kill her.

The creature reached out and took her head in its elongated fingers. Then it reached its free hand deep into her chest and seized hold of the beating organ. She felt her heart racing as the creature tugged. It was stealing her soul away bit-by-bit, layer-by-layer. The coldness grew, and she embraced it.

As if realizing her willingness to surrender to death, the creature had grinned at her. Its pointed teeth glistened in the moonlight as it drew more from her, faster and with such urgency that she felt herself slipping away. When she had been nearly drained, her head bobbed and focused on the horizon, somewhere beyond the creature. Out there a light blipped off and on. Red then blue, and white, the light spun along the road, racing to her position. Other lights followed, all of them bleeding into a surreal landscape, illuminating the trees as they neared her.

She glanced up at the creature and saw concern in its expression, as it too noticed the approaching lights. Then, to her dismay, it withdrew its hand without finishing.

Weakly, she managed one word. "Don't . . . "

The creature looked back at her, and in that moment she saw its greed, its need for her soul. How empty it was without her, and how awful life would be for her should it not finish what it started.

She blinked, hoping that when she opened her eyes again, the creature would still be there. But it had vanished, and in its place a dozen or so lights near blinded her, forcing her eyes shut. Unable to see, she heard a radio crackle. Whoever had been out there, they had hurried to her. The radio buzzed and someone spoke. A man standing close by said something, and she hadn't been able to understand him.

Still, she nodded and managed a weak, "No."

Dozens of people surrounded her. They discussed the magnitude of her situation with voices that bled into one another. Their words confused her. Despite her wooziness and failing eyesight, she had recognized the desperation in their eyes. Her anxiety deepened, and she very much had expected to die.

They removed Tom first. She had despised him for that.

They tried to encourage her, their fuzzy voices still difficult to comprehend as they worked meticulously to remove large sections of the car. The long wait allowed for insanity to shroud and consume her.

Her right leg had been crushed. She remembered thinking how amusing it was that she couldn't feel the pain. When they freed the pressure on her leg, the pain rushed in without end or limits, and she couldn't stop screaming.

"Come back," she had said. "Kill me."

She had squeezed as hard as her hands would allow on the crushed metal, the air being expelled from her lungs faster than it entered. She gasped, and her world shifted. Blind to it all, she had felt the darkness creeping in. Somewhere deep inside her, a new hurt formed for the first time. It seized her with a tight grasp similar to that of the creature. With all its might, it propelled her headfirst into a void she fully embraced. She had known then what she would do if she were ever capable.

Among the chaos of that night, her hazy eyes had followed a single figure among the crowd before she passed out. She saw how patient it looked; waiting for any opportunity to finish what it had started. And she had wanted it to. That was when the darkness took her.

Returning to the moment, she grasped the sides of the bathroom mirror. She stared at the stump of her leg in the mirror. Observing her scars, the sadness and anger returned in full force. Tears streamed down her face, rounding over the scars in thin trails of wet warmth.

He did this to me.

How had he suffered in return? A mild concussion? A two-inch scar down the middle of his back.

She saw the creature standing behind her, and the calmness returned. It nodded to her. She knew then she was on the right path.

Sitting on the toilet, she slid the sock over her stump. Used the sink to support herself while she reattached the prosthetic limb. It didn't feel right, never would again.

Afterward, she ventured out into the bedroom naked, walking to Tom.

"There," she said. "Much better."

He clutched a pillow to his stomach. His fingers gripped the pillow, pulling it closer, and then released. He didn't hide the fact he had been crying, and that made her happy.

She smiled. "There, there now."

This made her feel better. And that's the only reason she had stayed with him.

It's not enough.

She needed more than a whimper. What she needed was for him to feel all the pain, the detachment, the madness, the hand of death as it took everything it wanted. But that would take time. Before she finished with him, she would make sure he felt every bit she had and more. Only then would he appreciate what he had put her through. Then she could be free of him.

The creature grinned, and she smiled, too.

PREY

IT FELL ON a mother to watch over her children, to educate them on the ways to survive in an ever-evolving world. That task proved increasingly more difficult for Jada in regards to her Juno, though. Her eldest daughter ran unrestrained at her side, lacking focus and fear and discipline.

Sometimes it felt like she had given birth to Juno only yesterday. She was still so young, so inexperienced. But the illusion always faded, encouraged by the realization of Jada's own aging body. Soon enough, Juno would have no choice but to continue this effort alone.

But she isn't ready. Not yet.

Juno and Jada stopped short when they encountered two beings. Both of these two beings turned their slender faces to them at once, surprised by the intrusion. Their long ears angled back and they raised their spears.

Jada refused to flinch. She glanced to her side, and her daughter's resolve matched hers.

Good, Juno.

Wicked snarls formed on the beings' elongated faces. Tiny bumps pulsed on their milky white flesh.

Tufts of coarse hair on their knuckles, arms, and legs went as straight as the reeds of the marsh waters. It was their eyes Jada watched intently, seeing the hunger in those bloodshot orbs, and how they tracked her and Juno's every step.

Jada backed away.

Juno followed a few steps, and then froze.

Shouting erupted around them, filled with over-enunciated vowels and wispy consonants. But Jada didn't need to understand their words to know what they were saying. Inarticulate grunts preceded each thrust of their spears as they crept toward Jada and her daughter.

Jada recoiled, noticing Juno's hesitancy. She pawed at her daughter's shoulder. A startled Juno glanced her way, and only then did they move together.

Both bipedal creatures sprung for them.

Juno sped left.

That's my girl.

Jada went right, forming a large gap between them. Still, she kept a careful eye on her daughter.

The beings split apart, one went after Juno and the other followed Jada. She and her daughter came together, crisscrossing paths. The two beings stumbled past one another, nearly colliding. A moment later, they were on their trail again, Juno leading one far left, and Jada led the other to the right.

Juno and Jada crisscrossed again, causing another moment of confusion. The two beings faltered. These beings were a speedy bipedal species, so Jada wanted to keep them at a distance. Each time they intersected each other's path, the beings were quick to steady themselves, but it did serve to slow them down some.

Howling cries escaped one of the beings. In the distance, Jada perceived footfalls and cries that echoed her pursuer's effort.

Jada and Juno adjusted their course to avoid running headfirst into the approaching horde.

Soon, a group of hunters would chase her and her daughter. As if realizing this, both beings grew bolder in their actions, each frenzied and reckless. Twice their spears came close to piercing Juno.

Foolish girl.

Jada and Juno sprinted for the thickest part of the forest, hoping to get ahead of the beings. Juno came up beside her and pride filled Jada. Although there remained much to do, Juno had proved herself agile and intelligent enough to make it through this unscathed. Jada imagined Juno with her own husband and children to nurture. Nothing would please her more.

With the two beings still chasing them, they altered their course again, and then again. In this way, any newcomers would have trouble ascertaining their current path. Jada had encountered this breed before and knew their hunting strategies. They must avoid being caught at all costs. These people would clothe their young with Juno's skin. Feed their entire tribe with her flesh. Wear her teeth as jewelry.

It was too late to protect her child from this bedlam. They were in it, and the sudden appearance of a third being made survival all the more challenging.

Juno took the lead. She turned fast and ran hard.

Jada followed, as did this trio of hunters.

Thankfully, their white skin stood out among the overgrown foliage and canopy of trees, making them easy to see.

The stony ridges of the Calliope Mountains reached out far into the distance, ending their escape. Juno reached the rock walls and turned, with Jada doing the same.

The beings reached them and spread out, wicked smiles appearing on their faces, closing in with patience now. Two of them were males, the third a female. All had obvious strength and agility except for one, the lanky male who barked out orders, their apparent leader.

A guttural sensation reverberated deep in Jada's throat, but it was Juno who growled first, loud and enraged. Antennae alert, Juno swung her tail back and forth, rattling it as she took a defensive stance. The folds of skin under her neck gathered and formed an intimidating fan of quivering quills. For the first time during this altercation, these beings wavered. This was the moment Jada had been waiting for, the one she would record in her memories and dwell on for years to come.

Still the hunters closed the gap. A spear thrust to Jada's left and then to her right. Cool rock stung her backside, their plight now at an obvious end.

Juno growled again, this time sharper, calling out too early.

From the corner of her sixth eye, Jada spotted him soaring through the air. Her mate, Kyuta, pounced upon the tallest of these three beings. It necessitated a grunt, in part due to his age, but also because of the longstanding injuries he had suffered over the years. Kyuta wasted no time in tearing out the man's throat.

Seeing this, the others turned and fled.

Juno leaped for the female's back, digging her razor-sharp claws into the woman's shoulder and pulling her down. The woman struggled forward, no doubt driven by fear, but Juno held tight.

Jada chased after the other male, who had somehow managed to hold onto his spear.

If he gets away, he'll alert the—

The stocky man spun, lifting his spear to a leaping Jada. The ground between them shrank fast, and the spearhead bit deep into her flesh, causing the shaft to snap.

Jada collapsed, her weight striking the man, causing both of them to topple to the ground. The man scurried back to his knees, then to his feet. Again he fled. Juno tracked him down this time, and Jada could only watch.

Through the brush, Juno sped up beside the man. Some fifteen lengths later, he tried to duck away, but she clawed at his stomach and pulled him back down. She sank her fangs deep into his neck and held him there until the man no longer moved. Then she dragged his corpse back alongside the others.

Because Kyuta was in such bad shape, Juno maneuvered one of the bodies back to the lair by herself while Jada stood guard. More beings were coming, so when Juno returned, Jada helped conceal the other two corpses beneath some brush near the stony walls. They worked together to kick up whatever leaves and dirt they could, hiding any visible signs of a fight, and made new tracks that led away from the bodies.

Afterward, Jada climbed a tree. When she faltered,

Juno pressed her forehead against Jada's hindquarters to help her up. They perched high in the gnarled tree watching the others arrive.

For a long moment, the hunters poked and prodded around the area. They came close to discovering their fallen companions, but when they spotted the tracks, they hurried off in pursuit. Only when they were well out of sight did Jada allow Juno to relinquish her post.

They dug up the corpses and dragged them back to their lair. There, Juno presented one to her father, who at first refused the offering. She snuggled in beside him, nuzzled him with her snout and encouraged him to eat. He soon accepted, chewing the flesh with obvious pride.

With interest, Jada observed her daughter.

Juno barely ate at all. But those who provided often didn't eat much.

She's learned well.

Juno's eyes were big, trained on the little ones.

She'll make a good mother. This thought pleased Jada. *But she'll make a better hunter.*

PASSING TIME

IN THE MORNINGS before Jonathan woke, Paula would stare out their front window, waiting until the sun sparked the horizon. It ignited the sky with red and orange hues that colored their neighborhood, serving as her cue to wake her husband.

She always woke him before the alarm clock sounded, humming into his ear until he stirred. But waking him this way so early never made anything better between them. The emptiness would still be there.

Their days together were often uneventful, no longer any need for the exchange of words. That didn't mean she didn't love him. Most of these problems were her fault because she had somehow lost the knack of expressing her love to him. Some people claimed that happened when you had a child together, but she wasn't so sure. Due to her uncertainty, their relationship had evolved into something rather devoid of life these last few months since Heidi's birth.

He rose, stretched his lanky body, palms opened to the ceiling. After a quick glance to a photo of them together on the dresser, back when they were happier, he made his way to the bathroom. She followed, laughing to herself when he scratched his ass and yawned. He ignored her merriment, never fully conscious until he had his two cups of coffee and was about to walk out the front door. This also saddened her.

The bathroom light flicked on and he stood in front of the mirror, forcing his eyes wide. There had been more life in those blue eyes several months ago. They had lost the glimmer they had, back when they spoke of their dreams and possible futures. Now, he was but a shadow of that man. The scruff on his chin strengthened this visual, as he no longer shaved daily. She never would have thought having a child would bring him such sadness, and that also made her feel guilty as she had pressured him to have children.

Each day she missed his body next to hers, his sweet embrace when he kissed her goodnight. They were distant now, sleeping on opposite sides of the bed. Her side always felt so cold, and she rarely made it through the night without waking. She longed for the days when he kissed her goodbye each morning and again when he arrived home. They never kissed anymore, not since Heidi came into their lives.

Their cat, Chester, curled his tail around her calf and mewed. She smiled, and she snuck a peek at Jonathan, wondering if she would catch him grinning. His expression remained solemn these days, but he did look her way. She felt uncomfortable standing in the bathroom doorway under his gaze, shifting in place. He said nothing.

Chester sped to her other leg, looked up at her and cried. The poor thing must be hungry. She ignored the cat for now, focused on her husband. She was glad to see him shaving today. The process mesmerized her; he looked so handsome clean-shaven. Meticulous with each stroke, he sliced off the stubble without nicking himself. And she loved the way he smelled after he splashed cologne on his neck and cheeks to keep from getting a rash.

Today, his eyes were too dreamy, and he did cut his chin. A red pearl of blood trickled along his jaw and dripped into the white porcelain sink. He stared at the droplet, watching as the running water ushered it down the drain. There he remained, gazing into the steaming sink while another droplet formed and fell, swept away in the swirl of water.

A loud meow drew his attention, and his gaze moved from Chester to her. He opened his mouth, as if to say something, but stopped. The discomfort returned, and she had the odd sensation he hadn't been looking at her. Still, she waited, hopeful. He forced a half-hearted smile and went back to shaving. This, too, would suffice.

If nothing else, he had continued being a snappy dresser. He still wore dress shirts, although they had grown more wrinkled since the baby came. Even the pleats of his slacks were uneven. The jacket could use a good dry-cleaning, but he kept his ties knotted neat as ever. She expected no less, and it made her proud. Now and then, while they enjoyed prime-time television, he even took the time to polish his shoes a brilliant black. Regardless of how flawed their relationship had become, she still thought him so handsome after all these years, even on days when he wasn't so clean-shaven or sharply dressed. Maybe this was why she had stayed.

She sat at the breakfast bar, watching him prepare the eggs. He made the most delicious omelets. Even Chester meowed with approval. She and the cat watched Jonathan eat. He ignored them for the morning paper, engrossed in the day's affairs. Before he finished his food, he rose and placed the plate in the sink. Chester whined a complaint, but Jonathan had already left the kitchen and would not return.

Together, she and Jonathan stood in the doorway of their daughter's bedroom. They took a moment to observe the baby breathe. Heidi was so young, so new, so beautiful. Paula could not think of a single accomplishment in her life that could compare to what they had created together.

After stepping into the nursery, he stood over Heidi, but wavered. He picked her up, propped her against his shoulder, and finally did grin. This had been the first real smile Paula had seen this morning. A sleepy sigh escaped their precious little one, and Paula followed when he passed her in the hallway. She lifted herself on tippy toes behind them, trying to catch glimpses of her daughter's face.

He rocked Heidi for a bit, changed her, and then placed her in the car seat while he gathered supplies into the diaper bag. She took note of what he grabbed to make certain he forgot nothing. He was such a good dad and hadn't missed a single item. After slinging the bag over his shoulder, he lifted the car seat with his free hand.

She trailed him to the door. He opened it and stood in the doorway, gazing back at her. His eyes fell to their baby, and his smile returned, although briefly.

"Maybe after work we can stop by and say hi to Mommy," he said.

This made her both happy and anxious.

The door closed, and she hurried to the front bay window. Jonathan set Heidi in the backseat and locked her into place. He climbed into the driver's side and sat behind the wheel where he stared up at their house. She could see a frown form on his face. Tears leaked from the corners of his eyes as he backed the car out of the driveway.

She tracked their progress, all the way down the street until the vehicle disappeared around the corner and out of sight. Afterward, she stayed by the window for a long time, reflecting upon their marriage. It occurred to her then he hadn't bothered to kiss her goodbye. That was how most days went, always together but so very far apart. And she worried about him being so sad all the time.

She decided to wait in this exact spot for them to return. If she had to, she would spend an eternity trying to make things right again.

WHAT MAMA NEEDS

PORKCHOP HELD THE knife to the pusher's neck, but the guy fought to get loose, leaving nary a nick when he ran. And Porkchop gave chase.

+—•—#—•—+

"Take it, baby." Mama held out the crumpled up foil to Kenny. "Please, Porkchop. Take it for me. You know Mama can't deal with this sort of trouble."

She often called him Porkchop, although he never asked or understood why.

Her eyes drooped, round and sorrowful. "They'll take you away from me for good if they find out. Come on, this is what Mama needs."

And there it was; the words she had said to him so many times before. Life was always so hard for him. That's what Kenny had thought when Mama held out her keys that first time, back when he was ten. He took them, of course, for Mama's sake. Having played so many driving video games, he had thought he could handle the Olds. Besides, Mama couldn't drive in her condition.

While Mama slept it off, Kenny did his best to stay between the lines. He had been glad to get out of that smoke-filled dive anyway. What sort of ten-year-old hung out in bars with nothing more to do than watch people get drunk?

They had made it home safe that first night, save for a few scratches on the side of the car when Kenny drove too close to a row of hedges. At least it hadn't been a person. That's what he had always told himself after the fact. He hadn't been so lucky the next time, a week later, when he clipped a car.

Before the police got there, Mama ran for some nearby woods. She had left him all alone with her stash. And Mama had been right. With no priors, he had gotten off with a slap on the wrist, but he kept on doing whatever she asked because he loved his mama, and this was what she required of him.

Mama always gets what she needs.

By the time he turned twelve, Mama started shooting up, among other vices. On the bright side, Kenny no longer had to worry about driving her anywhere. Besides, it hadn't been long before she sold the car for extra cash, all of which she used to buy drugs. He had been too young to understand how these new drugs made her feel, but he had gained some insight over the years through observation.

She always looked so frazzled after popping pills. Wild-eyed after she dropped acid, though he never understood why she called it that. She had never dropped anything he had seen. After smoking a joint, she mellowed out. When she shot up, she fell into a peaceful bliss. Most of the time she would fall back on the couch or bed or wherever she had been, and start babbling stuff he couldn't make out. To him, she sounded like a baby, and that made him laugh. She would laugh, too, until she had drifted off into that other world she always spoke about. Whenever she went there, she looked so much happier and more at ease. That, apparently, was what Mama needed most of all because she started shooting up more often. But that was okay.

The pills made her awful sick. She threw up so much once he had needed to roll her onto her side just to keep her from choking on her own vomit. The clean-up afterward hadn't been fun either. And the acid always made Mama say the strangest things, sometimes even scary things. She would talk about people or creatures he couldn't see and that couldn't possibly exist, yet she always made them sound so real. Pot made her paranoid. Kenny would have to sit up with her whenever she got too high to make sure she didn't hurt herself.

Her medicine, as Mama started referring to the heroin after those first few times, seemed the easiest for Mama to endure. She would spend all day preparing for a good cook, asking Kenny to help out where he could. That was okay because he no longer attended school anyway. So, by the age of thirteen, he had known all there was to know about Mama's medicine, and without his help she might not have made it through some of those days.

This particular time, like many others, he took the crumpled up foil. Balled it up tight and shoved it down deep into his jacket pocket, among some gum wrappers. Seconds later, the door busted open and Mama fled to the bedroom.

When the police searched her, they found nothing but the scars on her arm. They hadn't thought to search Kenny; not right away. They almost hadn't when . . .

The bearded cop pushed through the doorway, looking frustrated. He glanced back at Kenny. "Hey Chuck, what about the kid?"

"Sad, isn't it, Jackson?" said Chuck.

"No, I mean, shouldn't we search him?"

Chuck raised a brow at his partner. Then he moved in and stood over Kenny, eyeing him up. Seconds later, Jackson had Kenny up against the wall, patting him down. He checked under Kenny's arms, down his sides, and his pockets, too.

"Bingo," Jackson said.

They didn't even read Kenny his rights, being a minor. And Mama, she never left the bedroom, never put up a fight. Not even when they hauled Kenny away.

Kenny spent a year in juvie. Did his time and learned a lot in doing it. He believed he had discovered just about everything about his life he could, all the ins and outs and everything in between. But life had a funny way of proving him wrong.

The taxi dropped him off in front of his row house. No lights were on, and all the windows had been left open. The front door hung on rusty hinges.

He opened the door and pushed his way through a pile of rotting garbage. The smell assaulted him, the foul stench of human waste. Despite the darkness, he found Mama in her bedroom like most nights, staring up at the moon through her bedroom window.

"Mama?"

A stark draft made him shiver.

"Who's there?" she said, sitting upright with some effort. "Who is it?"

"It's me, Mama."

"Porkchop? Is that my Porkchop come back home to his Mama?" she said in a raspy voice.

When she turned to him, he saw her face well enough. Her skin was wrinkled now, her throat sagging, lips cracked and bruised. She wore dregs of clothes.

He regretted being taken away from her.

I should have been smarter.

A tinkle alerted Kenny. He spun in time to see the bathroom door creak open. There, in the doorway, stood the figure of a lanky man. He said nothing, which made Kenny feel helpless. Then the man, which he realized was naked, stood over Kenny and raised his fist.

"No, don't. It's okay," Mama said. "He's my son." Her expression was worrisome. "Can I have some time alone with my boy, please?"

His ominous form looming, the man grunted. He pulled on his jeans and tugged a shirt off an open dresser drawer. Kenny saw his face: the scar running down his cheek, the rotted teeth and wicked grin that said: *I don't give a damn about your boy.*

Though he was scared, Kenny knew what all of this meant. Mama wasn't getting what she needed. She hadn't in a long time because Kenny hadn't been there to take care of her. In his absence, this man had assumed the role, and he was a bad man.

◆ ——— ✦ ——— ◆

The man came again the next day. Mama let him right in and they hurried to her bedroom.

She turned to close the door. "You leave us be now, Porkchop. You hear me, baby?" She hadn't waited for a response.

He heard noises, grunts and groans, things he sort of understood. An hour later, the man left without a word. When Kenny checked on Mama, she was passed out with the strap still tight around her arm.

Kenny rushed to her and eased it loose. He put everything away and sat on the edge of the bed. From there, he watched her eyes roll back in her head. The bloodshot orbs passed back and forth as if caught in a deep sleep. He saw her arms up close for the first time in a very long time. There were so many marks now. Even her legs were bruised badly. And she was way too skinny.

For a brief moment, he considered calling someone, but didn't know whom to contact. Mama's closest friend was this bad man. Before him, she had mostly kept to herself.

The man came with more frequency as the weeks passed. Kenny came to know him as Scar. Sometimes Scar left behind cash and other times he left drugs. A few times he spent the night. Scar rarely said anything to Kenny.

When he looked into Mama's finances, she no longer received much aid. That meant Kenny had to get creative with what little funds they did get, using the money for the basics, like milk and bread. Life wasn't good, but it was manageable. He learned to appreciate what little they did have, and that made him happy as long as Mama got what she needed. More and more, it was his struggle to satisfy those needs that troubled him most.

+ —— ∗ —— +

Scar slept over that night. Later, while Mama lay passed out in her bed, the man sat in a chair out front, smoking a cigarette. Knowing he was around made Kenny restless. So he joined Scar on the front porch. He said nothing, but stood beside the man. Together they stared off into the night. In that moment, observing Scar in the dim glow of the moon, he loathed the man for what he had done to Mama, and something inside Kenny snapped.

While Scar was looking at the stars, Porkchop removed the knife he had tucked under the back of his shirt and pressed the blade under Scar's neck.

"Da fuck—"

Scar never finished his complaint. Porkchop drew the blade across Scar's neck. The man collapsed to the ground, gurgling.

Kenny grinned for the first time in a long time.

+——◆——+

Porkchop led the pusher in and walked him down the hall. "What did you say your name was again?"

The pusher remained quiet, staring up at Porkchop's handiwork, a detailed aluminum foil TV antenna that ran across the ceiling from one room into the other.

"Art," he said.

The television was barely audible. Mama sat in her rocking chair beside the window, facing away from the TV.

Porkchop closed the door behind them.

"Mama?" he said. "Art's here with your medicine. He's got what you need."

Art moved closer.

"She can't do it herself anymore. I don't even bother with a hose. Some of her veins are just always popped. It worries me some, 'cause they're purple and all. Plus her skin is discolored. But whatever makes her happy. You understand?"

Art stalled, so Porkchop ushered him forward. The closer Art got, the more disgusted he looked. Much came thanks to the smell, always the first thing any pusher noticed.

"Don't tell Mama," Porkchop said, whispering in his ear.

Art offered a worrisome glance.

"Even a good sponge bath doesn't help much anymore."

Porkchop stroked her hair with his fingers. Coarse strands gathered between his knuckles. Many pulled away in his hand. He dispensed of the loosened hair in a knitting basket he kept tucked away behind the rocker. Then he held a forefinger to his lips to hush Art.

Art nodded, although he didn't look comfortable with any of this, which was okay with Porkchop.

"It'll be okay, Mama." Porkchop tilted the needle upward, flicking it with his finger. "We all have our needs, don't we?"

Art's eyes watched the needle. Porkchop pressed it into her arm, producing a sick noise similar to a pin being pushed through a leather cushion.

A curious Art moved closer.

"The way Mama looks sometimes, I think she takes to liking that magical world a lot more than the real one." He sighed. "Can't say I blame her. I wouldn't fault her much if someday she decided to stay there."

Art shifted to the side of the rocker and his eyes widened.

"My deal has always been the same, Art. You gotta be nice to my Mama."

Art searched Porkchop with troubled eyes, then his eyes went back to the old woman and he hobbled closer.

Porkchop prepped another shot.

"Mama was always so much happier back then. You know, when her man friend made her giggle some. That man, whose name I won't say, used to make her pray to God whenever they spent time together in the bedroom. But he won't be coming round here no more."

Art nodded, moving in closer. Gathering by the look on Art's face, he saw everything now: the awful wound on her arm, the decayed flesh, the pus-covered sores. The edges of those sores had encrusted to the point it looked like someone had burned them into her skin.

"I think you can make Mama happy again, Art, if you try real hard."

To this a ghostly grin appeared on Mama's face, shriveled and unnatural.

"Oh my God," Art said.

His eyes twitched back and forth from the horrid face to the even more disgusting wounds on her arms. Before Art could do anything, Porkchop stuck him.

Art succumbed fast. Porkchop leaned over and hiked up Mama's skirt, warranting a bony *crunch* as she shifted her hips. He pressed down on Art's shoulders, forcing the man to his knees. There, Art would do what Porkchop wanted; he would make Mama happy again.

"You make her pray like them old days. You do it

now." Porkchop hummed, breathing heavily. "We all have our needs. Yes sir, we all do. And *this* is what Mama needs most."

✦———❖———✦

Art burst out the front door and glanced around with urgency. Porkchop had seen it all. He took the back door and waited for Art out on the porch. He had him where he wanted, and drugged to the point he wouldn't put up much fight.

Porkchop hooked Art's arm. "You see that up there, them stars?"

Art said nothing.

"I used to think I could be better than this, more than just some boy who takes care of his Mama." Porkchop grinned. "But Mama has special needs and when I turned my back, a snake just like you slithered in right behind me. I had to rid myself of that snake."

Art tried to escape, but Porkchop yanked him back.

"See, it's not enough to rid myself of only that one snake. I know if something happens to me again, there'll just be another. And then another. There's a whole nest of them out there." He patted Art's back hard. "Point is, I gotta take care of all you snakes once and for all."

He brought the knife around fast. Slid it across Art's throat and pushed him into the grass. Porkchop watched as Art bled out on the front lawn. Because this was what Porkchop needed.

MY BROTHER BIT YOUR HONOR ROLL STUDENT

CLAIRE DOBSON COULDN'T get over the tire tracks imprinted across Denny's face. Same with the glazed pasty-white look in his eyes. No, it was more than that, because that had been his everyday appearance for a while now.

She sighed. "Mom, Denny's back."

Mother's hurried heels clacked along the floor on her way to the front door. She came to an abrupt stop in the foyer. "What?" She rubbed her tear-stained eyes with a balled-up fist of tissues. "Denny? Is that you, honey? Have you come back to me?"

She raced to the doorway and embraced Denny, bloodstained T-shirt and all. "Oh, Denny. We've missed you so much." She held him at a distance, her smile beaming. "Haven't we, Claire?"

"No doubt. Yay for Denny coming back from the dead."

Mother was too busy hugging her undead boy to notice the sarcasm.

Does she not see what he is? Did her generation completely miss the whole zombie thing?

Denny snapped at Mother's ear, missing by an inch.

Not a clue.

Things hadn't been the same since Denny died. They had been *better*. Quiet enough, she could focus on school. Even some of the boys she liked had started paying attention to her. So what if it came out of pity, as long as one of those boys was Lane Myers.

Denny will ruin everything.

A rancid stink emanated from him. It didn't seem to faze Mother.

And I thought he smelled bad before.

Mother had mourned Denny for an entire day. In that short span of time, Claire believed something had broken inside the woman. She had jumped off the deep end and embraced the madness of losing a child. And yes, all of it made Claire jealous.

Given enough time, Mother would have recovered from losing Denny. Maybe she would have gained back some of that much needed common sense. Now, as a result of his return, she didn't think Mother would ever be her old self again.

"Come on," Mother said. She pulled Denny's wrist. "We need to get you cleaned up."

Denny staggered behind her. Eyes sagging, he looked at Claire. He still had that same vacant stare.

No one is going to believe this.

Then she remembered how accepting the people of Eastwood could be, how hard they worked not to offend anyone.

So many weak-minded fools. It makes me want to stab my brain.

"We have to get you to bed." Mother led him upstairs. "Tomorrow will be a busy day."

He banged his shins against the first step,

struggling to comprehend the need to lift his leg. After a couple attempts, he caught on and followed Mother.

"We'll have to enroll you in school all over again," Mother said.

The school board fought her tooth and nail, but Mother had the support of several friends and neighbors. That's what being a respected citizen of Eastwood warranted. After sitting through all four hours of the meeting, Claire couldn't help but glare at her confident mother.

My idol.

At least the woman hadn't lost her determination. But she had never doubted her mother's perseverance. Given it was an election year, Mother had no problem spinning things to her advantage. Some of the board members started agreeing, her influence obvious in their rattled appearances.

That same day, Denny rode the bus home from the middle school. Claire couldn't stop staring at him, the way his head bobbed along with the movement of the bus.

Denny turned to face her, eyes foggy. Only he wasn't looking at her, but beyond her, out the window. At what she had no idea. Nor did she care.

No one sat next to Denny, maybe because of how he smelled. Most would've seen all the same movies she had and known what the undead could and would do. Not that Denny had been popular prior to today, and returning from the dead shouldn't have changed his social status, but somehow it had. Two girls, a few rows back, smiled at him, but he didn't seem to notice.

Give me a break.

How ironic Denny should be wearing his 'Chicks Dig Me' T-shirt, which depicted a cartoonish hand reaching out of a freshly dug grave and a female stick figure shoveling away a scoop of dirt.

Prior to his death, Denny's biggest foe had been Blake Hawthorne. Blake had been the most popular kid at school for as long as Claire could remember. He dressed in the most expensive clothes, shirt collars up, shoelaces always untied. As a lawyer, his father could afford anything Blake wanted. That was a fact Blake never had any problem showing off, either. He could be the cruelest kid in school, and Denny being undead hadn't changed anything.

Blake leaned over two seats and swatted Denny across the back of his head. "What's wrong, dead kid? Something in your hemo-goblin?"

Wow, not the least bit funny.

Everyone still laughed. Even Claire.

<hr>

The following day was Denny's first full day back to school. Claire observed him shambling down the hall, moaning and snapping at everyone who passed. He seemed oblivious to Blake's teasing, but then again, Denny always had been a bit out there.

Blake ran up behind Denny and yanked on his books. They spilled to the floor, various papers sliding out and fluttering in a wide circle. Worse yet, Blake's prank had altered Denny's path, and her brother walked face-first into the lockers.

Oh joy.

Everyone laughed.

"Look at him," Blake said. He cackled so hard it forced him to hold his stomach.

A snicker tickled her lips, but she denied it. Denny bouncing off the lockers did amuse her, but there was a bigger issue.

This is so embarrassing.

She felt like hiding. Her little brother had a bad habit of making her uncomfortable, even before he had died. She had never gotten used to it, like Mother promised she would. But then, something else came over her.

Oh God, what's wrong with me? Do I actually feel bad for him?

She rushed over to Denny and spun him around. He took a few steps and stopped.

"What do you think you're doing?" Blake said.

She began picking up Denny's books, gathering the papers and stuffing them inside. "Gee, I don't know, Blake, I guess I'm cleaning up some idiot's mess."

Blake seemed unsure if she had meant this insult in reference to Denny or himself, and she liked that.

"Leave him be," Blake said.

She held the books to her chest and stood. "Um, let me think about it. How about no? Does no work for you?"

"You'll do as I say if you know what's good for you." Denny snapped.

She ignored them both. "What will you do, huh? Are you gonna hurt me? Is that what you do? Beat up girls?"

Denny moaned and staggered down the hall. He dragged his left foot behind him and seeing this really did make her feel bad.

That bastard hurt him.

She spun to Blake, fuming. Blake's devilish grin

forecasted the fact he had also noticed Denny's retreat. He looked quite proud of himself.

"Wow. You're so strong picking on the weak," she said in her best mocking tone. "You're such a tough guy, Blake. Will you marry me?"

Those around them stifled their laughs, but Blake heard them all. He glanced back and forth as if trying to single someone out, his face flushing. Unable to find what he wanted, he stormed off through the stairwell door, his shoes stomping down the stairs.

What's wrong with me? Denny deserves this.

Yet, she wasn't so sure that was true anymore.

＊——＊——＊

Dinner was mostly quiet that night. Mother drank wine, a great deal of it, in fact. Claire poked at her food with her fork. Denny gnawed on a rare steak.

Mother broke the silence. "So, how was school today?"

A dribble of merlot trickled down her chin. Sensing it, she wiped it away with her napkin. When Denny didn't answer, her head lolled to Claire.

"Oh, just dandy," Claire said. "I *can't* wait for tomorrow. I get *so* excited." She grinned. "Hey, did you hear Denny's getting bullied again?"

Denny slurped up a piece of fat, still attached, causing him to drag his steak off the plate. It dangled from his mouth. He looked at them for a moment, and then shoved what was left of the steak into his mouth.

Her stomach crawled. The squashed meat had nowhere to go but down or out. A trail of blood raced down his chin and dripped to the table. She sat her fork aside. "May I be excused?"

Mother ignored her, sounding both tipsy and surprised. "A bully?"

Denny moaned.

"Yeah," Claire said, getting up and standing behind her chair. She tried to ignore the relentless gnashing of teeth. "Blake must have some sort of man-crush on him or something. You know how guys can be."

Mother took a long sip of wine. "Not that awful Hawthorne kid again?"

Denny groaned, still munching his steak. His hands dripped with grease and blood.

"Well then, I'll email Denny's guidance counselor and we'll just see what we can do about that."

Claire laughed. *Yes, mom, that sounds like a fine idea.*

"We can't have him bullying your little brother," Mother said, slurring her words.

— ✦ —

Blake was a picture of confidence the next day. He sat behind Denny, flicking her brother's ear. Denny never flinched. Not even when a piece of that ear came loose and sailed past his nose on its way under the seats.

Claire tried to ignore Blake, but she couldn't help but say something. "Smart. They should give you an award or something. Maybe it could read 'World's Biggest Idiot'."

Blake leaned forward and wiggled his fingers close to Denny's mouth. "Look at the biter. Go ahead. Bite me."

After the third failed snap, she couldn't bear it anymore. Blake must have expected this, too, because he turned his attention to her.

"How about you, girlie?" Blake said. "You got any bite in you?"

She didn't want to answer. Shouldn't even, but the words exploded from her mouth despite her effort to hold them back. "Get too close and you might find out." She regretted that comment right away.

Blake's smile grew. "If any part of me gets that close, I might just want you to bite."

A wave of laughter erupted.

She ignored Blake and his arrogant jokes, but his teasing persisted.

* * *

After school, Denny didn't show up. She had her suspicions as to why.

Mom's gonna be ticked.

"Where's your undead butthead brother, Claire?" Blake grinned his usual smile, mouth full of straight and perfect teeth.

What a jerk.

"I think you know," she said. "You told someone, didn't you?" Her scowl returned. "Coward."

"Oh, so you think your brother might be in after-ghoul detention."

Everyone laughed.

She remained quiet. When Blake followed her off the bus, she ran. He caught up to her and pushed her down to the grass where he straddled her, pinning her arms under his knees.

"Get off," she said, wriggling back and forth.

"Or what?"

Blake hocked up snot and let it drip down in a long gooey strand. It dangled an inch from her nose. If it hadn't been for Mother's car turning down the street,

Blake might not have slurped it back up. But he did, escaping through their neighbor's yard before Mother pulled into the driveway.

Mother exited her car, saw her lying on the lawn and said, "Claire, honey? Are you okay?"

Claire stood and walked to the door. "Oh yeah, Mom. Couldn't be better? Thanks so much for asking."

Her mother assisted Denny out of the car and into the house. Denny shuffled around the living room, stopping at various items while Mother detailed her discussion with Principal Addison. She had argued how all the kids were tired of Blake's incessant harassment. It hadn't done much good, of course, because Mr. Hawthorne's generosity in regards to fundraisers overshadowed any and all bullying.

Denny crossed to the birdcage and snapped at their pet cockatiel, Buster. Mother saw this and laughed.

Claire frowned.

What a great family I have.

Blake caught up with Claire the following day in the stairwell. He pushed her up against the wall. The few kids who passed did so without a word, each of them keeping their head down. They all knew tattling would bring retaliation.

My heroes.

Three goons often tagged along with Blake: Jake Dillinger, Matt Schreiber, and Greg Harleton.

Not a single one of them smarter than a flea.

She thought Blake chose them for that exact reason. They would do whatever he asked without question.

"Get her," Blake said.

They took her arms and held her against the wall.

"What are you gonna do to her?" Jake said. His pubescent voice crackled.

Blake wore a sinister grin. "Anything I want."

She kicked out.

Blake seemed to relish in her action, as he batted her legs away. When he found an opening, he pressed himself against her. His breath was hot on her neck, and he licked her.

"*Please*, you're getting me so excited." She laughed. "I can barely contain myself."

Blake slammed his hand against the wall. "You'd best quiet down if you know what's good for you."

"Or what?" She beamed. "Are you gonna lick my shoes next? You have some sort of disorder or something, a fetish maybe?"

Blake grimaced. "You—"

She heard someone stumbling down the stairs.

Blake glanced back without letting her go. "Stop him."

Jake tried to punch Denny. He spun away seconds later with a bloodied fist. He held the wounded hand to his chest as he slinked to a wall where he wallowed in pain.

The others teased Denny, jabbing pencils at him and hooting. Denny didn't look impressed. He attacked, arms raised and jaws snapping.

Seeing Denny coming for him, Blake shoved Matt forward to block the attack. Doing so threw his friend off balance. Matt didn't stand a chance. Denny tore a strip of flesh from his shoulder, and Matt went down fast.

Seeing this, Greg and Blake ran. Only, in his haste,

Blake tripped over his untied shoelaces. His face struck the stairs, and he slid back down.

Denny was on Blake instantly, biting down hard at the back of his neck.

Okay, so maybe my brother's not all that bad.

———※———

Denny got off easy after Claire explained what happened. Mother threatened charges, and that helped matters along. Friends championed her cause, too, despite Mr. Hawthorne's efforts. In the end, Denny served a weeklong suspension, which seemed fair enough punishment. Perhaps the best part was that Blake no longer picked on anyone. Sometimes Jake, Matt, and Blake even joined Denny on their way to class.

A few weeks later, Lane asked Claire to a school dance. It had been hard to contain herself long enough to accept. When Lane's mom pulled up, and he came in to get her, Denny snapped at her date. That seemed to worry Lane. Not Claire, though.

He's only looking out for me.

That's what good brothers do, and she loved him for it.

OUTCASTS: THE SICK AND DYING
1—HENRY WENTWORTH

THEY SAID HENRY would get better, especially out here in the unknown, an outcast of his planet, suspended in perpetual orbit. They said the cancer would eventually go into remission, part of their effort to rid the planet of disease, communicable or not. He was told it would prolong the life of those with critical illnesses, and they had been right in his case.

But they also said they would bring him back home, to the surface, to his family, to everything he had left behind. They had been wrong about this last part.

Henry's trajectory brought him back around to North America. Seeing the country this way made him gasp. The blues and whites had become vast masses of reds and grays.

Must be fires.

The meteor shower that had pounded the Earth would have brought instant chaos. It would have devastated the planet in ways he could not fathom nor see with any clarity from this distance. And it all happened right before his eyes, so he knew it to be true.

"CDC ground, this is pod #176523, requesting status update. Do you read?" he said into the intercom.

Static filled his speakers. Ate its way into his brain and had done so for hours, days, maybe even weeks. He wasn't sure which was more maddening: the silence, the static, or the not knowing.

"Repeat, CDC ground, do you read?"

The static broadcasted louder, then wavered as if something had tried to get through, but couldn't. Careful observation of the surface made him believe he was witnessing huge explosions.

He gripped the handles of his pod tighter, his frustration boiling over. The need to scream rose in his throat. *Do you read?*"

Only static hissed through on his end, abrupt and unforgiving. Henry would do something about that if he could, but these pods weren't capable of anything more than basic survival. The pod controlled his waste production, expelling it into the atmosphere whenever required. Daily injections of medical cocktails improved his health, while unseen massage devices helped with the atrophy. The lack of gravity had shown significant success in treating cancer, as had the magnetic field created by the pod. But he would feel a lot better once he was back home. The CDC had agreed to bring him home weeks before disaster struck Earth. They had been too busy preparing for the impending meteor hazard and hadn't gotten around to his return yet.

Sadly, the pod had no function for him to control reentry himself. With the CDC not answering his transmissions, all hope had diminished. Even if he were able to return, would there be anything left to go back to?

Frustrated, he ran his hands across the dashboard, inspecting anything his fingers found. There were no functions beyond these controls, a series of handheld devices meant to monitor and entertain him. They kept him abreast of daily events back on the surface, but even those broadcasts ended a week ago. Despite their ineffectiveness, his hands searched each with purpose, but in the end only one made him optimistic.

He seized the joystick and pulled hard. "Come on."

These pods had been crafted well. Yanking on the joystick did nothing but bounce the cursor around on the screen: left then right, and down.

Pulling harder, when it still didn't come, he dug a fingernail under the edge of the rubber casing. He continued to pry, using a second nail, and then a third, until the rubber started to give. Once he had the rubber sleeve loose, it popped off with little effort.

Staring at the bare joystick, it looked quite secure. He balled up the rubber sleeve in his palm and pressed that hand against the joystick handle. Placing his other hand behind his elbow, he thrust his forearm forward.

Crack.

Anxious, he surveyed the damage.

Fractured it.

He tried again and the joystick came free. In the process, his hand rammed into the front shield of the pod, jamming three fingers.

He shook his hand. "Ouch."

Afterward, he examined the severed joystick, recalling the many futile hours spent trying to contact the ground. He loathed his recovery in the wake of this disaster. His thoughts raced over all he had ever loved, how it seemed so far away from him now, feeling like there would be no return at all, ever.

And so it's come to this.

Tears stung his eyes, welled and then floated away from his cheeks like tiny clear balloons. He turned the severed handle in his hands and then, without any further thought, he lifted the broken joystick to his left eye. Angling the joystick just right, he pounded on the end with his fist and drove it as far into his skull as he could manage.

The pain was instant and overwhelming. Death slipped in like a cool winter night. The weight lifted from him, the crushing loneliness and grief faded. He leaned back in his pod, and right before the lights went out for good, he heard something.

"176523 . . ." *Static.* "This is CDC ground." *Static.* "Do you read?"

But Henry was already drifting into a whole other void.

THE SANGUINE WARS

THEY HAD TRANSFORMED Hellinger into a monster, but he refused to become some sort of freak because of it. He would beat this like he had everything else in his life, with guts and determination. Forever, he would be the man he should have been all along, before any of this happened.

He bolted left to avoid being vaporized. Dove and landed flat on his belly, the soil musty and damp beneath him. The ground rumbled and shook when the bomb exploded, his teeth gnashing together. Bright-white flashes formed arcs behind him, lit the ground in every direction. It brought back memories of the sun, something he hadn't seen for many years, and he somewhat wished he could stay in that moment. That he could linger in its unnatural glow and perhaps pretend it was the real thing. But this wasn't real, and he knew it.

Scrambling to a half-kneeling position, he gaped at the beauty surrounding him. The light devoured those closest to the blast. When the arc reached its full potential, tendrils of lightning zipped out like electric snakes, winding across the earth, hungry and eager for more. A light breeze rushed out from the blast zone, bringing with it the smell of death. This was an odor he had grown accustomed to over his many years in the corps.

He dug his heels in the ground and kicked, scooting out of reach of the light. Even then the electricity licked at his boots, tasting him, as though wanting to consume him. The light could be insatiable where his kind was concerned.

Others weren't so lucky. The lightning seized them by the legs and dragged them down. Caught in its imperceptible grasp, the luckiest were reduced to trembling masses on the hardened earth. Others weren't so fortunate.

At least they tried.

Not everyone had. Some yielded to the light first chance they got. Uncertain why, he believed it might be the shame that came in knowing what they had become, what they did to survive. It was a horrifying reality, but he would be damned if he would ever go out like that. He wasn't about to surrender to anyone or anything.

He had been the first, a pioneer for a new breed of Marine. In truth, these new Marines were only weapons, more so than ever before. They weren't even pawns, but the swords pawns fought with, and, as such, their lives meant little to anyone of importance. The government could and would create more of them if they needed to. Now that they had pried open Pandora's Box, no one was anxious to close the lid.

As the arc dissipated, he assessed their losses, frowning.

This isn't war. Not anymore.

This was a sadistic means to an end. It troubled

him the way these Marines sacrificed themselves. Perhaps what bothered him most was that he thought he understood another reason why they did it. In a way, they had all become prisoners to this war, led to believe they had a stake in the outcome. In reality, they had nothing. There were no assurances beyond this night, and no one had made them any promises.

Their sole task was to hand out death as if it were candy being passed around to children. They were to follow orders like any good Marine should, and ask no questions. So, when their country asked them if they could inject them with an experimental serum, any Marine worth his salt sucked it up and said, *Hell yeah, sir! Oorah!* They adapted like any good Marine would. After all, despite the obvious truths, there were those who still wanted to win this war, Hellinger among them.

I'll see an end to this even if it brings my dying breath.

The fallen troops seized, pulling him out of his thoughts. They chattered incomprehensible words. Most of those who survived would be out for hours. Soon, they would be transported back to base, fed and given time to mend. Once they could stand on their own again, they would be redeployed. Whether or not they survived was no concern to anyone.

They should have expected this. These grunts were on the fast track.

Like any other war, they rushed the freshies through boot camp. It left them ill-prepared for the very real horrors of war. The death they would see on a regular basis would, no doubt, define them in many ways.

Hellinger knew this well. He had served in the 124th Regiment during the North Korean conflict, and even signed on for two additional tours. Having witnessed things on the battlefield that could never be erased from his memories, those images were going to haunt him to his grave. Yep, he knew what real war was, and he missed it like a baby misses a mother's teat.

Stupid bastards and their super Marines.

He lifted himself and slinked along a row of parked cars. In the distance, the enemy had begun the arduous process of reloading their light cannons. Soon, another barrage of bombs would ignite the night sky. More Marines would fall victim to its splendor. If they didn't make some headway soon, all would be lost. If these attacks continued to break down their forces, retreat would be imminent.

Can't lose this front again.

He scanned the landscape and spotted a few Marines. "Porter, Dillon, Hanem."

They recognized him and hurried to his position. Forming a tight semi-circle around him, they awaited their orders.

"If we don't take out those cannons, they're gonna kill us all." Hellinger used hand signals to pump out his plan while he spoke. "Hanem, you and Dillon make your way around them foothills over there. See if you can't get them to focus on that left flank."

Hanem and Dillon snapped off salutes.

"Porter and I will take up the right side. Try to blindside those bastards." He stared off at the cannons. "They're gonna fire those blasted cannons again soon. We'll need to withstand at least one assault." His eyes narrowed on them one by one.

"Make damn well sure you aren't standing around gazing off into space when those bombs strike. Understood?"

"Yes sir," they said in unison.

"Let's take out those cannons and get back to the *Crotch* in time for an early drink. Right?"

Together, they yelled out a new slogan they had adopted over the last few years, "Cry freedom!"

Every time he heard that battle cry, it saddened him. That would never be true, not for the likes of them. Sure, they were king-shit when it came to fighting on the battlefield. As long as they won, they were treated like royalty.

But what comes afterward?

He had his suspicions.

Returning his thoughts to the war, he led Porter right. They ducked under a fallen bridge and skulked among tattered remains of iron and concrete. Porter stuck to his tail, never more than a few yards away.

The onslaught commenced. Dozens of bombs filled the sky. At their apex, they cast a wonderful luminance. Porter started lagging, slowing and staring up at those lights.

"Porter? Get your lily-white ass over here."

Porter stayed, though.

"Now, Marine," Hellinger commanded.

He could see now Porter would never follow another order. He had gone AWOL in his brain, mesmerized by the glow like a moth drawn to light.

Not his fault.

Like so many others, the kid hadn't known a damn thing about the serum they had shot him up with after he chose to sign those papers.

At least he made it this far.

Porter's eyes widened on the approaching light.

No way I take those cannons alone. Hope the others make it in time.

The time fast approached to put distance between himself and Porter. He sprinted several yards ahead, spinning in time to watch the light swallow the Marine. Porter's awful cries made him shiver ever so slightly. This time Hellinger made sure he was well out of reach. The light arched and tendrils swept out across the ground in search of flesh, living or otherwise.

Now that Porter had met his end, Hellinger refocused on the mission.

There were others nearby who had evaded this last attack. He considered replacing Porter, but too many of them still looked shaken by the assault.

I'm better off on my own.

That had often been the case. Minutes later, he advanced on the right flank of the cannons. It pleased him to learn Hanem's charge had succeeded, as well.

Hellinger dug in for a brief second, took note of what opposition remained. Their faces turned away from him, caught by surprise as Hanem attacked. They were also unsuspecting of the terror racing up behind them as they reached for their handheld light blasters.

Speeding to the closest technician, Hellinger sank his fangs deep into the man's carotid artery. Blood splashed over his gums, a divine sensation. Forcing himself to release, Hellinger moved on to the operator of that same cannon, slashing his throat with his clawed fingers.

One by one, Hellinger assaulted the enemy, drinking their blood and tearing out their throats. He moved with such immense speed they could not defend against him. With each renewed assault, it became more difficult to pull away from the thirst.

His eyes met Hanem's, and he saw that he, too, had come alone. Hanem's fangs pierced the thigh of an adversary, ripped it open and went back again. The man screamed. He was nothing but a toy to Hanem. Seeing this forced Hellinger to look away.

Hanem sped toward Hellinger, ripping out the throats of two successive enemies on the way. Together, in mere minutes, they lay waste to more than two-thirds of the forces occupying this post. Then, Hanem stayed too long while drinking from one of his victims. Before Hellinger could warn him, they got the drop on Hanem and riddled him with a burst of gunfire from their light blasters. Each round left a bright white hole in Hanem's chest.

Wounded, Hanem released his victim. He tried to fight back and managed to take out two more before the light ate away his insides. Seconds later, he came to an abrupt halt, his stomach bursting in a blinding light. Electric fingers shot out across his remains, eating away at him until only a bloodied stump of a torso remained. His corpse teetered, and then collapsed.

He was a damn fine Marine.

Angered by this loss, Hellinger turned on those who had killed Hanem. Even when one foe remained, he refused to stay and feed. There was a time and place for such needs, and that moment did not come on the battlefield. He remained alert until he had ended every last life.

He withdrew several charges from his backpack.

After he wired timers for the charges, he placed them around the base of each cannon. Then he retreated back to what surviving forces were left and watched.

Fire filled the night sky as much as it did the red irises of the Marines. Hellinger observed their indecision shift.

"Cry freedom!"

Focus renewed, he led their charge to win a hard-fought battle. Tomorrow would be another day and forward command would send human reinforcements to the frontline. The dead would be replaced. It was a vicious cycle Hellinger could no longer escape, but for tonight, at least, it was his time to shine.

+———✦———+

"Hellinger?" Dirkain said.

Hellinger snapped off a salute. "Sir?"

He stood wide and crisscrossed his hands behind him. Following Dirkain down a dark tunnel, several pairs of red eyes tracked their progress from the shadows of the barracks. Some of those eyes were familiar to Hellinger, others not so much.

They entered a dimly lit conference room.

"Sit," Dirkain said.

"Yes, sir."

"Congratulations are in order, Marine."

"Sir?"

"Your men have shifted the momentum of this war. It won't be long now before we regain control of the lower States. We might even secure America by daylight."

Hellinger grinned. "Oorah!" He should have been proud, but he wasn't.

Why is it Dirkain can't look me in the eyes?

Hellinger had heard rumors of a special bomb they kept stored in this facility, often referred to as a precautionary measure. He believed the day would come when they used that bomb to celebrate America's new Independence Day. To rid themselves of the monsters they had created in order to secure that freedom. If ever a new threat arose, they would just make more, but the country had no place for monsters in times of peace.

"You'll be commended for your effort, of course," Dirkain said. "Medal of Honor, I suspect."

"And Hanem, sir? I couldn't have succeeded without him?"

Something felt off about Dirkain, the way he tried to suppress a grin. "We'll find something fitting for Hanem, as well."

Hellinger tried to listen as Dirkain detailed movement in the Carolinas and the final push to secure Georgia, but his focus drifted back to the North Korean War. It had started in the spring of 2017 and lasted six grueling years. He had watched children sacrifice themselves and picked up pieces of his men from the muddied ground. Hellinger had left so many tears on that soil. He often wished he could let go of those memories, but they had stuck with him all this time.

In the fall of 2024, scientists researched a serum that would end all warring. With this power harnessed, the United States became a fierce nation. Guns were no longer a necessity, as they had little effect on this new breed of Marine. If only he had known then, he might have thought twice about agreeing to the injection.

He had been genetically engineered. Designed to end wars, but had in fact only ushered in a different form of warfare. This conflict was being fought on American soil against their own countrymen. The enemy didn't care for what he had become, and he couldn't blame them. It disgusted him, too.

No matter who won this war, North or South, East or West, his kind would be exterminated. Knowing this meant he could never be free again.

"Got that Marine?"

Of course, he did. He scanned Dirkain's face; let his eyes move over the map as he studied the strike points. It was all easy enough. Perhaps, too easy.

He stood and clacked his heels together as he snapped off a tight salute. "Yes, sir."

Now Dirkain did grin, but he still wouldn't look him in the eyes. Hellinger spun away, his concern about Dirkain's awkward behavior filling his thoughts. He headed off for some much-needed rest.

＊——＊——＊

The *Crotch,* as they called it, was an old mess hall. Deckhands had cleared the room of tables and chairs. They had fastened metal spikes to the floor, the tiles around them all fractured. No one cared so much about aesthetics when it came to this area. The humans tied livestock to these spikes: horses, cows, sheep, any living creature having outlived its purpose.

Hellinger entered, warranting a sideways glance from a few others. No one saluted here. Insatiable appetites overruled formalities, took precedence over any regulations. He didn't mind, knowing how easy it was to get lost in the thirst.

One woman looked too thin, her red hair buzzed

close to her skull. Another, just a boy, couldn't have been old enough to fight yet. There were half dozen others, still in their teens. The rest had barely reached drinking age, save for a handful of familiar men and women. Most of these Marines wouldn't make it through the night. Some would sacrifice themselves. A select few would survive and prove themselves as valuable as Hanem.

He stood beside the horse, observing two Marines as they drained the creature's life force. Their hands pawed at its sides, their mouths greedy at its flesh, and their eyes closed as if caught in a dream state. The sounds of sucking filled the room, blood trickling to the floor beneath the mass of Marines. Then he was beside them, fangs deep in the creature's flesh. Rich blood flowed over his tongue and down his throat. It warmed him, a sensation of renewal, of being born again into this bleak existence. The smell, sweet and sour, thrilled his senses.

Soon, the horse collapsed. Its chest expanded one last time, expelling the air in a long hiss. A dreadful silence followed. One Marine, a woman he hadn't met yet, turned and vomited. Half-digested blood spewed from her mouth, a kaleidoscope of red and orange on the white tiles.

She won't make it through the night.

After a long moment, the Marine stood and gathered herself. Seconds later, she fed on a sheep.

Then again, maybe she will.

✦———✦———✦

A carrier transported them to the frontline come dusk. The smell of fuel filled the vast area of the docks, as well as the slight odor of burnt rubber. These were the scents of what lay beyond the doors, captured within this chamber, intensifying the anxiety of every Marine in attendance.

Hellinger readied his troops, conveying the strikes Dirkain had laid out for them. The sheer number of new Marines unnerved him. Some listened, their attention full. Others stared right through him. He identified them one by one, meeting their empty gazes. Those would be the first to surrender to the light.

Kachink-kachink.

He glanced to the back of the vehicle. The large metal door rose and the evening air assaulted his face, warm and fresh, smelling of war and decay and life all at once. Hundreds of vehicles lay scattered across the battlefield, some overturned and others burnt to a crisp. A large dilapidated bridge filled much of his view, its silhouette haunting with smoke twisting around the broken suspension cables. He inhaled deeply, filling his lungs before leading the Marines out.

Even with these obstacles, the initial field offered little concealment. They were out in the open and already a cascade of bombs rained down upon them like fireworks. More than half the Marines stopped, some unable to keep from viewing a beauty they had not seen in a long time, himself included. Others had lost the will to live like this, a struggle even he had gone through. These latter soldiers huddled together, tears streaming down their upturned faces. They maneuvered as a unit to meet the descent of a bomb. A flash struck at their core, driving their arms apart and upward, their backs arching outward. The light formed a dome around them and devoured each Marine it touched.

Tendrils of lightning crackled along the ground, discovering those who hadn't escaped the blast zone, and slithered over them with ferociousness. Some of those fallen spat out white foam tinted with blood. Most wouldn't survive.

Hellinger surveyed the damage, observing his troops and assessing how many endured the blast. Soon the cannons would fire again. When the light erupted, more would die.

"Move out. Move out," he shouted.

They found cover among the wreckage of several vehicles and hunkered down while he reconsidered their strategy. If they took Atlanta, they would no doubt win this war before night's end. He glanced to his left and then his right. Pasty faces gazed back at him, the black paint doing little to conceal their true identities. He held out a fist, looked to his left, and beat out his orders.

That flank broke off in two groups, one for each cluster of the cannons along the left perimeter. The Marines on the right followed him toward the enemy's barracks.

The sky lit again, but this time no one stopped. They could taste the end, driven by the previous night's victory and having been told they were close. Hellinger himself now hungered for it in the same way he did blood, and seeing them respond like this made him beam with pride.

A light bomb struck the tail end of his unit, taking out four Marines. Five were left by the time they reached the barracks. What was left of the other two units rejoined the group. Only a few remaining cannons stood in the way of victory.

They split up and attacked the cannon operators and their technicians, moving between them. Tearing open throats and arteries, they left them to bleed out where they fell. With his heart pounding and his voracious appetite, Hellinger hadn't noticed how little opposition there had been, despite having visualized this much in his briefing. Seeing it now, he lagged behind while his troops broke through the doors to the enemy barracks. A force of two-dozen anxious Marines pushed past him, including the woman he had questioned would make it through the night.

He remained in the hallway as his Marines poured into the barracks. They appeared bewildered by the emptiness of the room, and disappointment showed on their faces, believing their attack a failure. They studied the large object in the center of the room of which Hellinger had only heard rumors. Uncertainty showed in their eyes when the doors slid shut.

Hellinger was too late. *"No!"*

Light flashed out from beneath the door. His Marines screamed for a brief moment, and he couldn't do a thing about it. Still, he pounded on the doors. Even when the tendrils of light trickled under the door and ran over his toes, he kept on pounding.

This is their goddamned reward?

It disgusted him. This wasn't war, and he would not be party to it again. For now, he would hide among the shadows of night. His ultimate goal would be to track down Dirkain and make him pay for his wrongdoings. He would become the monster they had wanted, the very thing they should fear.

"Semper Fi."

THE HUNTED

THEY HAD NEVER ventured this deep into Jenner's territory before. Now they did so with purpose.

He threw back his dusky robes and fled from them. A quick scan of the night sky revealed a tinge of orange on the horizon. Behind him, the light of two torches altered their path to match his.

What do they want?

He thought he knew.

Feet splashed in ankle high waters, trailing him. Their flames flickered in the wind, as they intensified their pursuit. No words were spoken between them, only heavy breaths as they pushed themselves. He would need to lose them before arriving at his dwelling.

Ducking through the woods, he kept his eyes on his trackers. Limbs snapped off against his physique and scraped at his flesh, but he barely noticed. He pushed through a group of trees and stopped to view their current position. Their fire wavered in an early morning breeze. There were three of them now, and something else, too. He detected the scent of an animal on the wind.

They've brought a dog.

Confirming this fear, the smallest man called out to the distant torchbearer. "Get that dog over here, Jake."

Jake's silhouette appeared, looking more formidable than the others. "Where do you think he's going?"

"Over yonder is my guess," the small man said.

The men remained stationary for a moment. As if sensing Jenner's presence, the dog growled. One of the men, he could not tell which, bent and dangled his fingers in the water, as if observing Jenner's wake.

"I think you're right," he said and stood.

At this, Jenner took flight with more deliberate footsteps. He altered his course, so as not to divulge any further details of his escape. They followed with fervor, assuming they were quite near. Jenner kept them at a distance, wanting to ensure he lost them before entering the cave. The dog wouldn't make that easy.

When he reached the cliffs, he rushed to his domicile and ducked inside the cave unnoticed. There, panic seized him, as he knew the dog would soon sniff him out if he wasted too much time.

Already, the dog's barking invaded his ears, escalating his sense of urgency. Hints of daylight sparkled on the foliage outside, and then on the entrance to his dwelling. Their torches also illuminated the area outside of the cave, indicating their proximity.

He shrank away from the opening and scurried to the rear wall where he lay down in a pile of moist soil. This comforted him, the dank smell pleasing his nostrils. He reached out and hauled large masses of soil over his legs, then his waist, and continued to bury himself in this manner until fully obscured by dirt. Afterward, he remained dormant, his breathing easing in one last gasp.

Outside, their voices neared. Their foul pet was first to breach the entrance. It raced about the cave in search of his scent.

Their intrusion distressed him, and if there hadn't been so many of them, he might have risen to end them for invading his tomb. Breath held, he waited, in hopes they would relinquish this insanity. But while the earth diverted their animal, it did not fool the humans.

One of them dug with eagerness, and upon revealing Jenner's face, the man hurried to excavate the rest of the soil. Jenner opened his eyes and beheld the men standing over him, all of them startled. He observed their sullen faces, his anger at its boiling point, and bared his fangs. Before he could attack, they were upon him. The dog tugged at his right leg while the two largest men pinned him to the ground. The third man straddled his waist. With hammer and stake in hand, this man jammed its point to the left of Jenner's breastbone.

Some inhuman noise escaped Jenner when the man drove the stake deep into his frame. Pain surged through his chest. His blackened heart struggled against the cleansing sensation as it washed over his entire being. He wanted to hate them but could feel nothing but indebted for liberating him from this cursed affliction.

With one last gulp of air, he exhaled with a light wheeze. Life fled him before their fire took to his flesh.

HER LIVING CORALS

ANDREA THOUGHT IT only fair those people who most often contributed to the destruction of the ocean reefs should be forced to witness the long-term effects of their transgressions against their planet. Earth deserved some form of justice, as it had long suffered at the hands of ignorance. So why not this?

Her anger toward these people did not come unfounded, and she did her best to set an example, to live her life as she thought everyone should. She joined several environmental organizations, took care in separating her trash, recycled anything she could, even rode her bicycle to work despite the weather. It was her goal to conserve energy whenever possible. She practiced what she preached and expected no less from anyone else, as it took so little effort to make mindfulness part of one's lifestyle. When those closest to her showed no signs of caring and refused to heed her warnings, she had been forced to resort to more impractical tactics.

Initially, her husband, Tom, had shared in her appreciation for the environment and the concerns over its continual ruin. They paid attention to the effects of global warming and what they, as a couple, could do to make things better. His interests had shifted over time. Now they revolved around unimportant matters such as football, reality television shows, and his position at the law firm. Those were his primary concerns when he wasn't too busy detailing her every flaw. He made sure to carve out plenty of time for that task, powering some ceaseless need to relay these particulars to her with such vitriol and animosity.

She often wished him dead for those verbal lashings. As a result of it all, not only had their union grown stale over the last year, since their wedding, but she had also begun to realize she would someday leave him. How could she save their marriage? Even their love life had soured, which proved one of the saving graces for many couples. She needed a fresh start, yet she lacked the conviction to follow through with her desire. Perhaps she required some time to consider matters.

If she could round up enough confidence, she would also like to leave her job. Being a telemarketer was an awful occupation, placing a constant barrage of phone calls to people who didn't want to hear anything she had to say. Every hang-up was like a hammer against a tin bucket, denting her inner-being and further weakening her will.

There was also the matter of her boss, Gerald, a man with a nasty habit of asking her to work every single weekend. He was an opportunistic pervert, often trying to position himself so he could get a peek down the front of her blouse. The fact he would go through so much trouble to check out her cleavage sickened her, and she felt like slapping him each time he did.

When she finally worked up the nerve to relay this offense to Tom, her expectations had been that her husband would rally to her defense. Instead, he had only laughed and told her she was being silly. That it was all in her head. He lectured her about spending less time worrying about what her boss did and more time dedicated to actual work.

So what did any of this mean? For one, both men deserved to die. They had worked hard at making her life miserable. In fact, her life had become unbearable, and she walked about like some undead creature, unsure where she should be heading or what she should be doing. She no longer valued life. The world she once viewed as a parallel existence to a vast reef in the ocean suffered a fate equal to that of the corals, all of the harm coming thanks to mankind's meddling hand.

Life had once been so full of wonder, so full of surprise. She had seen things that took her breath away. Things that moved her to the point she shed tears. But that life was ages ago. Now she believed this existence uninhabitable, a sea devoid of all life. She shouldn't feel the slightest bit guilty for wanting them dead, but still, she did.

Cubicles filled much of the open space at work, each of them singular habitats. When she passed by and looked in, she saw the denizens trapped within, almost as comatose as a bunch of belly-up fish. They, too, had lost their passion for life, and as a result, they might as well be dead alongside Tom and Gerald.

After work, she would retreat to a home she had worked hard to fill with dozens of lifeless corals: snapshots held in black wooden frames, drab paintings that hung on earth-tone painted walls, all of it with token sentimental value. These objects were windows to a past she could no longer appreciate and had even begun to loathe. The drab furniture that filled much of each room did nothing to provide her any comfort, serving as mere perches from which she could view these meaningless possessions.

Then there was the mindless television hung on the wall over the fireplace mantle. They gawked at it most evenings, each from their respective end of the couch. She sat through displays of bogus worlds, while Tom drank and complained of her shortcomings. Those were the nights she felt most lost, the times when she considered hurting herself. No wonder she sought refuge in the ocean.

The slight pounding of the waves against the hull of the boat alleviated her anguish. A steady rumble from the motor, the spray of ocean, the wake trailing out behind her, the cackle of seagulls hovering above the boat as if escorting her out . . . All of it humbled her and brought her some much needed peace. Soon after, with the shore far behind, she calmed.

She ventured out past the reef to a drop-off where people sometimes came to fish. Below, she would scuba dive and visit a wondrous beauty she believed undiscovered by anyone but herself. She had found it by accident after she damaged a coral and descended to retrieve the broken pieces. There, she found an opening hidden beneath the water's surface and a cascade of fallen rocks. This was a portal to a place she had occupied as her own, her garden, her own special reef.

She adjusted her regulator, dove into the sea, and

let her body drift down to where others would begin their exploration of the reef. Here, she adjusted her angle and headed down along the rocky slope to the ocean floor far below. She found the gap beneath two mammoth rocks and slid inside.

Light crept in through unseen cracks in the ceiling, brightening the underwater cavern with unnatural hues of blue. It reminded her of concerts she had attended in her youth. She could not help but feel a hiccup of elation as she lowered herself to her garden. There, she swam among her earliest attempts: small grafts she had nurtured back to healthy corals, structures she had brought here to help form a man-made reef where she could continue to place corals she collected. This place, in its entire splendor, lay hidden from mankind by the Earth. Therefore, it had sat untouched by man's intruding hand for so many years until she came to make it whole, to mold it into something more than some clandestine grotto.

A school of brilliant fish burst out from a gap in an old tricycle, one of the first objects she had brought here. Their bodies flashed a brilliant silvery blue, moving as one as they swam just above the sandy floor. A crab appeared out of nowhere and snapped at the fish when they passed. It came up empty-handed and resorted to grazing on the garden floor. She moved in close to observe the creature, but it saw her and burrowed out of sight, its hunger left unsatisfied for the time being. A laugh bubbled on her lips, muffled by her scuba gear.

Anemones riddled the surface of her structures, caught in the slight movements of the ocean outside the cavern. They were doing so well, and each waved hello as she moved over them, welcoming her back to the land of the living to which she felt such a strong attachment. What a contrast this was to her real home and to work. If possible, she would stay here for all eternity. But that was unreasonable, as she could never afford the equipment necessary to keep her alive underwater for that long.

She happened upon a familiar structure, one from long ago. Her smile faded. Dennis had been a stocky man. He stood unmoving with his limbs extended outward in an animated muscular flex. She once thought those muscles quite attractive. Had felt a stir in her stomach whenever she watched him workout. He had been neglectful of this planet to the point where she could no longer stand the man. When she tried to leave him, he had used those arms to hit her.

His lawyer got him off with some bullshit excuse, and even once the divorce had been finalized, he continued to harass her. When the police stopped coming, this place served as her last defense. A sneer crossed her face as she remembered him striking her. It bothered her, yet she felt some triumph seeing him here now. She swam away, still worried after all this time he might find some way to assault her.

Farther down, she stopped at another person she'd brought her. Andrea once thought the bright colors and unique patterns in the clothing store would help stimulate her senses. While the brilliant colors did make her feel more alive and resembled the many picturesque fish of the ocean, this woman had proved a relentless thorn in her side. According to this woman, Andrea never smiled enough. Andrea had never been one to fake happiness, and she supposed her sales reflected as much, warranting her being reprimanded. It had come more often than she expected, and Andrea soon grew tired of this woman's persistent bitching. After witnessing her former employer's other wrongdoings, she had all the excuse she needed to leave this woman frozen in time with a permanent view of this garden.

Andrea gazed into the woman's encrusted eyes, saw her former employer's fate and felt some of her annoyance wash away. Then she saw the man beside this woman, and her irritation returned. They belonged together, caught in their infidelity, arms and legs forever entangled. The mere sight of her second husband with this woman still aggravated her. Seeing them stirred up all of those old emotions she had kept bottled up for so long.

Goddamn that bastard for hurting me.

Unless she chose otherwise, they would go on living in this place forever. She gazed at them together a moment longer and then moved on.

She reached a neighborhood boy who had overcharged her for the morning paper. Yet, that hadn't been what bothered her most about the teenager. It was the way he handled his extra papers. How he never bothered to return them as instructed by the agency, and instead dumped them in the woods.

At the next structure, she saw the face of an old college friend who had joined forces with a medical waste company upon graduating. She had never expected the woman to amount to much, but summer after summer this woman ruined beaches. Next, she came across her brother's first wife and then her second cousin, both of them litterbugs who refused to listen.

All the most hateful and destructive people in her life were in attendance, present to remind her of the damage they had done to this world. That also meant the two biggest culprits were here. Her parents had punished her one too many times for having radical beliefs. She gazed at her mother's arm, still raised as if ready to slap Andrea. Then she saw her father, his pants down around his ankles. A vicious reminder of his crimes, seeing him like this revolted her. Her cheeks burned, and if not for a tiny fish darting in and out of the hollow of her father's eye socket, she might have lost it right then.

A sense of normalcy returned to her as she focused on the playful dance of this fish. She had come here to make a decision, and after seeing these people, the light bulb flashed brightly in her head.

I will leave Tom. She reflected further on the matter. *And my job, too.*

She studied her garden, picking out the perfect location for both Tom and her peeping boss.

They will make excellent additions.

Pleased with her decision, she swam to her third husband. Doug had never wronged her like these others. His wrongdoing had been his awful clinginess. He had been environmentally conscious, which once delighted her. They had even planned to have children together. Now he stood in solitude in this section of her garden, separate from the others. He had done his part, but still gone too far by smothering her with his affection.

She gazed into his eyes and imagined him staring back at her, his voice still alive and pleading in her head.

I'm sorry, but I can't stay.

How dreadful it had been when he discovered this place and confronted her. He never should have followed her. How could she have explained a thing like this to him, a man who always worried she had been cheating on him? Not even a man like him could understand. He had almost ruined this garden for her, and she had no other choice but to bring him here, regretting even now how their relationship ended because of it.

She glanced about at all of her living corals.

Maybe I did cheat on him after all.

She could not dwell on such unpleasant matters.

I'm sorry if I hurt you, Doug. I never meant to.

She would try to visit again soon, maybe spend some extra time with him. Perhaps when she brought the new additions. He deserved that much.

Bidding him a fond farewell, she blew him a light kiss from behind her mask and then winked. When she turned to leave, she could go nowhere. Her face wrinkled with confusion. She glanced over her shoulder and found her lower leg stuck between Doug's arm and body. How had she snagged herself? Or did he move?

She watched him, waited to see if he showed any signs of having moved.

No, he couldn't have.

Yet she remembered everything down here remained alive, for now and ever more.

She wriggled, trying to free herself, but his grasp seemed to tighten in response. Her eyes widened, and her heart strummed out a steady beat, a loud *thump-thump* even she could hear through the ocean depths.

Then he did move, the decaying flesh of his empty eye sockets stirring as some unseen life shifted inside of them.

A crab maybe? Or a fish?

She stared at his distorted face.

Was Doug smiling when I got here?

She traced the edge of his encrusted lips, could not remember whether the years of accumulation had only made it look as though he were smiling or if he had been grinning the day she placed him here.

His smile grew, and as she witnessed this change, she jerked away. Panic struck, her heart fluttered, and she found it difficult to breathe. She yanked hard, trying to free herself from his grasp. Pain seized her leg as the rocky growths on Doug's arm cut through her wetsuit and carved a deep wound into the meat of her lower calf.

A flush of red stained the water around her, and curious fish sped to her side. They dared to come closer for a taste, darted at the blood, through it, and then back around for more. Soon it would draw larger fish, the sorts that hungered for more substance, perhaps something meatier.

She peered into Doug's eyes, pained that he would hurt her this way, and could swear his grin spread wider in that instant.

Let go of me, damn you!

Her mask fogged, making it hard to see. She gasped, her breath uneasy. With determination, she pulled hard. The tugging brought more pain and more blood, which seemed to please Doug.

Glancing to his eyes, she felt wounded by them.

How could you?

She thrashed, knowing it would further tear her leg, but it would not matter once she made it back to the boat. There she could mend herself, and once she completed that task, she could return to deal with Doug. He was no longer welcome here in her garden.

She heard an unexpected clang. Felt a release of pressure from the puncture. Something had pierced her tank, and the oxygen escaped with a steady stream of bubbles.

"Is this what you wanted?" In this mask, her voice sounded weak and hurt. "Even now you can't let me go?"

His smile grew, grip tightened. Yes, she thought this was precisely what he wanted.

With one final attempt, she yanked, careless of her gear because it no longer mattered. The rock tore at her flesh, dug deep into the muscle, and a lightning bolt of pain shot through her leg. Blood stained the waters around her a bright red, a beautiful contrast to the typical blues she had grown accustomed to. On any other day, she might have appreciated its magnificence, but with her current situation she could not. She flailed her arms, thrust her legs, and heard a distinct *snap*.

Her body stiffened as cool water touched her cheek. Icy water crept along the inside of her broken mask, around to her other cheek, and rose. She convulsed with anxiety, her breathing irregular as the last of her air tank dwindled. She tried to reach the nozzle of her tank, hoped to get one last tug of air before it was too late, but to her horror it had already been depleted.

Her eyes pleaded with Doug. The ocean water

blurred her vision as it stole her life away. The smaller fish darted about her; so glad she could join them. Some larger fish appeared, swimming in circles around her, altering their courses here and there to come close enough for a taste of what she had to offer.

As her body numbed and her vision darkened, she realized her fate. An amused smile formed on her lips. Doug and she would be together always, decaying in each other's arms, here in this special garden where she would live forever.

PUPPET STRINGS

THERE WAS NO escape, not for a woman of Marianne's means. Not in this city, in these days of war against Germany. Here, the rich didn't have to fight for their freedom. They were viewed with star-struck eyes. And no man, wealthy or otherwise, was worse than a politician, always instructing his wife how to live her life.

She had been trained, or rather prepared, to be a proper lady from an early age. She had known of her father's plan to marry her to the right man from the start, the kind of man who had money and an equally heavy hand. He had meant to get something in return, too. Wealth or fame, it was all the same to her father, since he had never amounted to much.

She loathed all of it, the entire process of being groomed for marriage. Except for the dancing, which her father allowed. He even paid for lessons when he could afford it. She had learned to rely on men, to trust them, to know her role, to perform her womanly duties when called upon. All of it weakened her resolve, and she had become nothing more than a puppet to their will.

As a child, when her father got drunk, he often

reminded her of her place. He would take out whatever frustrations he had in his fruitless life upon her. At times, he had even scarred her, though most of those wounds were deep and concealed. He had made her feel worthless. As if she had no mortality at all. It was in those times she first became lost, going through the motions and performing tasks for her father, then for her husband in due time. Leo was no different than her father, equally as rough around the edges and just as quick to strike her. She had grown numb to it all.

Yet, her father had taken care of her. He had provided for her up to and including the day she had been married off. In some small way, he still supported her by means of these letters he sent, tape spread across the edges of the flap to ensure no one but Marianne read them.

She hadn't always been a puppet, refusing to fight back as she did now. As a teenager, she had mouthed off to her father enough that he struck her more often. The more she had fought back, the harder the blows came, open-handed at first, and eventually with closed fists. She had learned to mind her place, and she did so now for fear Leo might strike her in that same way. Leo had already proven he was more than willing, having left scars of his own on her olive skin.

What happened to that confidence she had shown as a teen, her sense of self-importance, having her own opinions?

If I could go back, I would, but . . .

But what? She hadn't been able to escape her father's wrath. What made her think it would be any different now? What more could she do?

Like most drunks, her father had grown bolder

whenever he imbibed. Leo hadn't been much different. Where her father laid the tracks, Leo now threaded the needle, especially these last few years when he had finally started to make something of himself. He had been the one to cement her transformation into what felt like a marionette, dangling from many strings. She performed for him on cue, playing to his every whim, just as she had been instructed. And she despised herself for relying on him, as she had never believed herself capable of true independence.

Often, she cried, but always in secret, and never in front of Leo. She didn't want him to visualize the effects of his handiwork. The letters from her father also made her sad, seeing his words now and knowing he wasn't a good man despite all he had claimed to do for her over the years.

She tilted her jewelry box, slid a hand underneath, and found what she wanted. Retrieving one of the lengths of tape from the edge of her vanity, she fashioned it around the handle of her creation. The shiv was no longer than her pinky finger, and she had some reservations as to how much damage it could deliver. Far too short to hold, she did her best to sharpen the edges with her nail file. She hoped she could muster up the nerve to use it someday. Though, even if she did, she would need to hide it on her person for an entire night.

She felt that pull again, the need to regain control and prepare for the show. He would come for her soon, and she dared not be late.

In her youth, there hadn't been any need to perform. She had been content with her rather plain existence. Perhaps that comfort was the reason Leo first referred to her as "a diamond in the rough" when engaging her father in discussions of marriage. He had spoken then of his master plan, how he would turn her into a trinket, a mere accessory for his purposes.

Her father never had any interest in Leo's plans, though. He only cared about what he got in exchange. And Leo kept her father fat and drunk enough that he never came around much. Even when he did, it was brief, and usually he was only looking for another handout.

Leo never tired of tinkering with her. The changes were slight at first, the color of her hair or how much blush she used. What brand of mascara she applied. The various makeups and perfumes she kept on her vanity. It wasn't long before he demanded more of her. He became ever critical of how she walked, requiring she maintain a proper posture. These were the things her father had briefed her on, but there was always room for improvement in Leo's eyes.

Like her father, she could never live up to Leo's expectations, either. Her failures angered him, but she didn't care because she knew the truth. Whatever dignity, innocence, and sense of purpose she had left, he had stolen it away from her. All of it snatched away the day she let him start changing her into . . .

Into this.

He had turned her into something despicable, far worse than anything her father could have made of her. She had become what she had dreamed of as a young girl, but despised as a teenager, wearing a skin she could no longer shed.

Leo was so much stronger now, too. Like a terrible spider, he had woven her into his web and there would be no simple means of escape. He had drained the life from her and left her for dead.

Her eyes stole a glance at the shiv.

I better put that away.

Instead, she slipped the weapon into the hem of her dress.

In the past, whenever she had tried to ruin his plans, he had been quick to repair the damage. He always spoke in his calm manner in front of company, offering reasons, as if he had thought of every possible outcome beforehand. The punishment would follow swiftly, so she had learned not to interfere in his business matters.

At least he still let her dance, sometimes into the wee hours of the night. She enjoyed the dancing, especially when left alone. Never had she danced more than she did these days. Her father had paid for ballet lessons and for a few popular dances of his time. Leo knew many new forms and had taught her all of them. Dancing was so therapeutic; the spinning, jumping, and leaping, all of it made her feel so . . .

Free.

When each new day dawned, their show remained unchanged. It had for seven excruciating years, eating away at her soul like the eroding banks of a small stream. The only detail that did change was the scenery and sometimes the audience. Theirs had become a show without end, starting afresh even before the end credits rolled. Each time she found herself counting away the minutes in her head until everyone left in her head.

Tonight, everything proved characteristic. Here they were at their house, in their ballroom, with alcohol and myriad of expensive hors d'oeuvres, music blaring. She moved about as expected, feeling much like an exhausted and frightened butterfly. Leo strutted around in full display, like a peacock spreading his feathers. These people bore witness to his creation, the awful things he made her do. Any deviation from this performance tested Leo's patience, and he must have noticed how forced her presentation had been of late. Even the most sophisticated spectator should be able to see right through the paper-thin veil of her recital. Identify it as a farce.

Yet, it never fazed a single one of them. Not one iota of compassion was spent on her. Not a single eye batted in the face of depravity. And like any good masquerade, Leo's admirers never tired of the charade, of the entire circus he put on for their benefit.

But surely they noticed something.

The way she carried herself. How she had let herself go. That she refused to keep up appearances or use the cosmetics he insisted upon, having them shipped all the way from Paris.

They did not. All these inconsiderate people in attendance this very night and not one of them saw anything but the show Leo intended. They wore eager smiles pasted to their perfumed and powdered faces like children come Christmas time. She despised the way their beady eyes tracked her every move. How they undressed her in their thoughts, licking their lips as their eyes penetrated her clothing. How they laughed in the face of her unease.

After the parties, there were always stragglers. Those were the people most inclined to ask the personal questions. Tonight, as usual, she declined to answer. But the liquor loosened Leo's tongue, and he was more than forthcoming. He detailed aspects of their marriage, revealing things so private it made her blush a fiery red. She endured his talk of undergarments and her breasts, and although she hated him for it, she flaunted both when instructed to do so. Standing there with her dress lifted, she thought not of the shiv, but of the red-hot gaze of their eyes on her bare skin. The electric touch of their fingers when Leo allowed them to prod and squeeze. How each time they did they stole away a little more of her soul. And they kept touching her, long into the night.

Leo was one to take what he wanted when he wanted. On the rare occasion he desired her, everyone left before things progressed too far. Tonight was such a night, which sadly made her thankful. He kept drinking, instructing her to dance for him. She did, only because she loved to dance. But on these nights he sought a different sort of dance, one that left her feeling depraved and violated. It made her nervous, her back to him, her dress still lifted, him sitting in a chair behind her, the loud music, and his hands on her arms. They slid to her breasts and squeezed. Ashamed, she ground into his lap. Like most nights when he drank, his manhood did not respond.

His frustration rose, his hands greedy and kneading at her flesh. Just when she thought matters would deteriorate, he fell back in the chair, screaming with pain.

She stumbled away, seeing the stain of red on her white dress. That was the first time all night she thought of the shiv.

He threw something at her, and she ducked. A

shatter of glass rained down upon her. She froze, unsure whether she had lost the shiv, and worried she would be punished. Then she found it still caught in her bloodied hem.

No. Not this time.

She withdrew the shiv and pushed it under the band of her wedding ring. Made a fist that allowed the tip of the shiv to stick out, barely visible beyond her knuckle. By the time she had gotten it in place, he was already at her. He shoved her hard against the wall, shattering her like he had the plate. But she didn't feel it, because he had already broken her in so many ways.

A drunken grin spread across his face and . . .

Now. Do it now.

He slapped her, sending her into a whirlwind. She lost her balance and landed on the floor. Lifting herself to her knees, she watched as he stormed away from her.

Good. Leave.

Only he didn't leave. He spun on his heels, and if she hadn't leaped to her feet, he might have hurt her bad this time. She slid into the shadows of the room and hid among large statues and luxuriant furniture.

He threw glasses and plates, some pinging off metal and others shattering. Shards of glass spread across the floor, crackling beneath her high heels.

"Why?" he said. "Why would you hurt me like this?" Slurring his words, he stumbled after her, knocking over an expensive vase, which crashed to the floor.

She jumped away from his clasping hands, gnarled fingers that meant to hurt.

He sputtered out something incomprehensible and lunged for her.

Somehow, she ducked out of the way and ran straight into a pillar. She spun, dizzy and not knowing which direction she faced.

His hands seized her shoulders, his body pressed against her. He wrapped his arms around her and squeezed, hurting her now. "Why, babe?"

She pressed her eyes shut. Her fist opened, closed, and opened. The smell of alcohol on his hot breath sickened her. She felt his penis swelling, excited by her fight and the idea of hurting her. When she tried to wrestle away, he twisted her, forcing her back against the pillar until she screamed. She felt his grin against her cheek. She took a deep breath and punched out, eyes closed and teeth mashed together. Felt her fist in his gut, and the shiv scraped against something hard, maybe a rib.

He staggered back, grasping for her with one hand. His other hand pressed into the folds of his stomach. Blood oozed out between his fingers. His hand found her shoulder, but she pulled away. Grabbing her again, he shook hard, shoved her back, and she crashed against the far wall. He blundered after her. Fell into her, smothering her with his rancid breath and the odor of other women. His hold tightened.

She lashed out again, trying to punch him twice.

He dodged both attacks and shoved her hard against the wall. Her shoulders, her ribs, all of her bones ached. To make matters worse, she nearly lost the shiv.

He leaned in. "Grrrahhh!"

Droplets of sour spit sprinkled her face. Her heart beat faster as she lashed out again, the flesh of his belly wet against her fist. Still he pressed against her, even when she punched his gut again and again. As if empowered by her determination, he continued to attack. Yet, each time her shiv met his assault and stung him, as he had her on so many occasions. Warm blood now covered her fist, feeling sticky on her knuckles.

Soon, his attacks slowed, coming with decreasing effort. Wounded, he turned away from her, wavered, and slumped to the floor. There, he begged for mercy, for her to call someone, get him help, and for her to not let him die. She couldn't even stand to look at him, wanting his silence more than anything. When the dreadful calm came it was beautiful. He inhaled a deep breath, struggling to let it out. His body hitched, and when that final breath reached his lips, it escaped him in a long snakelike hiss.

How fitting.

She removed the shiv and the ring. Dropped them both and stepped over his body. She ran for the horizon of a new day, for whatever tomorrow offered, and knew then the choice was hers and hers alone.

THE TRYING OF MASTER WILLIAM

NO MATTER WHAT happened to them prior to passing, the dead always returned to these fields. They had done so for as long as Aisha could remember. Not as vampires or ghouls, but something else—a faded version of their previous selves. She could tell who had reached their end by the way they carried themselves, as though they had suffered a good whipping.

When her mama had been alive, she used to tell Aisha how Master plowed over some burial ground when he built this place. She had said, *'Ain't no surprise those dead can't get no rest. They done turnt up that soil wrong. Wrecked all them markers and smashed up their bones, for Heaven's sake.'*

Aisha never could understand why they would want to return to such a godforsaken place. *God knows Master and his men are plenty generous with them whips.* At this thought, she sighed. *They're better off just stayin' dead.*

Not that Master ever noticed when one of them came back. It was a rare occasion she ever saw him out in the fields, and no one told him about the dead they saw, either. Perhaps because Aisha's people seemed the only folks capable of seeing or hearing the departed anyway. And today, by gosh, all them ghosts stood around being mighty noisy.

Everyone started singing in an effort to drown out the cries of the deceased.

"Lord, hear our praise," they sang. "Hear us sing your name. Lift up thy weak. Carry them to the river. Cleanse their souls."

Birds chirped. A horse clomped along behind her. The man atop the steed observed their work. The locusts buzzed, their sound rising and falling. Beads of sweat trickled down their faces. Her fingers, long blistered and callused over, stung with each plucking of a tuft of cotton. She couldn't help but acknowledge the dead, one by one, seeing how they mouthed the words at first. Then the dead were singing along with them, sounding like mad howling winds behind their chorus.

They sang louder. "God's chariot comes rushin'. Come roundin' that corner. Bring us this day, thy bread and water. Rest our weary heads. Hear us sing thy praise. Walk among these meadows."

The ghosts' wailing intensified, too. Their song sounded something awful, like someone beating a dog to death until it yelped and whimpered. Only it was hundreds of dogs crying like that. She could see it on the others' faces, too, how it bothered them as much as it did her. So they gave up on trying to out-sing the dead, and hummed instead, to which the dead quieted, perhaps finding some peace in the gentle noise. And that was so much better.

They spent the most sweltering days picking in these fields until the white tufts were all but gone. It offered plenty of time for reflection, too much. After all those hours listening to them voices, hearing loud and clear the whispers of the dead, it made Aisha feel like she was going insane. Only she knew she weren't the least bit crazy.

What do they want?

The slaves never spoke about the dead to each other, either. They kept it hush-hush around any of the white folk, as they would be mighty pleased to string any one of them right up to a post and whip them hard. Aisha had suffered such a fate twice. Both lashings taught her to keep her mouth shut, but that didn't make it any easier to stomach the truth about what they saw. If not for the humming now, all those whispers might have driven her right off the deep end. At least the harmony they created made things peaceful enough for her to focus on her work.

Ain't life just funny like that?

Then, all at once, she grew faint.

The rule had been known from day one: All here in the fields best pick their share. If not, they would pay for it come day's end. Old Miss Mazy eyed Aisha, as if she could tell something wasn't quite right. Not a word passed between them, but even Mr. Gaines, and that fool, Peko, showed some worry for her.

The voices of the dead filled the valley then, even when the living stopped humming altogether. Their song bathed them in supernatural melodies of howls and whispers. They walked among the living, a flickering image here and there, moving with lightning speed. A few of them lingered around her, witness to her suffering. Seeing them made her skin crawl.

Her desperate eyes searched the faces of the living. The noise from the dead seemed to have weakened them, too. They continued picking and wouldn't stop for fear of the whip. Aisha wavered on uneasy legs, her world slanting.

What's happening to me?

A few glanced her way, offering brief flashes of concern. She imagined they would assist her if they could, but they had no choice. Aisha dropped to her knees.

No, please. Get up. Get up.

White puffs spun all around her, looking like a heavy winter snow. The blue sky swirled, shoots of brown and yellow stems darting across both soft and stern faces alike. A lash from a whip brought her temporary clarity.

She stared up at the man, not angered, but sad. Her throat felt dry. As if it had all but closed up for good. "Help."

The callous bastard ignored her. The whirling sensation forced her to the ground, where she clawed at the earth with crooked fingers. Her eyes ached so bad she wished she could pluck them out like a tuft of cotton.

Miss Mazy nodded to Aisha, offering encouragement. Seeing this, Aisha tried to push herself back up. She reached her knees before collapsing again. The whip flashed out not once this time, but twice.

What's happening to me?

Rolling onto her back, she stared up at the blue sky. She heard the faint chirps of birds, the song of the locusts, and the dead gathered around her, their whispers more audible now. She pressed her eyes shut and breathed in the smells of these crops she had known for most her life, recalling the days when she played in these fields as a child, long before her first day of picking. Death came with such a whirlwind that it left her breathless, a bright and shining light blinding her, and the sounds altering into one long droning ring.

—————◆—————

Aisha woke to the night sky and sat up fast. She found herself in the fields and observed her surroundings as if seeing them for the first time.

It's late.

The others would be asleep by now. Not her, though. She felt anxious.

Ain't got no choice.

She stood and walked toward home. When she got there, she stopped out front of the big house. After a long moment of indecision, she entered. Not because she wanted to, but because she had to.

The entrance was peaceful and grander than she remembered. Seeing it now forced her to take in the vases and wooden scrolls along the banister among the darkness. Dim lanterns lit a few areas she could see from here, but most everything was dark as night.

As she climbed the staircase, she gazed at each painting she passed, recounting the specifics of her master's lineage. She saw Master's father, a man she had never known, but one that he spoke of often, mostly when cursing. There was a painting of his mother, too. More paintings along the way offered glimpses of Master's extended family, people who had only visited from time to time. Their pasty white faces adorned with cynical smiles. Paintings of the children followed.

Most visitors would have believed these paintings cost Master a small fortune, but she knew they hadn't. Master had Bony Joe paint all these portraits. Or rather, he had forced Joe to paint them. Old Joe died in the fields the very day he finished the last one. His death had been a trivial matter to Master, which had bothered Aisha as well as the others, though they never spoke of it.

She headed up the rest of the wide twisting staircase into darkness, wondering why she had never braved the upstairs before. Although ominous, some mystical force pulled at her insides, churning them around like butter in a barrel. The closer she got, the more that feeling intensified.

She approached the last step and stopped to look at the painting of Master's wife.

That woman don't smile like that no more.

Master stopped spending nights with his wife after the birth of their last child. He would wait each night until she got all liquored up. Then, while she slept matters off in the downstairs ballroom, Master had his way with any number of young ladies he would sneak upstairs in the wee hours. He kept the ballroom stocked with liquor for this exact purpose, though Aisha doubted the missus would mind his infidelities much anymore. That woman had been lurking around the slave quarters long before Master ever wet his whistle elsewhere. Apparently, she had a thing for the stable hand, and it was a wonder her last baby wasn't born colored.

At the top of the stairs, Aisha came to the room where young Master Mathias slept. What a wicked little boy he was. He had used his slingshot more than once to launch rocks at Aisha. And he had done the same to all the other women, too, but never the men, 'cause he was 'fraid of them.

The boy's covers were pulled up snug to his chin. He remained oblivious to his company. Bony Joe and three others glanced up at her. None said a word. This wasn't a time for words.

Bony Joe entered the boy first. Young Master sat right up and got out of bed and started across his bedroom floor. Aisha backed out of the doorway and into the hall to clear a path.

Behind the boy, the others followed. Not one of them flinched when young Master slid open the hall drawer and removed a letter opener. The boy wielded it like a knife, shuffling his feet down the hall as if dragging sandbags. The boy froze as Joe faltered and his ghastly form vanished in a wisp of smoke.

Lightning fast, Miss Elderton slid into the boy, replacing Joe. The young Master continued on his way, with the last two still trailing. One after another they entered the boy in this manner, the last offering Aisha a desperate glance beforehand. But she didn't like the idea of being inside that boy, feeling what he felt and seeing things through those eyes. She shook her head.

The boy slowed and fell limp at Master's bedroom door. As a result, the letter opener slid across the floorboards, kissing the wooden baseboard under a small table.

Not until an hour later did Master wake and happen upon the boy. He picked young Master up and carried him back to his bed, then returned to his mistress.

In the next room, little Miss Sally slept. There

weren't as many of Aisha's people in this room because the girl had always been such a kind soul. Both visitors looked to Aisha with hopeful eyes, but Miss Sally had brought her food once when she was sick. The girl had tended to a few others from time to time, too. She was a good person and didn't deserve any hurt.

It seemed there weren't enough of them to do the girl any harm, which made Aisha glad. She turned away, seeing their frowns, but she didn't care.

Aisha returned downstairs to the ballroom. She observed the woman sleeping on the worn couch, still decked out in a frilly dress. With her left leg thrown over the armrest, she offered a clear view of her undergarments. None of the men in this room bothered a peek. Those things were of no concern to them.

One entered the missus, and she rose and stumbled. Her hip bounced off a table, nearly upsetting it. The vase on the table wobbled and spun on its base. All of them watched as if willing the vase not to fall. Fall it did, though, and with it so did the missus. Her shrill scream followed the abrupt shatter. Footfalls raced down the staircase and Master's menacing silhouette appeared in the doorway. After a brief pause, he rushed into the room and helped the drunken woman back to the couch. With a scowl pressed upon his face, he stormed out of the room and back up the stairs, mumbling some profanity.

They observed his departure and then each other. None said a word.

After a while, Aisha ventured back upstairs to Master's bedroom. She became one of many standing over the man. His stern face judged them even in his sleep, though she no longer feared the man. None did, despite him having broken most of them more than once.

Beside Master slept one of his girlfriends, Master Dengue's daughter from around the bend. A brief smile crossed the young lady's lips and she whimpered. She yanked the covers up to her chin and wriggled her golden locks against the pillow. Her mouth opened and a light snore emanated.

Byron Smith entered her first. The young woman rose out of bed and walked straight for the window. Faltering halfway, another entered her, taking over. She reached the window and slid it open, wavering again.

Betty, Byron's wife, entered her next. She forced the woman to climb up on that windowsill. A second later the woman plummeted to the ground below, striking the earth below with a *thud*.

Master bolted up from his sleep and ran to the window. He stared down at her. "Martha?"

When he ran down the stairs again, many of Aisha's people followed. He threw open the front door and stood over Martha's motionless body.

"Dear God!" he said. "Are you okay? Can you hear me?" Seeing the bone protruding from her shin, he winced and turned a little blue in the face.

Martha let out a faint moan.

"We need to get you inside." Master raised his voice. "Mazy? I need you now." He bent and carried the girl back inside and lay her on the living room couch.

Miss Mazy entered the room. "Now then, what's all the commotion?" She had no doubt expected to find someone else. Seeing him, she corrected herself with a single question. "Master?"

His tired eyes searched the woman. "She jumped from the upstairs window."

"Oh my, my." Miss Mazy shook her head. "Why would she go and do a thing like that?"

Master looked worried, glancing to the door as if expecting his wife. But she'd had far too much liquor to hear much of anything. He offered Martha spirits to help endure the pain, which she drank greedily.

Mazy tended to the blood with a wet washcloth.

Martha cried at first, then seeing the bone, she wailed. Pain creased her face, her eyes glazing over.

Master stiffened. "When you're done have Peko fetch the doctor." He leaned in close and whispered something to Martha. "And have her parents notified." He sighed. "They'll want to know."

Aisha, among others, watched everything. Most of them followed Miss Mazy to the courtyard long after Master went back to bed. They beat Mazy to Peko, entered the man and hurried the old fool out of bed. Together, they took him as far out into the woods as they could, where he stood dumbfounded. This would delay him if nothing else.

The young woman would suffer, perhaps lose her leg or die. That would satisfy the dead for the night.

+———■———+

Daylight made it hard to see. She woke in the fields again, unsure how much time had passed. The living were an especially quiet bunch today. For a long time, she walked among them while they picked. Only Peko paid her any attention.

When she left the fields, he followed. They spent

the rest of the day walking side by side, saying not a word to each other. Come night they returned to the big house.

Master looks worried.

His pasty face appeared whiter than usual, as if he had gone weeks without sleep. Both his eyes had become dark pits, glossed over, but angry as ever.

The children and his wife had gone to bed early like most days. Some of the others entered the kids followed by Master's drunkard wife. None of those attempts proved effective. All were back in bed as quick as they were up because of Master's alertness and refusal to succumb to sleep.

Seeing this frustrated Aisha. She waited at Master's side along with a few others, staring into the fire until the man started nodding off. They remained patient, counting away the minutes. Soon, others joined them. All of them stood over him and followed when Master got up to turn in for bed.

The second he closed his eyes, Byron Smith took over. Master's body started for the window, but Aisha blocked the way.

She waved her arms and mouthed a single word. *No.*

He had barred the windows. Instead, she pointed to the door.

After a moment's hesitation, Master spun on his heels and advanced to the door. Faltering, another entered. This one threw open the door and stepped out into the hall.

Aisha led the way, directing them where to go.

Another entered Master and walked him down the hall, heading for the table at the end. The last soul to enter Master brought him within a few inches of the table. Only then did Aisha enter the man.

A powerful sensation came over her as if his blood pulsed through her. His anger invaded her essence as if staining her soul a blood red. She could feel his smooth hands, the heat on his rosy cheeks. Strong was the smell of ale on his breath and the sweat on his body.

She dropped the man to his knees. Bent and pawed under the table with his hand until she found what she wanted. Sensing his fear when she brought the letter opener around, she felt the power fading and knew she would soon be expelled if she hesitated any longer.

Turning the letter opener in Master's fist, she thrust his head forward. The cold sting of metal pierced her, followed by instant blinding light.

✦————✦————✦

She awoke in the fields, saw the others and heard them singing. With young Master in control, they had little reason to celebrate. He had been as cruel as his father, having many of her people whipped for nothing more than a passing glance. And he had been especially hard on the women, taking out the frustrations of puberty on the youngest and most helpless of them all. Still, her people rejoiced, including Aisha.

A whip snapped. So close she could smell the leather in the air. Young Master was there, watching over them, doing what he must. It angered Aisha to see him.

Now isn't the time, but soon.

BY THE CRESCENT MOON

CHESTER RUSHED OUT of the house into the dark of night, and Mike hesitated. The cat had been harboring an attitude ever since Mike packed him up and left the city for the foothills of North Carolina.

It would serve him right if I just left him out there.

He couldn't, though. Instead, he did what any loving pet owner would and followed.

A wall of thick fog met his exit, stopping him on the front porch. He ventured a little further into the yard and noticed how the eerie haze lingered across the adjacent field and up the hillside.

It'll be a bugger finding Chester in this mess.

Even the beam from his flashlight couldn't penetrate the cottony mist. The moon, no more than a crescent, didn't provide much help, either.

Determined to retrieve his cat, he mustered up his nerve and sprinted across the clearing for the wooded hills. Unseen marshy pools sloshed at his heels. The ground dipped and swelled, making travel difficult. Still, he made his way across in no time, stopping to catch his breath at the base of the hill. Only then did he see the weathered shack for the first time since moving here.

The residence couldn't have been any larger than his entire upstairs floor. Maybe it had a few rooms at best. The wood siding had rotted, covered with lichen and likely on the verge of potential collapse. Even looking at the small house seemed to cause it to groan and complain of its ill-cared for nature.

"You'd best mind the night, boy."

The woman's gritty voice startled him, and he turned. A small woman wearing ratty clothes and a thick red scarf exited the shadows. In the dense fog, he couldn't discern her features, but her pale wrinkled skin glowed like that of a porcelain doll.

Probably just as fragile, too.

He believed her to be well into her eighties, maybe even older. Despite her concealed features, he saw her eyes quite well. Two brilliant orbs, each bright as a full moon, condemned him much like the elderly often did when they didn't care for youthful endeavors.

Back across the field, hints of light hung in the fog. At first, he thought them fireflies or single-passenger airplanes. Now he saw them for what they were, glimpses of his distant neighbors' dimly lit houses. With each being so hard to see in this fog, he realized he could no longer see the front of his house. He returned his attention to this shack.

Are all the houses out here so rundown?

Not that it mattered. Nothing about this area held much appeal for the city boy in him. Already he missed the busy lights, the crowded streets, all the racket. While he considered himself lucky to have secured such a fine home in comparison to the others, he loathed the fact he had ever taken the job.

Maybe it's not too late to back out.

He eyed the woman. "I'm sorry, but I wonder if you might have seen my cat? His name is Chester, and he has—"

"Mayhap, sonny boy. Could be your cat wandered right up that old trail o'er yonder." She labored to speak. "But you'd best avoid chasin' after any cat on a night like this, especially if it done went up that there hillside."

After a brief moment's contemplation, he extended a courteous hand to the woman. "I'm sorry. My name is Mike Hayborne, and I'm your new neighbor."

She brushed past him, evading his hand, and opting for a position several yards away, closer to her front door. He still couldn't see her face, but those eyes stood out even in the shadows of her porch. They reflected what little moonlight shone in the night sky.

"I know who you be, boy," she said. "All the same, city people ain't got no right messin' round in country folk business. And on a night like this, you better mind yer nose and stick clear of them hills."

Her contemptuous tone somewhat amused him. He slid his hands into his pockets. "Oh yeah? Do tell."

"Trust me when I say this, leave that cat be. It'll either return come morn, or it won't." She stared up the foggy path leading to the hills. "I wouldn't want you goin' and pissin' off any of Madoc's descendants."

He had never heard of this Madoc. As such, it would be difficult to steer clear of him or his people. It was likely just a fable anyway, as this area was rich with stories, full of fascinating lore seeded throughout their history. He had seen pamphlets at every rest stop. Books in every store. These people were obsessed with such tales.

Not him, though. He didn't believe in ghosts or ghouls, let alone cryptic warnings that came from the mouth of some timeworn lunatic. He had seen far scarier things firsthand in the city: car wrecks, bloodied roads, bodies burned to a crisp, robberies, murder, rage over nothing more than a sideways glance. The country was a walk in the park in comparison to what he had witnessed in Chicago.

"That's an interesting story, Miss . . ."

She shook her head vehemently, seemingly annoyed by his determination.

"Well then," he said. "I should be off."

He nodded to her, but in truth he wanted nothing more than to put distance between them. He had far more important business to tend to. Chester needed him.

"Stay clear of them ruins, boy," she called after him. "What's out there ain't for yer eyes."

Offering only a bothered glance over his shoulder, he headed out into the clearing to throw her off. He had wasted his time with the woman, and the fog seemed to have thickened in that short span. His path led away from the hills, but once he was positive she was well out of sight, he altered his route, heading for the hillside.

Upon reaching the top of the first hill, the ground sloped down to a stream. Water trickled along, looking like frothy cream as it sped over the slime-covered rocks. Fog rolled off the stream like vapor from a hot cup of coffee, twirling and twisting among the rows of pine trees that lined the embankment. These trees were so full and tight they blotted out much of what little moonlight shone. If not for this, his flashlight might have been totally useless to him. Now it offered some light to guide his way.

Across the top of the plateau, near a rocky ridge, he spotted several white circles of varying sizes. Crossing to them reminded him of the old woman's caution, wondering if this was what she had been referring to. Upon closer inspection, these rocks appeared to have once been part of some wall. Over time, the wall must have weakened and eventually collapsed. No one had bothered trying to rebuild the wall, likely because it no longer served any purpose.

This must be the ruins.

He studied the fallen wall, how it ran along the ridge for several yards and ended in a large pile of rocks. He followed the rubble to the stack and examined it from a distance. A dark hole revealed itself at its center, perhaps harmless, but he remained cautious just the same.

No sense getting too close.

He considered crop circles, how some deemed those occurrences as pranks. He had seen shows about them and wondered if this too might be some elaborate joke. It didn't sound so farfetched that these people might try to play the new city boy as a fool.

That old woman made it plenty obvious she didn't care for me. Am I the goat here?

He scanned the area, seeing if he could catch anyone spying on him. Maybe they were having a hearty laugh over his bewildered gaze. But no one was in sight.

His eyes went back to the hole; a cascade of rocks surrounded the opening. By the time he raised his flashlight to the cave entrance, it illuminated a single object. Chester's ringed tail curled around one of the larger rocks that surrounded the hole. Before Mike could move, the tail vanished.

"Chester?" he said.

The cat ignored him. He waited a second longer to see if Chester would come out, but the cat didn't.

"Damn it, Chester. Don't make me come in there."

Even as he demanded this of his beloved cat, he knew how stubborn Chester could be. He approached the opening, shining his light into the darkness. More rocks spilled eight feet down into the hole at a hard angle, which looked difficult to climb. But he identified an earthen floor, which disappeared into a void. In that hole, a pair of crystal-blue eyes peered back at him from the darkness, glowing against the moonlight like two orbs, studying his every move.

Mike sighed. "Stupid cat."

With care, he worked his way down the rocks, slipping a few times and stopping to steady himself. When he came within a foot of the floor, he slipped again, this time landing hard on the ground. At least he landed on his feet.

He dusted himself off and examined his surroundings. Venturing farther into the cave, its dank aroma invaded his nostrils. The dry air made him cough. Phlegm gathered in his throat, made it difficult to swallow and hard to breathe. He wanted to leave, to get Chester and go home, but that proved more difficult than he had anticipated.

This is no place for him or me.

Movement captured his attention, and his eyes darted to it. He lit the ground near an opening to his left but saw nothing. Then something moved on his right, and he swung his light around. Again, he saw nothing.

Likely Chester's shadow. He's probably running back and forth between these adjoining caves.

"Come on Chester, I don't have time for this."

When the cat still didn't appear, he used his light to illuminate the rest of the small cavern. On the ground behind him, his beam discovered what he believed a long streak of red paint. It stretched out from his position in a wide brush stroke.

That's odd.

He tracked the path, following the red trail to its end. There, he discovered Chester's corpse, sprawled out and gutted.

He recoiled, overwhelmed by sadness, and crept forward. "Oh, Chester, no."

Feeling tears in his eyes, he studied the cat. Some evil bastard had cut off Chester's tail and used it to lure Mike down here.

Are they playing a trick on me?

If so, it was a cruel joke. Tears sprinkling his cheeks, he heard something behind him. He shone his light about, searching for signs of those responsible for Chester's death.

"Who's there? Come on, show yourself."

No one did, but an eerie sensation washed over him. It felt like he was being watched.

He hurried back to the rocks he had descended moments earlier and tried to push himself up. This was no easy feat, as his boots slipped twice. He made it halfway but slid back to the bottom when his grip faltered.

All he wanted was to get home and call the

authorities; tell them everything he knew about Chester's death. He jumped up and secured his hold on a rock. Once more his foot slipped and he lost his grip, sliding back to the ground below. The worst part was that he heard something moving about in the side caves, worrying now that Chester's killer might not have been human. His ears zeroed in on every sound, his hands trembling and making it more difficult to climb his way out, as the unseen creatures grew bolder.

Bears? Or maybe mountain lions?

Were there even mountain lions in North Carolina? Forgetting his flashlight for a moment, he stared off into the darkness. He imagined seeing the animals he feared. Considering what they might do to him if they caught him here in their lair, his thoughts whirled. He wasn't sure what it was, and he wanted to get out of here before he found out.

Breath held, he kicked one leg up and took hold of the rock again and angled his foot in this time to better secure his position. It was tough to keep his hand from slipping. The longer he held on, the more his fingers trembled. His grip loosened, so he clung with everything he had left.

The darkness moved again, and this time when he looked he saw a single pair of bright eyes blink into existence. His heart hammered in his chest so hard he nearly slid back down again. Forcing himself to regain his position, he clung there like a madman, staring off into the hollow of that dark cave, and trying to scramble his way up.

Then, beyond the first pair of eyes, two more appeared. Mike blinked in disbelief, but the image did not dissipate. Then another set of eyes, and another.

Suddenly, he felt claustrophobic, and almost let go. He shook his head, trying to set his vision right, and once more tried to scurry to the surface. In his effort, he lost the flashlight. It crashed against the ground and rattled across the cave floor where it dimmed, enveloping him in near total darkness.

A flurry of activity followed, moans and groans all around him. He ignored the chaos, focusing only on his escape. He pawed at the earthen walls, pulling himself up with the stones while his eyes scanned for the sliver of moon. Here and there he lost his grip, but he refused to let go now that it had gone dark. No way was he going to drop back into the hollow below.

With great effort, he pulled his way up and threw himself over the lip of the rocks. Managing the surface, he rolled away, free of the hole and inhaled deeply. A split second later he stood, staggered away from the hole, wanting nothing more than to put distance between him and whatever lurked within the cave. But he couldn't stop glancing back, seeing many eyes watching him from the darkness. Like hungry beasts anxious to seize their prey, those eyes tracked his progress. Then they were scaling the rocky wall with ease, several of them all at once.

Mike shrank back with deliberate steps, but still couldn't withdraw his gaze. He needed to see what had killed his Chester. When the first of them stepped out of the hole, his heart skipped a beat. Then the organ went silent for a long moment. When it struck its next beat, his entire body jolted.

What he had thought a boy upon first glance, he now realized was a small man. His scraggly, uneven beard surrounded the crooked teeth protruding from his slackened jaw. The pallid flesh of the man's balding scalp reflected what moonlight stole its way through the crowded trees, revealing long hair pulled back in a ponytail and painted a pastel blue. Streaks of this same colored paint covered the man's face, creating decorative patterns under his eyes, down his cheeks, and across his brow. The paint was so faint that it made it difficult to tell where it ended and the blanched flesh began. The skin hung from his body like soggy clothes that were a size too big.

And those eyes—

A woman joined the man, dressed and painted in the same way. Then another man exited the cave. Mike identified their crude weapons, how their fingers opened and closed on the handles. When a fourth and then a fifth emerged, Mike reconsidered the old woman's caution. She had known this would happen. That meant she might know how to stop it.

When he ran, the miniature people followed. They shouted and chanted, their cries echoing down the hillside and across the valley. In this way their peculiar calls surrounded him, making him feel vulnerable. All the while they wailed and howled, reminiscent of the Native Americans he had seen in old TV shows when he was younger.

There must be a dozen of them, maybe more.

Being larger than these indigenous people, he thought he could take out one or two of them if he had to. Without a weapon, he wouldn't be able to fend off the rest for long. If they meant to use their weapons to hurt him, he would never survive.

He took only a brief second to scan for a fallen limb. When he found one, he ran to it, stopping just long enough to secure the branch. In that brief instant, they gained on him. Two of them crisscrossed back and forth behind him, closing in fast. Their banshee-like screams intensified.

The first caught up to him long before the woman's shack came into view. Before the man could attack, Mike swung the limb wildly. By luck, he connected with the man's neck. The blow knocked the man's silvery blue eyes up to the sky. As if the sight of moonlight were too much to endure, the man squinted, causing him to misstep and stumble to the ground. The others ignored their fallen companion.

Over the crest of the hillside, he finally spotted the old woman's shack. She might be his only hope.

Two of them swung their crude weapons in unison. He dodged the axe, but the hefty hammer struck his ribcage. The contact rattled his bones and drove the wind right out of him. He gasped, staggering forward at an alarming rate. They looked more driven by his temporary inability to breathe. Winded, his lungs felt like fire in his chest, unable to suck in enough air. His world began to spin, making it more difficult to take that next running step.

Again, he gasped, finding some air, but not nearly enough. They prepared to attack again, weapons hoisted over their shoulders, readying to strike.

Air found him in a wheeze, and he didn't delay. Couldn't if he wanted to. His sole purpose to defend himself, he swung the limb out weakly. It pleased him to somehow trip up one of his foes. Another man brought down his hammer, but the limb continued on its upward arc, and with luck, knocked the weapon loose. Weaponless, the latter continued his pursuit, his rage obvious.

Nearly falling down the hill, Mike had almost reached the old woman's home when an arrow whizzed past his head. He glanced back and saw the woman reloading. She raised her crossbow again, and Mike leaned against the cabin. The shaft struck the meat of his left arm, penetrated deep into his muscle and out the other side. The pain in his arm was so intense.

"Owwww! Fu—"

The sight of the arrow in his bicep made him woozy, and he almost collapsed.

On uneasy legs, he threw his weight at the door. He seized the handle, turned, and twisted it with his weakened arm. His hand kept slipping off the knob. After switching hands, defeat consumed him as he realized he couldn't open it. So he leaned back and forced his weight against the wood again. This time the door gave some. Encouraged, he tried again. Despite his effort, the ratty barrier still held. One last time, he mustered up what little strength he had left and threw himself forward.

The entrance burst open, and he spilled in through the doorway. Seconds later, a third arrow quivered in the wall, less than a foot away from his head. He turned and slammed the broken door shut, bracing it with his body while he awaited a thundering onslaught of tiny fists and feet.

When no such commotion came, he slid his back down against the entryway and tried to catch his breath. Each time he inhaled, it came with a wheeze of pain. Something inside had broken.

A rib? Maybe a punctured lung.

"I warned you, boy," the old woman said.

He couldn't respond. His chest heaved, and his arm had gone numb.

The blade of the sickle in her hands glinted as silvery as her eyes in the moonlight that peeked through the curtains. She wasn't wearing her scarf, but the shadows of her dwelling hid her features well. Her steely eyes penetrated him even now, and he saw something inside of those eyes he hadn't before, something he had missed.

She hoisted back her sickle over her shoulder with ease as if she had done this before, perhaps many times. Now she didn't look so old. He slid to his side and scooted away on his butt, trying to escape her. The door crashed against the wall, but he ignored it. She swung swiftly, slicing through air and severed the tendon of his left foot.

"Argggghhh!"

He pulled himself across the floor, still trying to flee. Every time he tried to get to his feet, the tendon gave. After several failed attempts, his chin bounced hard off the wooden planks, ringing his bell enough to daze him.

He rolled over, trying to regain his senses. Standing over him, he saw her beside the rest of her tribe. Had he been so ignorant to this before? Or had the fog been thick enough to keep this secret hidden? Did she ever want to help him at all?

"Wait . . . " he said.

One of these people jumped on his chest. This man took Mike's ginger hair in his hand and yanked it taut. The steel of his blade came fast, quicksilver cutting through the air in a split second of time. It left Mike empty; unable to grasp what happened in the time it took for this man to scalp him with uncanny accuracy.

Together, these people ushered him to the gates of a darkness he had long feared. There, they left him to die.

MANTID

HOW WAS HE supposed to find a crawdad on a night like this, alone on Halloween? Nate Crawford wished he would have chosen *truth*, as opposed to this senseless *dare*, but now it was too late.

Having never cared for silly games to begin with, receiving this dare only intensified his loathing of the task. To think, they never would have concocted such a foolish request if not for his name. Thanks to that detail he found himself far from camp, marshmallow skewer in hand, and only a flashlight to guide him in his quest.

Stepping to the edge of the canal, he wondered if the water was fresh or otherwise. He wasn't even sure whether crawfish braved these waters, but supposed they were the type of creature that could live anywhere. Regardless, he moved his flashlight over the brook, scanning the murky waters for any sign of one. His effort slowed upon noticing the battered farmhouse. Though he remained at the edge of the stream, his light now focused on the structure.

Damn, talk about scary.

As if to acknowledge his fright, a groan escaped the dilapidated building, its busted windows like gaping mouths, the rotted siding covered with lichen and twisted barren vines. A whistle made him leap back, and he circled a large, dark hole in its side with his flashlight.

It's just the wind.

Although he stuck to this conclusion, he also knew it couldn't be further from the truth. The cool misty air sat motionless, and he soon realized just how much he missed the warmth of the fire. Once more, he wished he had chosen *truth.*

What do I have to hide, anyway?

His life was as unimportant as the next guy. He enjoyed sports, a good book, girls, and camping. What was so unusual about any of that? At worst, they could have inquired about his parents, the particulars of their split. Even that wouldn't have bothered him.

A splash drew his attention back to the canal. He lifted his skewer like a trident, keeping his eyes keen on the glassy night water. His vision sank into its depths and registered what his flashlight revealed while it crept across the surface to a swirl of water.

He sighed. *Nothing.*

Then he spotted something. A parade of crawfish sped by, and at first, he was too shocked to react. He thrust the skewer down into a group of twenty or so crawdads. The thin metal rod stuck in thick mud and an instant flurry of activity and pings against the skewer made it difficult to determine whether he had speared one. But, even with the waters becoming so cloudy, he believed there was a good chance he had completed his *dare.*

He eased himself down to a rock that stood just above the water and leaned out for the skewer. When he withdrew it, the impaled creature began to flap its tail. Reaching the shore, he stopped to examine the animal.

What the hell is this?

This creature was thicker than any crawdad he had ever seen, especially around its thorax and abdomen. And it had beady little eyes that seemed to follow Nate as he moved the skewer around to examine the creature.

Well, this isn't a crawdad.

A frown formed as he realized he might end up out here all night.

*Maybe I can pass it off as—*He studied the creature. *Wait a minute.*

He brought the end of the skewer closer to his face and saw the way the creature held its arms back as if preparing to strike. Then it did, pinged its clubbed appendage against one of the metal prongs of the skewer not once, but twice.

*Damned if this doesn't look just like a—*Excitement filled him. *It's a mantis shrimp.*

He had seen a similar one at the city aquarium and thought it such an amazing creature. The crustacean's eyes seemed to examine Nate right back. Its unique front appendages resembled those of a praying mantis. Two distinct types of claws defined these creatures: *smashers* and *spearers*. A *smasher* could strike with the impact of a .22-caliber pistol and *spearers* were more often referred to as thumb-splitters. This one was a smasher, and it flicked its tiny fists at the skewer again, bringing a quick series of dull plinks that vibrated the skewer.

What the hell is it doing out here?

Mantis shrimp lived in the ocean, and while he supposed this water might be brackish, he still didn't think even that proved a suitable habitat. He had read that these creatures lived in the depths of the ocean, where they could prey upon fish, snails, clams, and other small creatures. Yet, here it was.

"Weird."

The shrimp flapped, this time weaker in its effort. He considered letting it go, to head back to camp and inform them he had been unsuccessful in completing his dare.

What could they do?

Before he could decide, the swimmerets ceased altogether, and the mantis shrimp rested unmoving at the end of his skewer.

For a moment, he continued to observe the deceased shrimp. Turning the skewer in his hand, he wondered if it might be faking. He shook the skewer. When he did, he saw something beyond the dead shrimp that surprised him. Dozens of mantis shrimp had gathered at the edge of the canal, all of them staring up at him with their beady eyes.

He leaped away, dropping both his flashlight and the skewer. The light landed facing the skewer. Even now the shrimp remained unresponsive, and the light joined it, dimming to a dull faded glow. But it was enough to see the shrimp's brothers and sisters had started up the side of the embankment and onto the shore, where they formed a broad line. As if sensing his mounting fear, they marched toward him on their millipede-like legs.

At first, Nate could not fathom what they were doing. Considering those claws and the damage they could inflict, though, he thought it better to leave these creatures behind. He stared at the failing flashlight and then the skewer, and thought to grab the latter so he could complete his *dare*. Leaning for it, several of the shrimp rushed forward, thrusting out their club-like appendages.

Whoa, missed.

He slinked away and risked trying again. This time he darted forward, seized the skewer, and thankfully the creature remained at its end. Before he could withdraw his hand, though, a barrage of pings clanged against the metal skewer. Somehow, at least one of them struck his flesh. He nearly dropped the skewer when he yanked his hand away.

"What the hell."

The wound on his thumb produced a quick flush of blood. He winced and squeezed, skewer still in hand, and watched as red flowed out smoothly. It was a deep cut. He glanced at the end of the skewer, and that was when he noticed his capture had gone missing.

He turned, scanned the frosted grasses for the shrimp, but found it nowhere. Though he continued searching, he was unsure why he bothered. Perhaps he thought he might not care for what came next, maybe two equally senseless dares or worse. A piercing stab in his toe forced him to look down, where he discovered a sharpened claw stuck through the front of his shoe.

"Goddamn it!"

The pain nearly threw him off balance, but he was thankful to maintain his footing. He kicked the horrid creature away and several quick clubbing sensations struck his foot when he did. Wielding the skewer like a sword, he tried to fend off these pesky shrimp. Though he hated doing so, when their advance persisted, he retreated to the one place he could, the safety of the nearby farmhouse.

Darkness swelled around him as he approached the entrance. The door hung in shambles from a single hinge, looking as though it might collapse at any second. He slid into the shadows of the room but kept his eyes on the door. There, he heard the *pitter-patter* of marching shrimp on the hardened earth outside, and then the distinct *clickity-clack* as they entered the farmhouse.

Can they see in the dark?

He had no idea but believed they could. This meant they would find him. He stumbled around in the dark, bumping his shin on an old table. Doing so brought him instant pain, but he spun and staggered on, searching for the wall. Upon success, he felt his way across the room, the old sagging wallpaper and marred wall scratching against his fingertips. When he reached the edge, he determined how close they were by listening and turned to the next wall.

Maybe he could trap these creatures inside and get back to camp. In this moment of hesitation, they had already reached his feet, some clubbing and others stabbing. A crushing blow drilled his ankle, and he hobbled away from the wall. One pierced his shoe, striking the thin flesh between his two longest toes, and he screamed, wondering if it had been loud enough for the others to hear back at camp.

It doesn't matter, because I sound like a screech owl.

If he screamed louder, would they hear? Before he

could produce any sound, he tripped over some debris and was falling. He didn't have a chance to brace himself, and crashed hard against the floor, wood splintering under him with a *crunch*. The eerie *clickity-clack* of tiny feet steadily approached him.

He lifted himself to his hands and knees and began to crawl away. But they were fast, and one busted open his knuckle. A stabbing pain came to his left hand, and another at his ankle, then two more crunching blows to his knuckles. He sped away as fast as he could, breathing heavily, his anxiety at a paramount level.

His hand touched something, his fingers worked to define its edges. Their assault intensified at his ankles and shins, but upon identifying what this was, he pulled himself onto the stairs, mindful of their assaults as he kept crawling up. Three or four steps up, his feet cleared the floor. What shrimp had not managed to seize hold of him now gathered below the bottom stair, hammering their appendages against the old wood. Several had managed to crawl up his legs, some into the cuff of his jeans, and others clung to his clothing. They attacked again.

He kicked one away, left it on the first stair. He swiped another away with his hand and caught yet another with his back swipe. And he continued fighting them off until he found himself at the top of the broken stairway, his assailants all left behind, unable to clamber up after him. There, he mustered up the strength to stand, turning and staring down into the darkness where they waited for his return. No easy escape revealed itself that way, so he needed to find another way down. He spun to the first room, stood outside its door, wary of entering. He placed his hand on the knob, and when he did, the door fell away. A loud *bang* followed as the door slapped against the floor, exposing the room beyond.

The moonlight cascaded in through the broken walls. What few leaves still graced the limbs of a tree outside rattled and cast eerie shadows into the room. Among those shadows, he sensed movement. Something big *click-clacked* across the broken floor like well-trained militia. The largest shadow cast by the moon terrified him, beholding appendages bigger than even Nate. At the end of them were large clustered fists. This was what he saw first, before the giant mantis shrimp crept out of the dark.

With a quick flick of its limb, it struck him. The impact knocked Nate back down the stairs. He landed near the bottom with a *crunch*, his body sliding down the last few steps, limp and broken. He gazed to the top of the stairs, where the enormous mantis shrimp glared down at him. The smaller shrimps hurried over, their punches and stabs already riddling his body. Although he could no longer feel their attacks, his mind processed all of it.

They tore off bits of his flesh, the sound of their mandibles chewing away at him. He tried to scream, feeling the madness grow, but produced only a bubbling gurgle. They climbed up on his chest, were at his chin, and crawled about his face. One came close enough for him to stare into its small face, seeing how curious it appeared. When it turned away from him, he was offered a glimpse of the wound in its side where something, maybe a skewer, had pierced it. Seconds later, it pried its way into his mouth and crawled down his throat.

He felt intense pain at the back of his throat again and again, until the creature broke through to his sinus cavity. When it did, Nate Crawford did not just slip into darkness. The horrid pain wouldn't allow it, each blow making his eyes go wide until he could endure no more.

THE UNDERSIDE OF TIME AND SPACE

SPACE, TIME, OTHER dimensions, these things didn't interest Wylen. Kyle's wife, Alice, was the expert on such matters.

So why's he calling me?

Not that Kyle wanted his opinion. Whenever their conversations turned to monsters or the supernatural, Wylen tuned him out. He would start watching TV and even tended to turn the volume up a couple clicks.

Monsters? Who does he think he's talking to?

Those things had always fascinated Kyle, something he had picked up when they were in their teens. Wylen never understood why, as he had always preferred sports since he was old enough to swing a bat or throw a football. So despite Kyle being his lifelong friend, they had their obvious differences.

Kyle was what Wylen's wife, Mindy, referred to as an 'unfortunate' friend. She didn't call him that due to his lack of good fortune, despite a long run of bad breaks. Grief seemed to follow Kyle around, always popping up at the most inopportune moments. It was a big part of the reason why Alice had left him a few years back. Of course, she did come back, but to this day they still argued like cats and dogs.

Personally, Wylen didn't think it a fair assessment of his friend. Kyle hadn't always been unlucky. He had a way of getting caught in the middle, for better or worse. Sure, most of the time it had been bad, but what kind of person kept score?

Mindy, I guess.

She walked into the bedroom, slipped out of her robe, and got ready for bed. When she noticed he was on the phone, she raised her left brow like she always did. That brow judged him, showing her disapproval, especially at this hour.

Most of the time, Kyle only wanted someone to listen. The guy kept detailed notes regarding most of his paranoia in a series of spiral notebooks, but that had never been enough to sort through the issues. Wylen had perused the books on multiple occasions. They read like science fiction; again, not his cup of tea. But who didn't want to let off a little steam now and then? Wasn't it always better when someone listened in on your problems? Wylen himself had detailed every last issue he had with the Yankees game the other night while his wife listened. And she could care less when it came to baseball. Still, she had listened to every bit of it, which made him feel a little better about them losing the game.

Wylen picked up some papers and started crunching numbers. With tax time right around the corner, this took precedence. Numbers were a real thing. He offered a steady stream of indicators to clue Kyle in that he was still there.

"Uh huh."

Kyle went on.

"Got ya."

Then Kyle did something uncharacteristic. He screamed, and hearing it pulled Wylen out of his paperwork and right back into the discussion. This wasn't just an angry shout, either. It sounded terrifying, which caused Wylen to question whether it had come from Kyle or Alice. Whatever the case, the abruptness of it concerned him.

"Kyle?" He held his cell phone at a distance to make sure they hadn't been disconnected. "You there, man? You okay?"

Kyle didn't respond. The strangest sound emanated from Kyle's end.

Sounds like . . . static?

No, it wasn't static. It sounded more like several snapping noises in a row, crackling.

Mindy crossed to him, standing there, judging with that brow again. "What is it this time?"

"It's Kyle—"

She frowned. "Not again."

"No, hon. Just listen, please." He held the phone up for her. "He was going on about some Sci-Fi crap and—"

She hummed. "Sounds like the whole alien abduction thing again."

"No." He regretted the way he had presented the matter. "Not that. Dimensional type stuff."

Her expression tightened like a banjo wound too taut. She didn't look the least bit convinced.

"It's just that . . . he screamed." Wylen looked up at her with hopeful eyes, met only by a stone cold gaze. "I think we should—"

"Uh huh, no way. That man is Alice's problem. Not ours. We're not going over there at, what?" She twisted to the clock. "It's almost one in the freaking morning. Are you kidding me?" She cocked her left brow again. "You want to go all that way just to check up on our *unfortunate* friend?"

His eyes softened on her, weakening her resolve. "What if Alice left him again?"

She huffed. "Damn it."

Mindy didn't say one word to him the whole way there. Not until they were parked outside. "I can't believe you convinced me to tag along." She flashed a wry smile. "I must have been crazy when I married you."

"Yeah," he said, getting out of the car and rushing over to open her door. "Crazy about me."

She pushed out of the car and slapped his behind. "You owe me one, good lookin'."

"Always, my dear."

Wylen knocked, despite the door being cracked open a good three inches. He stared through the gap but saw nothing concerning inside.

"What the hell are you doing?" Mindy said.

He leaned in closer. "Checking things out."

"Oh, for heaven's sake." She threw open the door and the smell of stale food and body odor assaulted them. "Oh God, you must be right."

"I thought she may have left again."

"Good Lord," she said, observing the mess on the coffee table. "Does he do anything other than masturbate and write in those damn journals?"

Wylen shrugged. "Well, if Alice isn't around . . . " As if this explained everything.

"Has he never heard of Lysol?"

Wylen laughed. "Apparently not."

A noise startled them both. Mindy shuffled beside him. He scanned the table for a weapon, anything he could use to defend against an attack. All he found was the TV remote, which he wielded like a sword.

"Who's there?" he said, his voice cracking.

No answer.

"Say it louder," Mindy said, moving in behind him.

Annoyed by her demands, he did. "Who is it? Come on, show yourself."

A large shadow grew against the wall. Someone or something shambled up the hallway. Whatever it was, they did so with confidence.

Both he and Mindy shrank away from the shadow, observing its progress with wide eyes. He couldn't tell whether it was his heart pounding so hard or hers, or both in unison. Either way, it sounded loud and obtrusive in the growing silence, his anxiety mounting.

"That's it. I'm calling the police," he said, forgetting about the cell phone in his pocket and searching for Kyle's.

Seeing this, Mindy tapped it.

"Ah! What the—" She had surprised him, and he lost his grip on the remote. The sound it made when it struck the ground made them both jump, as the back flew off and the batteries rattled across the floor.

A second later he had his phone out but had a heck of a time dialing 9-1-1 on the tiny keypad with his fingers trembling so bad.

The shadow diminished fast as the figure entered the room. Kyle stood before them in stained underwear, his eyes blinking as if he had just awoken.

"Kyle?" Wylen said. His skin still prickled with goosebumps. "What the hell are you doing, man? You nearly gave me a heart attack."

He yawned, long and deep. "Sleeping."

"Really? You were sleeping?" Mindy stormed to the door. "I'll be in the car. Don't make me wait too long or you'll be sleeping . . . on the couch."

Once she left, Wylen turned back to his friend. Sliding his phone back into his pocket, he settled some. "You scared the crap out of me."

"What? Why?"

"Your phone call."

Kyle scratched his butt, smacking his lips as though he had been asleep for days. "I don't remember calling you."

Wylen surveyed the room. Empty beer bottles cluttered the tables. Maybe the odor wasn't body odor at all, but some sort of mind-altering drug. "Were you partying a bit too much tonight?"

"A little." He cracked his knuckles, looking uncomfortable. "Okay, a lot. But I still don't remember calling you." He looked Wylen up and down. "Hey, you want a beer?"

Mindy's gonna kill me. Still, he nodded.

While Kyle was in the kitchen, Wylen picked up the top journal off a stack and paged through it with indifference. There were several smears. Kyle had a bad habit of dragging his hand across the words as he wrote—a curse for some lefties. He caught glimpses of a few familiar conversations, ones he had tried to tune out but had somehow retained bits and pieces. Then he came to the last page, which detailed this exact night's events.

He scanned the entry, noticing stuff about some 'other dimension'. How it was the 'same world, only different'. How Kyle had met his 'alter ego' when the air 'unzipped' right before his eyes. All of it sounded so surreal.

The last words, 'Called Wylen', caught his eye, and he found himself staring off at the kitchen. *He lied to me.* Wylen closed the book and held it tight to his chest. *But why?*

He looked down at the book.

The answer must be in here somewhere.

He heard Kyle's feet plodding back. Wylen slid the book down the back of his pants, under his waistband. He yanked down his shirt overtop the journal.

Kyle stood in the doorway, more alert and staring at him. "You okay?"

Nervous, Wylen adjusted himself on the couch. "Absolutely. Just need a beer to take the edge off."

Kyle held the necks of both beers in his left hand and used a bottle opener in his right to pry off the caps. All the while his eyes scanned the room, the coffee table.

Does he notice?

Kyle's expression eased. "So, Mindy's kind of pissed, huh?"

"She'll get over it like always." Wylen chugged half the beer. "But listen, you can't go calling this late."

"But I—"

"Dude, seriously?"

Kyle grinned. "Okay, okay. Get off my case, will ya?"

It was an admittance of sorts, though not so convincing. Wylen wasn't sure Kyle remembered anything, which bothered him.

"Where's Alice?"

Kyle shrugged.

"Again?"

Kyle didn't seem fazed by this at all. "I don't know. Just not here, I guess."

"Listen, man. You need to get your shit together. If Alice hasn't left you by now she will once she gets a load of this mess."

He stood and edged toward the door, walking backward. After chugging the rest of the beer, he sat it on a table near the door. He bent and picked up the remote, tossed it to Kyle, which he caught in his left hand.

"You should get that fixed." From there, he observed Kyle a moment longer. "I better get going or I'll be in hot water, too."

Then he noticed something peculiar.

He looks different. Maybe somewhat more astute.

Kyle farted.

Wylen grinned. *I need to stop letting his paranoia get the best of me.*

"Clean up around here." Wylen opened the door and stood in the entrance. "And stop masturbating so much."

Kyle spoke in his mother's voice. "It'll make you go blind."

"Careful not to wear out leftie, too, because all you'll have left is good ole rightie. And we both know how weak wristed that hand is for you."

They both laughed.

＋ — ＊ — ＋

Sleep didn't come easy that night. He lay awake in bed, thinking about his encounter with Kyle.

Something had been off, and he couldn't quite decide what.

He reached over, slid the notebook off the nightstand and studied the cover. There were lots of doodles, evidence Kyle didn't always know what to write. Inside he found endless treasures, things he could use to embarrass Kyle with for years to come. His only concern now was this latest entry, the one detailing some of the strangest events Wylen had ever read, and he had read many.

Kyle claimed the hallucinations were due to previous drug use. When they were younger, Kyle used to cut lines of blow on the covers of these notebooks before summer league baseball games. As a result, most of the older covers were worn and tattered. Only the newer covers indicated he had stopped this abuse. However, Wylen believed Kyle still used drugs, just not the kind you snorted. He had seen as much this past New Year's Eve, walking in on Kyle in his garage and seeing the needle in his toolbox. He had never questioned Kyle about it.

This reads like some deranged dream.

All this talk of an opening midair and seeing a person inside that tear sounded ridiculous. It was like something he could find on one of the movie channels. He wasn't schooled in psychology, but for some clone to appear like that seemed rather Freudian. As if Kyle were confronting himself about his own drug abuse. For that clone to try and replace Kyle aligned with this thinking.

Damn if I don't sound pro.

But even if Kyle were coming down from a high, his head still hadn't been screwed on right. Something about his friend had been off.

No, that's not it. More like it was screwed on too tight.

He had expected Kyle to fly off the handle. For him to act maniacal, part of the reason Wylen enjoyed his friend's company. Kyle had come off as being uptight, and that wasn't characteristic of a guy like him. The guy always had been unpredictable, and anything but normal. He was the epitome of abnormal. If he had been coming down from drugs, he should have been all that and more.

Wylen sat the book aside and tried to get some sleep.

⁕

Her scream woke him, and he shot up in bed, stiff as a board. Seeing what she saw took his breath away. There, by the window, the air itself had a tear in it, as if someone had taken a chainsaw to reality. That wasn't the most terrifying part, though. Mindy, his Mindy, stood inside that hole in space, her arms outstretched and screaming for him. Something pulled her from behind, taking her away.

What kind of dream is this?

He rubbed his eyes, trying to force the nightmare to end. When he removed his balled up fists, the tear no longer remained. Still, he leaped out of bed and fumbled for the light. His frigid digits found the switch and flicked it on. Light burned his orbs, forcing him to shield against them.

Another scream erupted. *Mindy?*

Her tired eyes searched him. A brow lifted, judging him even now. "What in the hell are you doing?"

"I'm sorry." He walked to the end of the bed, knowing he must look delirious. "It's just that . . . I saw something."

She sat up in bed. "What? What did you see?"

Don't tell her. You'll regret it.

Nothing about what he had seen could be real. She would have no reason to believe him, and he could picture her cocking that brow at him a lot the next day.

Her brow.

He studied her face, waiting for that brow to rise again. It didn't, but that didn't mean he hadn't seen it. Uncharacteristic of his wife, it had been her right brow that rose. While he believed she could raise either if she wanted, it had always been her left. But that wasn't all.

Kyle's hand.

He had used his right hand to open the beers instead of his left. Also, he had caught the remote in his left hand. Sure, he could have used either hand for both tasks, but he had seen Kyle open hundreds of beers. Having played baseball with Kyle as a kid, he had witnessed his southpaw friend catch dozens of balls.

This evidence added up to something, albeit weak.

"Nothing," he said after a long moment. "Sorry. It's nothing really. Just a bad dream."

She slumped back into bed and yanked the covers up to her nose. "Fine. Let's get some sleep then. Come back to bed."

He hovered over his side of the bed. "I'm going to go get some water."

"Whatever," she mumbled.

When he got downstairs, he fetched a glass and held it under the refrigerator's water feed.

"What did I see?" he said, whispering to himself. Realizing this, he glanced around, paranoid.

No more talking out loud.

He drank half the glass in one gulp.

Sure, either of them might use the opposite hand or brow any day. But both in the same night? What are the odds?

He drank the rest of his water.

Either Kyle's bullshit is getting to me or it's too much of a coincidence.

He placed the glass on the counter and turned fast. A figure stood in the darkness beyond the kitchen, in the living room.

"Who's there?"

The figure moved, swaying back and forth.

Wylen grabbed the closest weapon he could find, his fingers wrapping around the handle of the broom. "I said, who is it?"

A noise startled him, coming from behind.

Mindy closed in on him. She wrapped her arms around him and used her hand to force the broom down. "What are you doing?"

Confused, he glanced over his shoulder at her, then back to the figure in the next room.

She giggled. "It's Kyle, silly."

He studied the gloomy figure and saw she was correct. "Kyle? What the hell are you doing here at this hour?" He scanned the front door. "How'd you get in?"

"Don't worry about it," she said in his ear. "See what he wants."

Since when does she care what Kyle wants?

Still, Wylen approached his friend, concerned and worried. He kept the broom down, but his hold on it remained tight.

Kyle stood unmoving. The white of his eyes

reflected the moonlight from the window. Behind Wylen, Mindy followed.

What's going on here?

All of this was too weird. Mindy would crucify Kyle for something like this, especially if he just showed up in the middle of the night. She loved her sleep. Besides, Kyle would have called first. This wasn't just out of character for him; it was improbable. Both of them almost seemed like . . .

Mirror images.

Tugging on the broom, Mindy almost freed it from Wylen's grasp. He struggled against her, shoving her to the side. His focus remained on Kyle.

With his finger, Kyle carved an incision midair. The rip flayed open and Wylen saw a face peering back at him with an awful wicked grin. An exact copy of himself winked at him, reaching through the opening and taking Kyle's hand. Kyle assisted the Wylen clone's upper half through the hole. Before his clone could pass through, though, Wylen rushed them, broom in hand.

He shoved his alter ego back through the hole. The clone righted itself and tried again. This time Wylen cracked the broom handle across the bridge of the clone's nose, knocking him to the ground on the other side. In that short span of time, Kyle seized Wylen from behind, pinning his elbows behind him and maneuvered him closer to the tear.

Kyle's hot breath tickled his neck. "Don't worry, it'll all be over soon."

"Get up, damn you," Mindy said.

The other Wylen sat up, rubbing his jaw and shaking his head.

"Now is the time," Kyle said. "I can't keep this open much longer."

The other Wylen prepared to cross over again.

Seeing this, the real Wylen came to a sudden resolve. This was not his best friend. Nor was this the woman he had married. They were both imposters. With that, he severed any connection to them along with any restraint.

Wylen lifted the broom handle high and thrust the jagged end back in one swift motion. The broom pierced Kyle's abdomen, forcing him to let go. The clone lunged forward through the opening, hunching over Wylen. He elbowed the fraud away, turned and drove the stick farther into Kyle's stomach.

Then Mindy was on his back, clawing at his face with her fingernails.

He spun, trying to shrug her off. She drove one of her knees into the small of his back. He charged a wall, driving her back into it. Her hold on him loosened, and he rammed the wall again. This time she fell.

Wasting no time, he seized his mother's old candy dish and brought it down on her raised right brow. She collapsed, unconscious and bleeding.

Wylen spun back around and located the fake Kyle, who had risen to his knees, bleeding out on the floor. The tear started to falter. The clone on the other side, however, hadn't yet conceded.

Searching for a weapon, Wylen found the only item available. He threw a candlestick hard, trying to wound the clone. The clone dodged this attack and clawed one arm through the hole.

Wylen rushed forward and seized the arm, trying to stronghold the imposter. It wasn't working. The clone had anticipated this and wrestled Wylen until he stood right next to the hole.

Wylen brought his elbow down on the arm and heard it crack. His clone screamed as Wylen pulled away. A familiar crease of anger showed on the clone's face. When the clone tried again, he moved with purpose.

It happened so fast, Wylen couldn't believe it was real at first. The hole closed, severing the broken arm with a clean cut. The limb fell to the floor with a *thump*, and a small pool of blood spread out beneath the appendage.

Fake Mindy roused, but this time he made sure to end it. He secured a bread knife and made sure neither imposter would cause him any more trouble.

With the task complete, he now felt empty. Everything about time, space, and other dimensions had been made clear. There were indeed other worlds, at least one identical to his reality. The mirror copies of that world bided their time, waiting for the right opportunity to replace the people of this Earth. He worried that nothing he had done so far would stop them from trying again and again.

He stared down at Mindy's clone.

What am I going to do with these bodies?

The doorbell rang, drawing him out of his thoughts. Through the small window, he glimpsed Alice.

Why now?

He had no idea what to do, so he did nothing. He hid, waiting for her to leave.

Once she had, he started cleaning up. Seizing the fake Kyle's pant legs, he dragged him into the kitchen. A piercing scream startled him.

"My God, what have you done?" Alice said.

He turned to her. Saw the shock on her face, the blushing cheeks. "Alice? Wait, listen."

Enraged, she stepped forward. "Wylen, how could you?"

He tousled his blond hair with bloodied fingers; unaware of the mess he made.

Just tell her the truth.

He wanted to. It would sound outrageous, unbelievable at best, but it was the right thing to do.

An arm seized him. He tried to see who it was, but he already knew by the feel of the bloodied stump pressed against his back.

Alice grinned.

A second later, Wylen felt himself being yanked back. He drifted among the remnants of a surreal world, one full of chaos and destruction and death. Right before the hole closed for good, his one-armed clone pushed through.

OUTCASTS: THE SICK AND DYING
2—GEMMA NYLE

GEMMA HAD SEEN it all. A huge meteor came close to wiping her out of existence, missing by only a few hundred yards. She had felt warmth as it passed, watching several smaller fragments pulverize Earth. The dark clouds formed almost instantly and remained for days to come. She had known at that precise moment there would be no return.

Despite the fact they had contacted her since the disaster, she wasn't sure returning to Earth would be any better than being stranded out here alone. Besides, they weren't going to risk bringing back anyone who was still sick with a transmittable disease.

Above all else, she felt the sickness moving through her body, evading their medicines in an attempt to hold on to every last opportunity to kill her.

She had once been optimistic about her chances. Not anymore, though. She had given up long ago. Besides, she had no family left on Earth, no friends, nothing. She had burned every bridge prior to this experiment, knowing even then the probability of return had been slim. This, all of the destruction and fire below, cemented her fate.

So why wait?
She knew that answer, too.
Because they gave you no way out.
There it was, out in the open for her to consider. She supposed she would have ended things sooner if they had given her the option. What did she have to live for?

⁕——✦——⁕

She woke, seeing another pod and thinking nothing of it. They crossed paths from time to time with so many of them in orbit. When the pod spun around, it offered her a brief view of something unexpected.

The man inside the pod had somehow removed the joystick from his dashboard. Her eyes examined her own joystick before returning to him. He had driven that length of metal right through his eye socket and up into his brain. Blood had dried on his face, one thick streak of red. What she could see of his skin, it looked gray. Despite all this, his expression seemed pleased.

"Yuck," she said.

His pod floated away. She watched until it became a tiny dot in the distance and could no longer be discerned from the rest of space.

"Okay, that's not for me."

She examined what other options she had, but there weren't any. At best, she might be able to smash her fists into her forehead, but she doubted that would do anything but produce an awful headache. Even then, the pod would do its best to rid her of the ailment.

"Oh my." The thought swelled up inside her without warning. "I don't want to die."

For once, it was true. She wasn't that old. Even if

she got back by the time she reached forty, she would have plenty of time to make a new life for herself. She could start over, and judging by the sight of Earth, others would be joining her.

She felt hope for the first time in years, closed her eyes and pressed the call button. "I don't want to die."

Nothing but static.

"Hello? I don't want to die. I don't want to die. I don't want to die. I don't *want to die.*"

More static at first and then, "212276, are you reading us?"

Elation filled her. "Yes." A giggle escaped her. "I read you."

"This is CDC ground. Please remain patient. We're working to bring the pods back to Earth. This will take some time."

"Yes," she said. She felt her heart swell. "I'll wait. I'm hopeful."

With that, she felt something else, something she had never expected. It was as if whatever dark shadow had followed her around for so long suddenly lifted from her like a black veil. Hope alone would carry her until the time came to return home.

THE GRIFFON

LIGHTNING HAD DESTROYED the griffon. Not just any statue, but one that had already been paid for and would be picked up tomorrow. He rushed out to the garden with only moonlight to guide him. Upon reaching the sculpture, he discovered three pod-like indentations at its core.

They look like eyes.

Each about the size of his fist, there was no apparent difference between them.

Fossils, maybe?

He supposed they could have been preserved in the granite slab for thousands of years. Maybe they had even weakened the statue. He wondered if he might find similar indentations throughout the rest of the shipment.

That's what you get for buying cheap rock.

Regret consumed Ian, knowing much of that shipment of granite remained in his studio. Would everything he created with the stone be ruined?

Refocusing on the indentations, he considered whether these oddities might be pockets of air formed over the years by creeping water.

Somehow, he doubted it. Their oblong shape was too perfect.

Could be some sort of fruit. Or maybe—
Eggs.

He ran a single finger along the inside of one hollow and detected a strange moss-like silkiness to it. For some reason, he held the finger to his nose. A pungent smell brought tears to his eyes. Bile rose in his stomach, difficult to settle.

Bending to wipe the finger on the damp grass, a rustle of leaves drew his attention to the garden. Without a flashlight, he saw nothing but the shapes of decayed plants. A burst of lightning crept across the sky, highlighting the gardens, but still he saw nothing.

Probably a rabbit.

He returned his attention to the sculpture.

Now, what can I do with you?

It disappointed him that more than five months of work had been reduced to this, a pile of ruptured rock. He recalled feeling elated when he had finished the griffon. Now, in its current state, the sculpture's cracked head seemed to sneer at him.

And I already spent the deposit. He kicked the stone. *Maybe I can convince them to take another piece.*

He had a handful of finished pieces. If nothing else, maybe they would permit him the time to recreate the griffon. Even then, he doubted he would be able to capture the exact look.

Well, maybe I can repurpose these scraps.

"Hoo, hoo, hoo."

Three identical sounds arose from another location seconds later.

A barred owl maybe?

Though he had never been much of a birdwatcher, it was a welcome distraction from his worries.

He examined the granite again. *Maybe I can sculpt an owl or two out of what's left. Maybe . . .*

A trio of hoots arose from the original location, followed by two more from the gardens.

That's a lot of owls. Must be some mating ritual.

It was best to chalk this loss up to bad luck. He decided he would clean up in the morning, and headed back inside. Unease escorted him to the door, as rustling noises trailed him. And they were gaining on him.

He quickened his pace. When he reached the door, once inside, he spun and slammed it shut. Staring out through the window, he saw nothing of consequence. Even then, it took a moment for his heart to settle.

In bed again, his mind drifted through the early stages of sleep. When something crawled across his thigh and leaped down from the bed, his eyes widened. He heard it scamper across the floor and forced himself up, identified nothing out of the ordinary and checked his clock.

Only got two hours of sleep.

His eyes refocused on the floor, thinking about what he had heard.

Must have been a dream.

He threw himself back in the bed, folded his hands behind his head, and started to drift off again. A strange noise startled him.

Gazing down his lanky frame, and then beyond, he explored the darkest recesses of the room. He checked every shadow but saw nothing.

This is silly.

Obviously, he wasn't going to get any sleep. He sat on the edge of the bed, sank his face into his hands, and rubbed his temples, hoping to encourage the life back into his skull.

"Ouch! What the— Fuck!"

The pain in his foot made him sprawl back against the bed. He banged his crown against the headboard and shot back forward in time to see an unidentifiable creature scurrying across the floor.

Anger filled him. "Goddamned rats."

The trail of tiny bloodied footprints on the carpet reinforced this belief. Only, he had heard something, too. And it hadn't sounded like any sort of rodent.

Was it . . . laughter?

He rubbed his foot, frustrated by the thought of such an infestation. Unable to stop thinking about it, he drew back his fingers and stared at fresh blood on their tips.

Should have never moved out here.

Holding a sock to his foot, he hopped across to the bathroom. There, he wet some tissues and dabbed at the wound, revealing a semi-circle of punctures, all of them together about the size of a quarter. The blood flushed back quick, oozing.

No rat did that.

At least he didn't think rats had so many teeth.

Do squirrels have teeth like that? Or possum?

From the safety of his bathroom, he scanned the bedroom, but whatever it had been, it wasn't showing itself now.

He sighed. *Dr. Siebel's gonna want to give me rabies shots now.*

The thought made him squirm, and his eyes

continued to scan the room, the floor, the bed, everywhere. Then he did see something. Two creatures, unlike anything he had seen, sped right for him. A third leaped down from the mattress and landed on the floor with a solid *thump*. It joined the others in their pursuit. Seeing this, he fumbled with the door, leaving a smear of blood on the tiled floor when he found the knob and leaned hard to slam it shut. He had closed the door just in time, too. Two distinct *thuds* rattled off the other side, indicating just how close it had been.

But that's only two.

From the other side of the door he heard, "Hoo, hoo."

Three similar hoots echoed from somewhere inside the bathroom. And he couldn't deny the sudden weight he felt on his shoulder. The hairs of his ear prickled, surprised by the creature's breath. Ever still, he observed himself in the mirror and saw the creature up close.

It couldn't have been much taller than a squirrel. Sparse stubbles of hair peppered its scrawny frame. Thin batwing-like ears saddled its knobby head, no bigger than a child's fist. Two enormous bloodshot eyes stared back at Ian's reflection. One of its paws clung to a tuft of hair and the other to Ian's ear. Then, seeming to grin at him before it did, the creature bit down hard on Ian's earlobe.

"Goddamn it!"

He flailed his arms, trying to throw the creature. Without caring what he struck so long as he rid himself of this monstrosity, of this pain, his elbow crashed into the mirror, shattering it. Glass tinkled on the sink and floor, all around.

He rammed the closet door, splitting the wood, and fell backwards, wrapping himself in the shower curtain. A smothering sensation fell over him as he struggled to untangle his body. Finally, he rammed his midsection into the sink, which shot him forward and thankfully dislodged the creature. The tiny thing landed in the sink among the shards of broken glass.

Tearing down the curtain, he left it behind and glanced at himself in the mirror. His earlobe was gone. Then he glared down at the creature, watching it scramble up the edge of the sink. To Ian's horror, it held the fleshy morsel of his ear to its mouth. Before Ian could do anything, the creature ate the lobe whole, leaving behind only a streak of Ian's blood on its pointed chin.

"Shit," he said, feeling woozy. "What are you?"

The creature sported a devilish grin.

Seeing this made Ian boil with anger and fear all at once. He brought his fist down, trying to smash the beast. It jumped away faster than Ian could bring his balled fist down on the Formica counter. Bits of broken glass embedded in the meat of his hand, intensifying his pain.

"Ye'ow."

He dug slivers of glass out of his hand one by one, cursing with each he freed. Afterward, he searched the bathroom, rummaging through the cabinets, the shower, throwing soap and shampoo and anything else he found about the small room. He found no signs of the creature.

"Where are you?"

A weapon will make this easier.

Wincing, he dabbed several tissues at his bleeding

ear. They stuck, turning an instant red and dangled there oddly. He braced himself behind the door, shrugged it open and stood in the doorway, waving his arms like a madman. The force in which he did this caused the door to rebound off the doorstop. It bounced off the wall and smacked against his back, startling him enough that he leaped several feet out of the bathroom.

All three creatures gathered in the middle of the bedroom, staring up at him with drooling mouths.

"Hoo, hoo." This one rushed low, sinking its teeth into Ian's big toe.

He tried to kick it away, but another assaulted his calf. This sent his body into an awkward pose. Unable to stop what had been set in motion, he fell, crashing hard against the floor.

Taking advantage of his collapse, the third attacked the small of his back. Ian flailed a hand at the one on his leg. Its sweaty skin cooled the back of his hand long enough to send the beast tumbling across the floor.

Dazed for a split second, it rushed him again, this time digging its tiny teeth deep into the flesh around his bellybutton.

The hurt was electric. "Ahhhh . . . "

"Hoo, hoo, hoo."

He lifted himself to his knees, seized the creature at his stomach with both hands and pulled hard. Relentless, the beast clung to his flesh, tearing away a thin strip of skin from his bellybutton when it finally came free.

Ian shrieked.

Staggering forward on his knees, dizzied by the pain, he observed how it nibbled away at his thumb. It gnawed the digit like a miniature ear of corn. When Ian shifted the creature to his other hand, it bridged the gap without pause.

Ignoring the other two, Ian reached back and threw out as hard as he could. The thing came free, but not without taking a rather large chunk of Ian's palm with it. A splatter of blue exploded on the wall. Cobalt droplets raced down beige paint, followed by its slumping corpse, which left a thick streak of the unusual blood.

Seeing this, the other two creatures retreated to the bathroom where he should have braced the door to trap them and called for help. Yet, with his anger consuming him, he sprinted into the kitchen instead. Distracted, he dug through the drawers, secured a meat tenderizer and a serrated bread knife, wielding one in each hand and tiptoed back into the bedroom.

Foreseeing their attack, it did not altogether surprise him when the bathroom proved vacant. Still, he listened for movement but was met with only dreadful silence.

He stormed farther into the bedroom, no longer concerned whether he stained the carpet or not. The smudge of blue blood had already dried, now an awful bruised purple. A pile of dust remained in the spot where the corpse had fallen. As he neared the bed, he noticed the open window. The after winds of the storm teased at the drapes.

Oh, thank God.

He rushed to the window, abandoning the weapons on the bed. Leaning his hand on the sill to shut it, the window slid down fast and hard. It crushed the fingers of his left hand, while the cord of the blinds coiled around his neck like a python. He pawed at the windowsill with his right hand, trying to free himself. Meanwhile, the pressure around his neck grew tighter, making him light-headed.

A swift blow to the back of his head sent his crown through the pane. A shower of glass exploded into the night sky, highlighted by moonlight and a burst of heat lightning.

"Hoo, hoo."

Another creature answered this call as if coordinating their strike. "Hoo."

One bit down hard at the back of his neck. He awaited the second assault, but it never came. As he regained some of his senses, he watched as his studio door opened and then closed.

He lifted himself out of the broken window with some effort. Jerked his hand free, creating awful scrapes of skin that gathered at his knuckles. This pain was nothing compared to what he had already endured. Seizing the creature at his neck, it revisited the handiwork of its fallen companion. A tender strip of flesh tore away in its teeth, bringing sharp pain.

Ian pawed at the bed, leaving streaks of blood on his sheets. When he found what he wanted, he brought it around fast and without thought. Blue blood sprayed in all directions as the tenderizer pulverized the creature he had pinned against the floor.

Afterward, he deserted the tenderizer. He stood and seized the serrated blade, his sights set on his studio. Staggering to the door, he opened it without caution and slid into the darkness of the room, letting the door close behind him. The absence of light swallowed him whole, but revenge consumed his every thought.

"Nowhere to run now, little piggy. I've killed all your friends."

He heard the feet scampering, but it sounded like more than one.

"So, you've got another friend, do you? Well, I'll kill him, too."

He swiped for the cord of the light that hung from the ceiling. When he found it, he yanked hard, which sent the light swinging in a pendulum-like arc, casting its warm glow here and there, everywhere. Each pass revealed the fate of his latest shipment of granite.

An avalanche of rock came from somewhere behind him. He turned and found several pieces of granite had been stacked against the door, blocking his escape. Within the shadows he heard slurping noises, the sounds creatures make when they're hungry and food comes within reach.

He dropped to his knees, dove for the door, and started throwing the pieces of granite aside.

Behind him, a chorus of creatures erupted, all of them hooting in horrifying unison. "Hoo, hoo, hoo."

ADAPTABLE

DAVIS HID AMONG unfamiliar men and women, though it unnerved him to think of them as such. Although humanoid, they were anything but Homo Sapiens. With grotesque bulbous eyes and hulking forms riddled with gills and fins, he believed them water breathers, but they endured this atmosphere as well as he did. In fact, he had identified a single weakness in this species in their aversion to sunlight, likely the reason they inhabited this underground city.

He had come to loathe this metropolis. One day, he would escape, but for now he remained a prisoner. Though he posed little threat to such formidable beings, they had kept the entrance guarded ever since the incident three months earlier, when he first arrived. He waited, loitering about the cobblestone streets to observe the path. Although he took care not to draw attention, he doubted he would be able to fool them forever. But as long as they continued to protect that gate, he had no other choice.

He prayed daily, implored God to liberate him from this place, which he also believed a feeble hope. Each day, he struggled to cling to what optimism remained. He had witnessed firsthand what happened to those who were caught; the precise fate of the young man who had accompanied him to this place.

His assistant, Edward, and he had uncovered this dwelling by mere accident and thought nothing of its seclusion at the time. It was what they spied in the darkness below that enticed them to proceed deeper into the cavernous opening. When they had nearly descended the entire way down the path, the gilled people revealed themselves. With luck, the large boulders scattered about hid him well enough, and they only spotted his friend. Upon Edward's capture, they ripped the man in half. Fleeing had proved futile, as they blocked the way out and headed his way.

Terrified by his friend's demise, he had been forced to search for an alternate escape. A hint of the waters flanking the elevated path had seemed his lone option. He dove without further contemplation. If not for the obscurity of its depths, they might have hunted him down and killed him as well.

Soon after, he clawed at the shore, choking on water and gasping to fill his lungs. There, he took shelter, secluded from their city. He fed off strange mushrooms that lined the ceilings of their sewers. When he grew tired, he took refuge on the decrepit shore, inside a section of one of the large stone pipes that had broken away.

Without the sun's illumination, he saw subtle grays and what black hues the shadows offered him. The only real colors he could identify were the forest greens and bruised blues of their aquatic flesh. This distinction of color proved his first challenge at blending in. Already, he struggled to maintain his humanity. Somehow, he always found the will.

Early on, he had been fortunate enough to filch an overcoat. He flipped up the lapels and knotted a tattered scarf around his neck to conceal most differences. Each day started the same, using the unpleasant clay produced by their waste to tint his pale skin. The mud had an atrocious odor, but he tolerated the stench for survival's sake. Their scent aided in his masquerade.

Staring at the exit, he stuffed his hands into his pockets and wiggled his fingers. Hundreds of tiny objects poked at his flesh. But what good were diamonds to him here, where creatures observed him with suspicious eyes? If he could not escape, collecting them would have been pointless. Today, luck favored his determination.

Once the last of them left the exit, he hurried with apprehension up the stone path. As he ascended the narrow ledge, he glanced back, expecting to see them trailing him. Because of this anxiety, he tripped and they heard him crash to the ground. Three sizeable gilled creatures bounded after him, and he shrugged off his cover to flee without limitation. In doing so, he had surrendered the diamonds. But he didn't fret, as his freedom had become more valuable than any treasure.

Beams of sunlight trickled down through the canopy of trees outside, the first light he had seen in a long time. His success all but guaranteed, he shielded his eyes and hurried along. All three pursuers came to an abrupt halt, hissing at him from a distance. They muttered words in a language he didn't understand, although their tone suggested much. After a long moment, they shrank back into their lair.

He clambered the rest of the way out of the cave. The sun felt unnaturally hot after so long without its warmth. A drizzle of rain cooled him, and he felt anxious for it to wash away his mask. Soon, the last tie to this dreadful place would be gone and with his confidence high, he crossed to the path that led away from this cave. There, in the clearing, he spotted three hunters and waved. In their eyes, he saw fear. They lifted their guns and fired without hesitation. Two shots whizzed to his left. A third penetrated deep into the meat of his thigh, grounding him.

He clutched the wound and dragged himself back to the mouth of the cave. With the sun teasing through the trees, only then did he notice the frightful change. His pink flesh had turned an awful green. He rubbed at it with fervor, but it would not fade. His greatest fears were realized when he retreated back to the precise dwelling he had only just escaped.

WHEN THEY COME

NOBODY BELIEVES IN monsters until they start showing up in broad daylight, their corpses lying right out in the open. Why should they? Monsters are mythical creatures, lore meant to scare children. That was Addison Parker's experience when one first appeared just off the turnpike, across from Ghost Lake.

She had helped gun down the creature—or at least she believed she had. In truth, she hadn't known what severity of weaponry would be required to do so. She just fired her gun into the horizon and prayed. Riddled with bullets, its silvery silhouette could be seen for miles. She saw it well afterward, down the street from where she stood. She had gotten close enough to stare into its bulbous eyes, but the CDC had marked the surrounding area off, so she stopped there. Only military had made it this far, and she found herself staring at the gaping hole where its trachea once resided, trying to put together what the wound meant. She observed its shimmering scales, the cavernous mouth with a picket fence of sharp teeth inside.

What an unusual creature.

At least, that was her first thought. The creature

had been a singularity like Bigfoot or the Loch Ness monster, until it wasn't.

A similar looking monster emerged a week later. Again, she had gotten a glimpse of the fallen creature and nothing more. Far smaller this time, she thought it somewhat reminiscent of a massive werewolf, only with gills and slick rubbery skin. It looked like . . .

The Creature from the Black Lagoon?

Kind of, she guessed. She found herself dreaming of another world. One where aquatic titans roamed the seas and smaller creatures ran wild through alien woods and over foreign knolls. She pictured herself among them, guns blazing, fighting the good fight. But no matter how much she wanted to go to war, she doubted it would ever become reality as she hadn't made the cut for the frontline yet.

More creatures of all shapes and sizes followed in the coming weeks. Some had fur, others scales, and then there were those that fell in-between. She had viewed each monster from a distance and learned what the armed forces were up against. But she had never gotten *really* close until this morning when she had been assigned to a post a few city blocks away.

Once the media caught wind of these monsters, the military quickly established a perimeter. Army reserves like Addison were to maintain that line, an unfortunate duty that kept her out of the action, though she did not take the job lightly. Together, they were the last line of defense, and she knew what that meant.

A lost dog managed to break through the lines and wander about, howling at the monster in the distance. She removed a stick of gum from her flak jacket pocket and chewed, watching the dog. Overhead, the gulls cackled, and the dog ran for the creature. For a moment, this surprised her, and then she found herself somewhat jealous of the dog. Even it would see more action than she did.

So goddamned bored.

A helicopter swerved in the distance, airlifting one of the deceased creatures to a local Air Force base. As a result of the 'copter's projected path, reporters were privy to a distant view. Anyone using a cellphone would capture nothing more than a speck. But those photographers equipped with long lenses snapped photos by the dozens, hoping to capture just one with any sort of clarity. Dressed in fine suits and carrying unfamiliar weapons, a different sort of soldier, men and women handed out money as if it were candy. They roamed freely, making other arrangements when one of the reporters couldn't be bought. Not one of those photos would see the light of day.

Addison could care less about what the photographers saw, though. Sooner or later this was going to get out. She imagined any one of the tall buildings that lined the city streets might offer a better view of that monster. No matter what they did, how much they paid or what force they employed, a picture would eventually make it out to the public. This had all transpired too close to civilization for that not to happen.

Just as entertaining as the monsters were the people. The military had shut down the local beaches. As a result, the boardwalk was devoid of business. Many purveyors of souvenirs had taken to the streets in an effort to sell their wares. They lugged around armfuls of T-shirts that depicted strange creatures, stuffed animals and plastic cups, all of this paraphernalia stamped with the title: '*Jersey Monster*' in easy-to-read bold lettering. It added to the buzz outside the taped-off circumference where she patrolled.

With the armed forces so focused on containment, several groups of people took advantage of the chaos. They ransacked local houses and stores, burned what they could, and left a wake of bedlam wherever they visited. She observed some of them off in the distance, a crowd of maybe forty men and women. They rocked a police cruiser back and forth, screaming and yelling while they worked. Several minutes later, the car toppled onto one side before rolling over on its roof. The crowd cheered, chugging beers and chanting nonsensical comments before moving on like a swarm of bees.

The young threw Frisbees or tossed footballs, playing any variety of tailgating games along the outskirts of the crowds. She heard elders speaking of days long past, telling stories of monsters she knew hadn't existed anywhere but in their aging imaginations. Then there were the Jesus freaks that stood on makeshift platforms and preached about the imminent end of the world. How only God's chosen would survive this atrocity and be permitted entry through the pearly gates. All of these people seemed more interested in each other than any monster. Despite the annoyance, they made an already tedious task somewhat bearable.

She swung back around and observed another monster in the distance, stumbling forward on shaky legs. Sure enough, they could all see it, every last one of them. Despite so many having their cellphones out and ready, few seemed capable of taking any actual pictures in light of what they viewed. Most were either too stunned or terrified to do anything but stand there, eyes wide and mouths agape.

What the hell did they expect?

One elder gun advocate drew a pistol. She turned to address the issue, but another civilian man came rushing for her. She spun, readying for his assault, but he sped past her and dove into the air, tackling the old man. The gun rattled to the ground and the man straddled the older man, landing blow after blow into his face. Leaving the elder man unconscious on the ground, the younger man seized the gun and hurried into the frenzied crowd.

This is getting out of control.

The *suits* tried to maintain peace, perhaps sensing no further need to conceal anything. That was when she spit out her gum, abandoned her post like many others had, and ran right for the creature. She lifted her weapon and fired off several rounds into the air, trying to scare off the pedestrians. As a result, people fled in every direction, screaming and running among the soldiers. Civilians found themselves being wrestled to the ground when they got in the way. Even she took down a few.

They're keeping me from my destiny.

Most wore dazed expressions. Some remained still, their eyes pressed shut, and breathing fast and heavy. At least a few of these people carried concealed weapons. Yet, like many citizens, when the time for bravery came, they cowered like everyone else who hadn't been trained in combat. Most wanted nothing to do with any part of this fight and sought refuge wherever they could. War, any war, had a funny way of doing that to people, defining the sort of person they were meant to become. Addison had long embraced what kind of person she was and had no problem charging in headfirst.

Four blocks from her target, the ground started to tremble. The shaking forced her to a stop, making sure she wouldn't have to abandon the roadway. She stared at the monster, the adrenaline rushing inside of her and coming to a boil. Then the creature burst into flames, and her elation deflated in an instant.

Damn. They're bombing it.

Nearly everyone slowed when they saw this. Those closest to the monster were firing mortar shells. Bombs cascaded around the creature, bringing more destruction to the surrounding municipality than they did the monster. One round struck the monster in its chest, fire bursting up its torso and rushing into its face. It roared, and then staggered as if losing control as it spun to face the dunes.

Every armed soldier, Addison included, chased the beast. However little their gunfire did, she felt renewed exhilaration and wanted more than ever to bring the creature down. At first, she heard only rifles, but soon, machine guns, too. Grenades then missile launchers added to the symphony of destruction. Somewhere off in the distance she identified a mechanical rattle. A tank settled into place and fired.

The large green monster swerved on uneasy legs. It crashed through an entire block of apartment buildings before falling dead.

No one prevented her from approaching the monster this time. She moved around it, getting as close as she wanted, observing every detail. Up close, these beasts no longer seemed like something out of an old kaiju movie. Dull colored scales about the size of a baseball cap covered the flesh, which felt cold and clammy to the touch. Sharp claws the size of skateboards intimidated her even now. With no scales on its underbelly, she believed that its lone weak spot. Then she noticed the sacs beneath its chin and how one of them had been blown wide open. Remnants of flesh hung from the carcass like meaty drapes.

Hmm, maybe they're gaseous.

The monster's mouth smelled like a field treated with manure. It had huge pointed teeth, the gums around each base worn. The eyes, large and gaping, gazed out into space, and she wondered if its brain might still be processing its demise.

"Christ," she said, not fully understanding she had spoken aloud.

A 'copter flew in fast, accompanied by two busloads of workers. It hovered over the creature long enough for the crew to secure the cables around its massive body. Several minutes later, they transported the monster away as they had all the others. She watched until the 'copter was well out of sight.

"You there," said a man.

Her eyes found the general, and she snapped off an instant salute.

"No, no. Stop that." He grumbled something under his breath. "Come here."

She hurried to his position, stiff as a board and her arms at her sides. "Yes, sir?"

"At ease. At ease." He looked bothered by her attention to detail. "There's no time for any of that right now."

She eased some.

"Gather what soldiers you can and reinforce this front," he said, staring off at a dust-filled horizon.

"But sir . . . " She glanced to the whirling storm, thinking it looked closer. Her eyes went back to the general. "What about the soldiers up—"

"Didn't you hear me?" He seized her shirt collar and shook hard. "Stop that nonsense." His expression turned grim. "There is no one else." He waved his hand dismissively. "This is all that's left now. There are no reinforcements. This is it, damn it." Worry flashed in his eyes. "Now get those soldiers and secure that front."

She hurried off, stopping here and there to pass on the order. Soon, other soldiers joined her and formed a line to hold back the swirling obscurity. Together, they marched forward, closing in on the winds that now roared around them. It became difficult to see anything.

"Good Lord," the soldier next to her said.

She echoed his concern, though she said nothing in reply.

He glanced her way. "They should have left it sealed."

"Left what sealed?"

His brow furrowed. "That crack back by the first one. Didn't you see it?"

She shook her head.

"They opened up some gateway. It leads straight to Hell if you ask me."

Mesmerized by his words, she stopped. He moved on.

A gateway to Hell?

Was there such a place? She ran back to him. "Are they gonna close it?"

"What?" He looked at her as if she were crazy, and then fired off a few rounds into the darkness before turning back to her. "How would they do that?"

She didn't know. All she did know—

Two creatures materialized on the horizon, their silhouettes moving among the haze. One of the monsters had a dreadful white skin tone, which stood in sheer contrast to the other's bluish-gray tinted flesh.

Gunfire broke out, the frontline raced toward the creatures, and she followed. Focusing their attack, the white monster went down fast, its hide somehow more vulnerable to their weapons, perhaps the milky white consistency related to its maturity. The bluish creature, on the other hand, reared back on its hind legs as if preparing to fight back. Many soldiers took defensive stances, unsure of what to expect.

The creature leaped into the air on unsteady wings. It flew high enough to vanish into cloud cover, reappearing a full minute later. It circled them in a breathtaking spiral, cutting through the air with awkwardness. Then, as if a novice with flight, it plummeted hard, crashing and decimating the local Burger King. Another building collapsed when the creature stretched out its wings and flapped them in an effort to fend off the ensuing gunfire.

It took to the sky again. A sudden blast from a tank ended the creature's brief, but devastating flight, taking out most of its left wing. The monster shrieked, ambling away as if trying to soothe the wounded appendage. This afforded the soldiers time to reassemble. Once they had shored up their lines, they opened fire again.

The tank discharged, this time gutting the beast. The soldiers applauded, hooting and hollering, all watching the monster sway. In a brief moment absent of gunfire, the monstrosity collapsed face-first, intensifying the cheers.

Addison didn't stop to celebrate. She gathered up what weapons she could find among the dead and wounded. Trying to ignore the overwhelming exhilaration that rushed over her, she stuffed clips into her flak jacket and strapped two guns over her shoulder before loading up with grenades. Seconds later, she charged deeper into the storm.

Two others followed, perhaps as interested as her in seeing this come to an end. She recognized Miles Batson, having gone through basic training with him. While they hadn't been friends, they knew each other well enough to have formed a semblance of trust.

He nodded at her, and she grinned.

The other could have been a civilian dressed in soldier's gear for all she knew. Enough of it had been scattered around. Then she saw the camera around his neck and realization hit.

As long as he fires that gun first and foremost I don't give a crap.

The winds dispersed as they neared the place where the second flank went down. Whatever crack that soldier had referred to couldn't be far from where they had spotted the first monster, and she had a good idea of where that would take them.

She found a Jeep and saw the keys were still in the ignition. "Over here."

Miles and the reporter jumped in the back. Miles manned the missile launcher secured to the roof. Turning the key caused the engine to crank out an awful whine. She tried again and the exhaust backfired, but the motor came to life.

After backing up, she maneuvered the Jeep onto the highway. She threw it into gear and sped down the road, over rubble and debris.

"Miles?" she said.

"Yeah?"

"You better hold on." She glanced to the reporter. "What's your name?"

"Dodson."

"Dod, you're up here with me."

He crawled between the seats and strapped into the passenger seat.

She pointed at his weapon. "You know how to use that thing?"

He glanced down to his camera.

"No, not that. The other thing."

He nodded, speaking loud now. "My dad owned a gun range."

"Good."

Most of the road had been left in ruin.

She tilted her head up so Miles could hear. "Gonna get rough up ahead."

They came to the gap in the road. Most of the left side had buckled, leaving the right side difficult terrain at best. She hugged the shoulder, but the Jeep bounded over rocks and potholes. By the time the right side ran smooth again, the Jeep had started to slide.

She pressed down hard on the gas, and the front tire struck a wall of crumbling earth. The Jeep skipped, landing at an odd angle that caused her to swerve out of control. She regained traction before anything more than a squeak escaped the tires.

"Close one," Dod said.

"Nah." She grinned. "Had it all the way."

Dod let out a nervous laugh.

Up ahead, they spotted a place where darkness gave way to light. Tendrils of black smoke gyrated as if caught in a light wind. They stretched out toward the Jeep like a long winding staircase.

She pointed off in the distance. "Must be out that way."

"What are we looking for?" Dod said.

She didn't answer, but Miles did.

"A hole."

Dod's mouth dropped open, perhaps wanting to inquire further, but he never got the chance.

Miles lowered himself. "I think I –"

She saw it, too, and slammed on the brakes before they got too close.

The pale creature plummeted down in front of them, its wings flapping so hard it became near impossible to see anything. She leaned forward and crossed her hands over her head, encouraging Dod to do the same. Miles spun the missile launcher around to a better angle. The beast reared back as if readying to attack when Miles fired.

The missile struck the monster in the esophagus. Its neck burst and although the creature fought off some of the flames, it staggered about as if blinded. When it breathed, the gaping hole in its neck flayed in and out, the monster gasped loudly as it tried to inhale. The creature twisted, trying to flee perhaps, but only wavered a moment before collapsing. The ground shook hard, and the enormous body heaved once more, its breath escaping with a hollow sound. Then the corpse settled for good.

She hit the gas and wheeled the Jeep around the mammoth carcass. Back on track toward the darkness, the Jeep edged over debris.

"I see it," Miles said.

The strange orange glow lit the horizon. Dumbfounded, she had no idea what to expect or whether they could do anything to stop it.

They abandoned the Jeep some fifty yards out from the crack. A closer inspection of the fissure offered a clear view of the other side. Through the red mist of what resembled rays of sunshine, she beheld something remarkable.

"Is that grass?" she said.

The blades were different shades of red and if it wasn't grass, it was at least some sort of ground cover. Miles and Dod saw it, too. A whole other world existed beyond this one, hidden for who knew how long, deep inside this crevice.

Maybe I can load this hole up with grenades. Blow it all sky high.

Doing so with such light explosives would also risk increasing its size. It must have been a tight squeeze as it was, but what creatures might appear if the hole were made larger?

A bold idea came to her. "I'm going in."

"What?" Dod grabbed her arm. "Are you crazy?"

She pulled away from him.

"I have to agree with the photo hound on this one, darlin'." Miles scratched his head and cocked an eyebrow. "What you're gabbin' about sounds a bit outrageous."

"How else are we gonna stop this?" She stamped her foot. "If we don't try, this might get worse. We have to do something."

She stepped into the hole and they let her go. Then they followed her, saying nothing more on the subject. Although difficult to traverse, with some effort they found themselves in a world similar to their own. Only this world didn't have a sun as she had first surmised. The orange glow resulted from the many fires. Flames rose high in all directions, as far as she could see.

In the distance, she identified a structure, which she believed a hangar at first. Wide trails of purple smoke wafted from its roof, indicative of some type of factory. She couldn't tell what material had been used to fabricate the building, though, as none of it looked similar to anything she recognized.

She waved them onward. They formed a tight line behind her and made their way to the structure. Then she spotted one of the creatures, and they came to an abrupt halt.

It exited the far end of the building, increasing in size an instant later. Its bony frame remained barren at first, but already she could identify flesh developing on its body. Its neck elongated, twisting out in a spiral. As if in pain, it groaned, mouth wide and straining. The outline of scales began to appear on what skin the creature had grown.

Seeking refuge behind some large rocky formations off to the right, she urged the others to follow without saying a word. They hid among the rocks, observing how the creature further matured on its way to the crack. Upon reaching the crevice, it squirmed up, but not without struggle. She hated to let it go, but she didn't think it wise to start a fight on enemy soil just yet. Not until they fully understood what they were up against.

Once the monster departed, they continued their approach. Now she could discern the skeletal framework holding the structure together. The entire building, comprised of discolored bone and sinewy mass, seemed to breathe as if alive. Bursts of fire exited through openings in the ceiling, accenting the billowing smoke. How any monstrous organism could be created under these conditions seemed impossible.

Closer still, several life forms moved about the perimeter of the building. The larger of these beings operated the machinery, most of them shooting pink fireballs into openings in the structure. She imagined this somehow gave life to the monsters, perhaps filling them with whatever gas they required to live. She seized Miles' arm without knowing. Seeing this, he grinned, and she yanked her hand away.

Another fireball soared into the structure and imploded. One after another, fireballs burst inside the building. When the bombardment ceased, a large creature exited, confirming her suspicions. This monster, a mass of bone and muscle, had not yet fully cured.

A telltale click surprised her. The bright flash drew all eyes to them. Dod stood there, camera to his eye, the look on his face one of surprise equal to her own.

"Really?" she said. "You used a flash?"

He let the camera drop to his chest and retrieved the gun. "Sorry."

No apology could reverse the damage. Smaller creatures already bounded toward them, bouncing up and down, and zigzagging. Each creature's eyes burned a fiery yellow. The closer they got, the better she could see their spotted red flesh and dagger-like fingers dangling at the ends of lanky arms.

What the hell is this place?

She shook out of her daze and lay down a line of fire. Dod and Miles did the same. Together, they clipped a few creatures, ending their attack, but the rest kept coming.

Addison fumbled in her flak jacket, removed a grenade and yanked out the pin with her teeth. She launched the grenade ten feet in front of the demon-like creatures' current position. The resulting explosion took out all but a few. She focused her gunfire on the remaining demons until they were a twitching mass on the ground.

Seconds later, something bright shot past them. She staggered back and saw one of the larger creatures readying to fire again. To make matters worse, their freshest creation had also taken an interest in the intruders. Seeming rather unfinished, its bony feet clacked along the rocky landscape, keeping its formidable tail poised and ready as it hurried to their position.

The creature brought its tail down. The bony point penetrated deep into the rock, creating tremors that sent her reeling.

Miles split off to the left. Dod remained close to her. All of them fired round after round into the creature, their bullets doing nothing more than rattling off the bone and sinew. It only seemed to further annoy the beast.

A fireball struck the rocks to their left. The momentary blast heated her face. Rubble showered them.

"Back. Get back," she said.

They all slid back toward the hole, closer to their world.

"It's not working. We need to take out those big ones," Miles said.

They aimed their guns at the larger demons. One rattled in its chair, and then another. They were replaced as fast as they could mow them down.

Once again a fireball rushed their way. They all dove. The blast missed by a few feet, and the ground erupted. Rattled by the blast, for a moment she watched, wondering.

Could that do the trick?

Another group of smaller demons sped their way. She readied another grenade, and this time the blast killed off most of the pack. They fired at the few survivors, but before they could take them down, the monster's tail struck again. The surface quaked hard enough to throw her off balance. Miles, too. The rumble threw Dod to the ground, carving a nasty wound in his leg. To make matters worse, the three smaller demons were close enough to attack.

Two went after Dod. One tugged at the camera strap around his neck, near strangling him. The other wrapped its arms around his waist and dug its fanged teeth into his abdomen. Dod screamed. Somehow managing to escape their hold, he hobbled for the exit.

Miles took out the third demon. He turned his attention to Dod, but a fireball kept him from doing anything more than shielding his eyes.

The blast devoured Dod and both demons.

Witnessing this, Addison gathered herself in time to avoid being struck by the monster's tail. As the bone spike thrust deep into the earth, she noticed the developing flesh.

Miles must have seen this, too, as he turned his gun on the monster and fired off a few rounds. She patted her palms in the air to stop him after considering everything she had seen.

She thumbed at the crack and although confused, Miles followed her. The monster trailed them, as did another wave of the smaller demons. Behind all of them, the fireballs roared on, crashing to their left and right. They weaved back and forth, losing their footing a few times, but recovered fast.

When they reached the opening, she stopped him again. There, they waited until the monster closed in on them. Only then did she instruct Miles to climb up.

Fireball after fireball assaulted the rocky earth surrounding them, the formation around the gap collapsing as they climbed. A few demons made it past these blasts and tugged at their legs. That monstrous tail crashed into the surface not once, but twice, each time coming closer than she liked.

Soon the monster had trouble reaching them in such tight quarters. This forced the creature to trail them. It clawed at the rocks, preventing them from gaining much ground.

They scrambled on their bellies. Pulled at roots and grass and rock, whatever they could find. For every three feet they gained, they slid back one. But they were succeeding, and although she held little hope for their survival, she believed the end was near.

She reached the top first and turned to help Miles. From far inside the other world came a barrage of fireballs. The monster had reached the bottleneck of the hole and scrambled up toward them. Its pale flesh now fully cured, she wanted to put distance between them and this portal.

Fireballs battered the monster. A burst of flames erupted, shaking the earth. They held tight, taunted by the lesser demons but clawing at the ground for support. The earth sloped, and a wave of dirt and debris rolled out beneath them. Then one of those fireballs struck the target she had been hoping for, the monster's gaseous sacs.

Earth, sticks, whole trees, the Jeep, everything shot up into the sky. The ground crumbled beneath them, collapsing some ten feet all at once.

Exhausted, and in pain, she rolled over on a huge slab of rock. The ground still complained of the explosion, rumbling even as they rose to their feet.

Miles scanned the demons for signs of life. As if unsure, he fired three shots into one of the corpses.

They walked hand in hand and stood at the edge of the chasm until the dust cleared. Rock had encrusted over the portal as she had planned. But she knew the war could never end here. The creatures had found their way here once, and they would find a way back. Next time, though, she would be ready.

THE REASSIGNMENT PROJECT

DISORIENTATED, JOSLYN DISCOVERED herself being lifted into the sky. She leaned against some invisible wall in an attempt to escape, but the barrier moved with her.

Lake Charlton had doubled in size. The surrounding woods were engulfed in flames. A gorge had formed in the distance.

What's happening?

To her left, she saw her brother but averted her gaze. She imagined his expression upon seeing her, believing he would be just as bitter now.

"Citizen," said some unseen woman's voice. "Please refrain from leaning against the pod substrate. Doing so could damage the digital lining of your temporary vessel."

There was a moment of silence and then, "If you continue to ignore this request we will be forced to pass a small surge of electricity through your body as a warning."

A large digital nine glowed bright red on what appeared a thin cellophane-like wall. The number transformed to an eight, counting down at a steady pace. The suspended numbers captivated her. When it reached zero, a dozen or so electric spider webs crept out from the extremities of the pod to her fingers. Before she could move, the charge forced her back. This shock alleviated some of her immediate confusion.

The voice came again. "Citizen, we have detected unnatural breathing patterns. We're providing an adequate source of oxygen to compensate. Please remain calm until the docking procedure is completed."

Joslyn scanned the ground below. The Earth grumbled and the dark gorge expanded, swallowing everything in its path.

This is it.

The underbelly of the enormous saucer had already docked several pods. Thinking back to the events that led up to this moment, she believed things would never be the same.

✦⎯⎯❖⎯⎯✦

Saucers arrived from the east, flying in a V formation, which reminded Joslyn of a flock of geese. The various news reports said the fleet of black discs had spread across the globe. They darkened the skies, shrouding the world with intense silence. These reports said "not to panic" and to "await further instruction," but then those signals were lost. At first, people looted stores, followed by homes. Men killed women and vice versa. Children started fires. Even the elderly wreaked havoc upon the town, crashing their canes or walkers into store windows and taking what they could carry. That was only the beginning, but the destruction had not come solely at the hands of mankind.

At night, the saucers were nearly invisible, but she

knew they were still there. She wondered who they were, what they wanted, why they had come? Were they the reason for all the destruction? Fires had ruined the surrounding forests, tornadoes had destroyed much of the adjacent neighborhoods, and even an earthquake had done its worst.

And now this.

The winter in Carbondale, Pennsylvania had been far colder than most. Spring had come too soon and a scorching summer trailed close behind. Clouds and storms were more common than sunny days, yet the rainwaters dried fast, steam always rising from the pavement. The intense heat made it difficult to breathe and everything smelled like a wet dog.

She had turned fourteen a week ago. With her mother dead, her dad had done his best to keep her safe. Without him and her brother, she might not have survived.

Joslyn's father insisted they remain in the basement to avoid being seen. He had heard many others were doing the same. There were bad people in the streets, those who tolerated the weather long enough to take out pent-up frustrations on whoever crossed their paths. She listened and did what he thought best.

Dillon, on the other hand, had developed some opinions of his own now that father's illness had worsened. Every few days, he removed the locks on the basement door and ventured up into their kitchen. They had barricaded the doors with furniture, but he always wielded the lone rifle just in case.

Sometimes she followed, carrying a knife and sticking close to him. Today, the kitchen reminded her of a spring day of old, with refreshing scents instead of the dank smelling basement she had grown accustomed to. A brief check through the window offered glimpses of the devastated town where she could see her instincts had been wrong.

In the background, the Civil Defense sirens bellowed an intermittent yet persistent whine. They gathered what supplies they could and retreated to the basement. After locking the door again, they parted ways, her going to her bedding and him to check on Dad.

Father had started skipping meals to conserve food, insisting his children eat and stay strong. Up until now that had been okay, because he had been strong enough to fend off any intruders. However, with him growing weaker, she had no choice but to rely on Dillon. That was a dismal thought, because some days she would swear he had taken a change for the worse.

He had once been a good brother. He chased off at least one of her bullies, spent time assisting with her math, and he even taught her how to ride a bike. He had been smart and caring, but these new responsibilities had transformed him into something awful.

He glared at her upon returning to the room. Starting her way, he cocked an eyebrow, studying her.

"Okay, what'd you take?" he said. "What are you hiding?"

She edged away. "It's nothing."

His eyes consumed her. The more she backed away, the bolder he grew. His face twisted with anger. "Show me what you took."

From another room, she heard Father coughing,

followed by a hoarse hack. It distracted them both. She stared at the wall until Father quieted, but her worry for him mounted.

"I swear Jos, if you're hiding something."

"What?" She stood her ground, as she would have on any ordinary day, even took a bold step toward Dillon. "What will you do?"

There weren't any regular days anymore.

Dillon's eyes widened, as if straining to contain his anger. He raised his hand. "Don't make me do this."

Another rattling cough interrupted them.

This time, she glared at Dillon's hand. *Is this what it's come to?*

Father settled and before she could say anything, Dillon's hand came down. It halted progress a fraction of an inch from her cheek. Although he didn't strike her, the shock that he could even think such a thing made her drop what she had been hiding.

The can rolled along the uneven concrete floor. She watched it stop against the far wall.

He looked up at her. "Is that all? A can of baked beans?" He sighed. "For Christ's sake, I don't even like them."

She had known that.

So why hide them?

He rubbed his knuckles as if he had struck her. "Damn you, Jos. You almost made me do something bad."

Something inside her wanted to scowl at him, but she didn't allow herself this pleasure. That would only worsen matters. She knew if anything happened to their dad, there would be nothing to interrupt them next time.

"Go." He waved her off. "Pick it up and eat it if you want."

Sometimes it was hard to believe Dillon was still sixteen. He seemed so much older now.

The look in his eyes confirmed her guilt. "But don't think you're gonna get anything more for dinner." One corner of his mouth turned up in a wicked grin. "Dad has to eat, too, you know?"

She wandered over to the can of beans and picked it up. Her stomach grumbled when she did. She glanced back at her brother and her facial control waned.

"What was that?" he said.

Great.

She stood, beans in hand. Regarded him with hopeful uncertainty. "What?"

His lips thinned. "I saw you snarl."

She fended him off with her palms. "Wait, what? *No.*"

"If I catch you mocking me, Jos, I'll . . . "

He lifted his hand again, acting as though he would hit her. "Don't make fun of me. I'm warning you."

Dillon thrust his fists down at his sides. He stormed off down the hall where their dad rested. She watched him go, wanting to follow, to make sure he didn't hurt Father. But she hadn't eaten in days.

She dug through father's tool chest, searching for a means to open the can. Dillon had hidden the lone can opener.

I wish I didn't depend on him so much.

She found a hammer and chisel and went to work. At first, she managed to dent the can and nothing more. As her strikes improved and her desperation deepened, she punched square holes on the surface of the can until she could dig the chisel in and pry the lid open enough to slide a single finger into the hole. Probing the inside of the can with her longest fingernail, she fished the beans out one by one.

Afterward, she retreated to her dark corner of the basement behind the furnace.

She jerked awake, roused by—

Nothing. Just a bad dream.

Then again, she didn't hear Father coughing. With bated breath, she listened. When it didn't come, she rushed to him, mindful of her step. She didn't want to alert Dillon.

If Father needs help, I can't have him interfering.

When she arrived, though, her heart sank. Standing frozen in the doorway, she witnessed a horror she hadn't thought possible. She wanted to scream but choked it back. And she wanted to help, but she had no idea what to do.

Dillon straddled their father, pinning the weary man to the floor. He pressed a pillow tight against Father's head. That disturbing evil grin spread across his face again, an expression she would not soon forget.

Father flung his hands into the air, as if grasping for some unseen object. His fingers opened and closed, then opened wider. They clawed at the air for a long moment before his body slackened, his aged hands slapping the cement floor as the life left him for good.

Dillon didn't ease up. He pressed the pillow down long after their dad had stopped breathing. A few seconds later, he noticed her standing there, but even then he continued holding the pillow over Father's face.

"What—" She tried again, but managed only one word. "Why?"

He didn't answer, looking more like an animal than a man. As if hearing her thoughts, his smile widened. She noticed his foot twitch. That was all it took.

Running for the stairs, she heard him gaining on her and couldn't help but glance back.

Thank God. No gun.

Dillon paused long enough to seize a section of metal piping and a wrench. He wielded both like some mad warrior.

The wrench swatted at her. She ducked. The tool clanged off the basement door.

She focused on the locks.

This time he brought the pipe around. Longer than the wrench, it caught on the wall, digging a long line in the drywall. Still he managed to land a blow.

The pain in her shoulder forced her to scream. But she ignored the pain, working with fervor at the locks and making some headway.

Please open. Please . . .

He readied to attack again, but this time she spun and kicked out with all her might.

Trying to regain his balance, he dropped the wrench and clawed at the railing. Before he could steady himself she kicked again. This time she landed a blow square in his gut.

He sprawled back, face wrinkled, gasping for air. The pipe slid from his grasp in favor of bracing for the fall.

She didn't stick around to watch. Didn't need to.

She finished releasing locks and escaped into the kitchen of their dilapidated home. There, she slammed the basement door shut behind her and breathed.

Need something to brace it.

She yanked the table towards the door. Already she could hear him clambering back up the steps.

Hurry.

With one leg missing, the table rolled onto its side, and she couldn't move it any farther.

Damn it.

She leaned back and drove her aching shoulder into the table, trying to maneuver it closer to the door. Afterward, she surveyed her work for a brief second.

That will never hold.

A loud *bang* surprised her. She leaped back. The door seemed to bend outward from the doorframe. A gap between door and jam grew to a full inch.

It's holding, but not for long.

His fingers crept out around the edge of the door. "Jos?" His tone sounded raspy. "I'm coming for you, Jos."

Run.

She rummaged through the blockade in front of the door to the living room, throwing chairs aside and toppling a bookcase. Managing to squeeze by, she escaped the house through a large hole on one side.

In the street, flames licked at the sky. The smell of charred wood and bitter grass assaulted her senses. The air was thinner now, hotter than usual. She glanced up to the sky and slowed.

Some of the saucers are gone.

She heard expletives from a distance and glanced

back. Dillon waved a length of wood, a nail protruding from its end, and charged her way.

Desperate for a place to hide, she ran for the old drainage pipe across the park, darting through a thicket of bushes on her right. Branches scraped her flesh, and this time she allowed herself to scream. One branch dug deep into her side, but she ignored the pain upon feeling his fingers clawing at her shoulder. She pulled free of his grip, and he tried again. This time he missed, and with him leaning so far forward in his effort, he stumbled to the ground.

She raced over the embankment to the drainage pipe.

He'll give up if I lose him.

She stood near the opening on her tippy-toes to confirm Dillon hadn't seen where she had gone. He knew of the pipe but hadn't come here since he was young.

Maybe he's forgotten.

From the high brush, she could see him running up the street, searching for her.

Breathing heavily, nerves shot, she slid down the swell of the duct and around the end where she entered. Three shadows moved in the dark.

"Well, well," said the shortest figure, a man with a thick southern accent. "What do we have here?"

She backed out and they followed. When she tried to flee, the three men surrounded her.

"Where you going, missy?" said a bearded man with a rough voice.

Flustered, she stuttered, "I'm just . . . I'm looking for my brother."

The youngest of the three scratched his chin. "Is that right?"

The short one no longer smiled. His eyes brightened. "Well, he ain't here. What you got to say about that, darlin'?"

But he *was* there. He stood over them on top of the drainpipe, his wooden weapon reared back.

The youngest saw Dillon first. He raised his fists and scrambled up the edge.

Dillon swung, snapping the wood in half and driving the nail deep into the man's temple. The man stumbled back, clawing at his face, looking as though he was unable to perceive what had happened to him. He didn't seem to feel the pain. After a few seconds, he slumped to his knees, and then flat to the ground.

Dillon's fingers caressed the broken end.

"Charlie?" said the short man. "Look what he did to Charlie."

The bearded guy rushed forward, and Dillon rammed the jagged wood right into the man's chest. The man staggered away, yanking the wood free of Dillon's grasp and leaving him weaponless. At first, no blood flowed. Not until the bearded man withdrew the wooden stake. Then it spurted out so fast he couldn't suppress the flow. It seeped out around each finger, staining the man's hands and shirt.

Dillon watched, a smile forming on his face.

The smaller man readied to attack. He carried something in his hands.

"Dillon, look out," Joslyn said.

Dillon tried to duck.

She closed her eyes but heard an awful *thud*.

Seconds later, Dillon lay in a pool of blood, unmoving and silent. She didn't know whether to worry about him or not. Feeling vindicated yet grief-stricken, she fully believed this man had killed her brother.

He tossed the rock aside. "You're gonna pay for what he did to my friends, whore."

She lurched away, but he shot forward. He seized her arm before she could escape. His fingers were like a vice on her bicep.

She screamed.

This made the man smile. He pulled her in close where she could smell his stale breath, his putrid body odor. His yellowing teeth were cracked, his face riddled with scars. He pushed her against the drainage pipe and slid the belt out of his pants. It dangled from his hand, swaying in the breeze. She thought she knew what would come next.

Then, something boiled up inside of her. Not fear, but determination. She had suffered, more so than any girl her age should endure.

No more.

She braced herself and attacked the man with her free hand. Her fingers dug into his cheek, and he let go of her. She jumped forward, throwing him off balance. When he fell, she was on top of him right away. The rock he had used to strike Dillon lay off to the side. She seized the rock and raised it high above her head.

The fear in his eyes empowered her. She brought the rock down. It made her feel whole again, capable, like she could survive on her own. Then some other sensation took hold of her, and she found herself rising into the sky.

PRESAGE

DOCTOR SAMI FAIZ Bhakta couldn't breathe. The weight of the moment struck him all at once when the adolescent boy opened the door and stepped out into a night blanketed by death and destruction. The streets lined with smoldering ash, the distinct smell of fire struck Sami. Bombs exploded. But the teen's confidence was obvious, as he lifted his palms to the heavens and spoke indiscernible words. It was all so surreal, even down to the blood red moon.

In October of 2021, Sami secured a single incomplete strand of DNA from the lauded shroud after much litigation. To think, they had nearly lost the source material in the process. If they had, it would have caused mass chaos. As it was, it still managed to spawn an onslaught of protests. The occasional religious fanatic, airing out their concerns for all to hear, joined them. Their words riled everyone in the streets outside the New Mexico facility.

Regardless of these interruptions, the cheers and the jeers, Sami's work continued without falter. He began the cloning process right away, but the computers already struggled to reconstruct the missing data. The cloning took two days with a complete DNA chain, but Sami could only speculate as to how long it would take in this case. This unexpected setback left Sami and his crew with little more to do than plan.

By November, the computers continued to baffle Sami, having not yet deciphered the missing genetic code. With reporters convinced his efforts had failed, only a handful of protestors remained. Sami's doubts echoed their assumptions. His financiers began to question the future of the program. This concerned Sami most of all, as the facility grew ever closer to shutting down for good. Only in their final hours did the computer finish the replication process.

The financers permitted Sami to delay the closure long enough to verify whether they could proceed with the cloning process. Details regarding this small victory were not disclosed to the media because the previous waves of protestors still made Sami nervous. He feared their interference prior to any clone birth.

Come January of the following year, matters still hadn't progressed as expected. Sami could not fathom why this data should process slower than any other basic genetic set, but this case proved unique. It remained a source of great frustration to both his financiers and his staff. Regardless, he pushed through and by the end of the month had succeeded in a clone birth. With everyone abuzz at the prospect of the dark-skinned baby boy, increased security measures were ignored. As a result, a fellow colleague of Sami's, one Kendra Dillinger, attempted to abduct the child.

The staff detained Kendra before she could escape the facility or bring any harm to the child. That same day, Sami fired her without contacting the authorities, believing that pressing charges would somehow bring more unwanted attention. That ended up being a grave mistake.

Ms. Dillinger stirred up matters among the local religious parties. She not only alerted them to the child's existence, but, due to her meddling, the protesters returned in force, intensifying their demonstrations and, at times, invoking violence. The ensuing mayhem forced Sami to take significant efforts to upgrade security to ensure the safety of the child.

In March of 2027, the United States attacked Syria to start World War III. The weaponry alone had vastly improved since the wars of old, so the losses quickly eclipsed those of World War II within the first year. Sami did his best not to think about the conflict, focusing his time on working with the child, trying to discern whether he had been successful.

He taught the boy everything he had learned, both theological and scientific. The boy proved rather astute and goodhearted. Discipline wasn't an issue, but the boy's thirst for education proved challenging. The entire staff took part in his schooling. There was an unmistakable air about him, as if the staff seemed to almost breathe easier around the boy. They felt comfortable in telling him the things he inquired about, knowing he would take every opportunity to discuss all matters whether they be social, physiological, mental or otherwise. Because of this desire for knowledge, Sami found himself growing rather fond of the boy.

With the protests outside of the facility branching to various countries, further fueling the heated battles,

Sami invited several influential leaders to inspect the facility in hopes of ending the disputes. These men and women expressed a strong desire to meet the boy, but Sami had grown leery of such visitations, in part due to the increased violence outside the facility. Therefore, he granted them a brief visual study from behind a mirrored window, if for no other reason than to ease any prior concerns these individuals may have had. Most of all, he wanted to refute any belief that the boy posed a threat to the future of mankind.

He didn't, of course, as he was only a boy, no different than any other child his age. The boy's build was no more formidable. Even his intelligence, though above average, proved no more than the most perceptive school-aged preadolescent. While the guests remained skeptical, Sami was hopeful these visits would pacify the media and perhaps the quarreling would end. If nothing else, it afforded him some peace to resume his studies.

By the time January of 2035 rolled around, the world outside proved far too dangerous for most of his staff to remain on site. Of those leaders who previously visited, many had sent armed forces to guard the facility at all hours. That meant they were safe to a degree. The financiers offered a reprieve to any employee who deemed it necessary to stay with family instead of at the facility. Many tests and further education of the boy took place mostly over Skype and through emails or on social media.

When hackers revealed the boy's Internet conversations to the public, attention grew. Some well-known leaders took to news platforms, professing to the country and anyone else who would listen that the boy was the very messiah Sami sought to disprove. Others debated the facts, appearing more skeptical than Sami. Few took the scientific approach, valuing the child no more or less than any other being.

It had become clear to Sami the child had no powers over anything. Yes, he was quite charismatic, the way he seemed to admire Sami and adhered to their schedule. That did account for something, Sami supposed. Yet, his genetic makeup was no different than any other human. He lived and breathed and comprehended just like any other youth. The boy slept and ate like any man or woman required. He had not affected anyone near or far in any sort of prophetic way. Therefore, Sami thought it improbable such a man had ever existed as foretold in the scriptures.

The war had gone on now for eight long years. Three years ago, smallpox had once more taken a toll on mankind. When Yellowstone's volcano erupted, it darkened the sky. Only the hazy red image of the sun glowed through the devastation. This all seemed to follow the very prophecies Sami wished to disprove. But Sami remained on the fence, undecided as to whether or not he had succeeded.

Perhaps what concerned Sami most was how the boy had taken to asking the most interesting questions. Why does a baby cry? Why does one feel sad when it rains? What makes one fear death? He had somehow picked up a curiosity about the inner workings of this world, though Sami often thought these the whimsical subjects of boyish fantasies. Therefore, he believed he would outgrow this nonsense given time.

Staring out through the window, the boy rested his

forearm on one of the bars of the window. They had moved to the ground level of the facility to survey the situation outside. Sami believed they were still safe here, but he no longer saw any of the soldiers. It dismayed him when the boy pressed his forehead against the metal.

"You shouldn't stand so close to the window." Sami pushed his glasses back up on the bridge of his nose. "Now, let's get back to our research, yes?"

The boy turned to him. Sorrow overwhelmed Sami upon realizing the boy had been crying. The boy sniffled and wiped away the tears. Doubt showed on his face. "Why do they war? Is it because of me?"

"I don't know, but in a small way it's the precise reason for our study."

A wrinkle formed on the boy's forehead. "What do you mean? Is our research meant to uncover the reasons why people fight?"

It was a stretch, but not an outlandish one.

"Somewhat. Listen, our primary goal has always been to replicate someone of such profound significance that we could either prove or disprove the past. This is all an effort to better comprehend our very nature, and as such, form a better understanding of humanity. If we can determine our beginnings, we can then put to rest one of the most heated debates in our history. We can better define our future and perhaps then all the warring will stop." He sighed, tapping his finger on his notepad. "But first, we must disprove you have any link to that past."

The boy skulked away from the window. "Tell me," he said. "What do you believe?"

Stunned, Sami thought for a second. "I believe you're one of the brightest children I've ever met."

"No, that isn't what I mean." The boy returned to the window and gazed out through the bars. "Do you think I am this Messiah?"

Sami wondered why the boy had taken to these questions, as his own foundation for belief had been shaken these last few years. He didn't want to admit that, though. Would never confess such a thing. "Not one bit." Puzzled, he stared at the boy. "Why do you ask?"

The boy shrugged. "Never mind."

But this intrigued Sami. Most of what had happened came as a result of this spectacular experiment, but one could not deny all that had occurred. The war had laid waste to more than a third of the world's population, and it would claim many more lives before it ended.

Only now the boy has suspicions?

Sami did feel responsible to a degree, though his work had been necessary for the salvation of a better tomorrow. If it had been the existence of Santa Claus he had wanted to disprove, no one would have batted an eye. No one believed in good old Saint Nick anymore, not even the children.

Why then such an uproar over this?

"No, tell me," Sami said.

"I don't think you'd understand."

Something in the boy's eyes captivated Sami, as if the kid had aged several years all at once.

"Besides," the boy continued, "nothing I say will change anything."

"What do you mean?"

The boy reached out and brushed Sami's cheek with the back of his hand. His touch was both warm and soothing. The boy stared into his eyes. "Your faith has been tested."

Sami shook out of his near spellbound state and stormed away. "This was never about faith."

"No, of course not."

"So why then do you bring it up now?"

"Because it's time." Again, the boy wept. "I fear I've failed you."

Feeling his work slip through his fingers, Sami trembled. He had given his entire adult life to this study and taken every precaution to ensure the boy would be safe and now, here he was threatening to leave. How could he just let him walk away? "Stop this foolishness. Come now, time for your lesson."

"No, Sami. These lessons no longer do either of us any good. This is long overdue."

The boy moved toward the door and Sami followed. Each entrance had been wired to shock anyone who attempted to open it. Yet the boy turned the knob without the slightest hint of pain.

A misfire?

Sami withdrew his handheld Taser and prepared to stun the boy. When he came within arm's length, he lashed out with the device. Before he could pull the trigger, the boy turned and seized his wrist. He was so much stronger than Sami, keeping him from finishing the job.

The boy's eyes softened but still welled with tears. "Is this what you'd do to keep me here?"

Sami stared into his eyes, weakened by the boy's gaze. "You can't leave. Not now. Not when we're so close."

"I must."

"Please don't."

Hurt spread across the boy's face. "Look at them out there. Do you not see them? You see it, don't you?"

And he did see it. Now, Sami cried. "Please, don't."

Sami dropped the Taser and fell to his knees. He let the boy go, and the boy walked with confidence. It was far too late now to disprove anything.

The boy headed out into the chaos with his head held high, and Sami watched until the Messiah vanished into the hazy night.

ONE HOPELESS NIGHT BY A CLAN FIRE

MATT STURGESS OPENED his mouth to scream, but what came out wasn't expected.

"... two down, man on first, full count. Jackson steps in and ... " said the voice in his mouth.

He pried his trembling fingers inside his mouth in an effort to locate the source. Perhaps, because of his surprise, he did not fully comprehend his immediate situation and see those around him until it was too late.

Then he found it.

My tooth. It's coming from my tooth.

Glancing about, he closed his mouth. Holding his hand over it for good measure, he gripped his fishing rod, preparing for the worst. Not only had his mere presence alarmed them, but he judged by their facial expressions he had scared the living daylights out of them when he opened his mouth and spewed out some baseball radio broadcast.

Run. Just get up and run.

His legs had become jelly-like, due to the uncontrollable shuddering. He couldn't run if his life depended on it.

One of them, the largest of the three men who was tall and lanky, stood and approached Matt's position. Seeing this made Matt's world sway with anticipation. His eyes searched the two women who watched from beside the fire and then the other two men who sat frozen in place. None of them offered any readable expression, seeming content with however the big man, their apparent leader, decided to handle Matt's intrusion.

The tall man retrieved his club and came face to face with Matt, who remained on his knees. Matt noticed the man's sizeable forehead, defined cheekbones, and the bushy eyebrows, which sat over squinted eyes that scrutinized his every move. His lips appeared swollen and his breath rancid.

Matt couldn't stop trembling.

The tall man grunted but said nothing. He seized Matt's hair and tugged hard. Looking amused, the others grunted, too. Matt felt small in the giant man's hands, so he let him do as he wished, hoping to de-escalate matters. But when the man sniffed his hair, Matt almost pissed himself.

Come on. Keep it together.

But there was no way he could remain calm. Not here, not now. If it had only been the odd radio thing that occurred, he might have been able to control his emotions, but so much more had transpired. All of it added up to something horrific.

One minute he had been fishing, listening to the baseball game, and ignoring the rising storm. Next thing he knew, the rain became torrential. There was a bright flash of light and the lake swirled beneath him. He felt a small prick and then he was falling into darkness, wondering if there was a bottom to the drop. And it did end, coming with an abrupt stabbing pain to his ribcage when he struck the ground, the wind driven right out of his lungs. He hadn't known where he had ended up, whether it be past, future, or some parallel world. He had scrambled to all fours and knelt to find himself among some clan of Neanderthals.

I shouldn't have stayed out there so long.

The smallest man hurried over to Matt. He snatched the fishing rod away. Matt didn't care. That was the least of his worries. The small man ran his hand up the shaft, over the eyelets, and around the tip. By accident, the hook lodged in his hand, and he let out an awful howl.

Matt pressed his eyes shut. He waited for it to come, the blow to his skull that would no doubt brain him. But no such attack came. He dared to open a single eye and saw the women had gathered behind the man. The third man of a thicker build also joined them. They all studied the hook, squinting to see the line that attached it to the rod. The small man pushed through them to get to Matt, who dropped and slid away on his butt. But the stocky man and the women followed. When the small man reached him, Matt held up his hands, but the man only extended his injured finger.

Matt wasn't sure what to do: Explain himself or try to help. " . . . reports at this time signify a possible . . . "

They hooted and hollered, seeming frightened by the news report erupting from Matt's mouth. He clamped his lips shut and ground his teeth together, but it was already too late. Still, he kept his hands raised to fend them off, worried when they still didn't attack.

Matt inspected the hook. After a brief second, he pinched the man's flesh and pushed the barb back through with extreme care. The hook swung free on the line.

Observing this, the stocky man seized the hook and yanked it free. He had been lucky not to suffer the same fate as his friend. The thick man studied the hook, running a finger along the small barb and poking at the eyelet. He retrieved a hairy matted hide from the folds of his odd rubbery looking skins and unfolded it, taking care not to spill its contents. Inside, there were several handmade items, each carved out of stone. Matt could make out at least one of those items.

It's a hook. This is his tackle box.

The thick man stared into the hide as if comparing. This seemed to satisfy the man enough. He placed Matt's hook beside the others and refolded the thick hide, replacing it inside his clothing.

The red-haired woman took the rod. She bent it nearly in half. Good thing Matt had opted for a quality rod because when she let go of the thinner end, the rod snapped back up and smacked their leader across his face.

Their leader growled.

She backed away, hooting in a submissive way. "Ooh ooh ah ah oh."

The others' eyes remained untrusting as their leader sprung toward them. He snatched the rod from the woman and snapped it in half. Inspecting both ends for a brief second, he tossed them into the fire.

Now they surrounded Matt, inspecting him, his hair, limbs, and eyes. They took whatever things they found on him without any conviction: keys, wallet, pocketknife, anything. They tried to determine each item's purpose, and when they could not, they tossed it aside. When they could, they pocketed these items in a way similar to how the stocky man had the hook.

They took turns passing around his fishing hat, wearing it atop their filthy hair, seeming to mock Matt.

Then they tried to take his glasses, and Matt attempted to protest. All that came out was, " . . . Now, appearing at the Kenswick movie complex, The Lord of . . . "

He shut his mouth again. Suddenly they weren't so interested in his glasses. Instead, they peered at his mouth, curious and close enough he could smell their earthy odor.

The brunette female seized his lip, pulled it out, and pried her fingers between his teeth, locating the troublesome tooth. The radio signal still came, although muffled by her exploring fingers. Her digits tasted like what he imagined raw meat would and he couldn't help but worry what diseases might come along with such uncleanliness. Bile rose in his throat, but thankfully she withdrew her fingers in time. She met his teary eyes with a big smile absent of three teeth.

Matt's mouth remained agape. " . . . and the mother swears her child dialing 9-1-1 saved her life." Followed by a man, saying, "Great story, Nancy." Then the woman reporter again said, "Quite a heartwarming moment. Back to you . . . "

He closed his mouth.

The leader ushered Matt back to the fire. There, they all sat and stared at him, as if waiting. He wasn't sure what to think. Then, it hit him.

I wonder if music would relax them?

He opened his mouth and let out a single word before closing it again. " . . . My . . . "

Not music.

He tried again and failed. " . . . name . . . "

And again. " . . . is . . . "

Wait a minute.

He opened his mouth for a single word and it surprised him. " . . . Matt . . . "

Blown away by the discovery, that he could somehow speak with his radio voice, he felt somewhat optimistic. Then he remembered his audience and discouragement flooded him. Still, he tried.

He tapped his chest. " . . . Matt . . . "

It seemed as though he had lost them.

After checking with their leader, the stocky man tapped his chest and said, "Joh."

Others followed.

"Ha," said the smaller man.

And the red-haired woman, "Cin."

"Laur," said the brunette.

The large man finished, puffing out and slapping his chest as if to display his role. "Kai."

All of this pleased Matt. He had made contact. This alone meant the likelihood of him being clubbed to death had diminished. They had welcomed him, at least for the moment, into their little clan. Only then, as his body and senses relaxed, did he smell something cooking, and it delighted his senses.

Cin turned the spit and Matt glimpsed a sizzling rack of ribs. Juices dripped into the fire, each time forming a tiny puff of smoke. Beside the fire, on a large flat rock, sizzled some liquid in a stone basin.

Laur tore a chunk of meat off with her bare hands and offered it to him.

Grateful, Matt took the meat, unaware how hot it was until it was too late. He lifted his shirt and dropped the meat into the fabric. Then he dug through the fire and retrieved a severed end of his fishing rod. He forced the rod through the meat and ate it from the stick.

Seeing this, Kai seized the skinnier half of the rod and attempted the same feat. The weight of the meat bent the rod. He kept lowering himself, poking his tongue at the meat, but unable to dig his teeth into his portion. This made the others laugh, and Matt laughed, too.

Kai didn't seem to appreciate the boisterous laughter, accompanied by some indiscernible news report bursting from Matt's mouth.

Matt held up his hands and patted the air. " . . . Sorry . . . "

Kai seemed to understand. He continued eating off this thin rod, his eyes rushing to any person who let out the slightest peep.

Feeling better now, Matt braved his primary question. " . . . What . . . is . . . this . . . place . . . ?"

They won't understand. Heck, I can barely communicate with them.

Kai did answer, though. Not with a word, but with a shake of his head.

Taking this as an opportunity, Matt observed his surroundings. Maybe he could figure this out himself or find a way out.

It doesn't look so prehistoric.

He didn't see any animals or other signs of life. In

fact, all he saw were caves, and lots and lots of rocks and dirt.

Surely there's more. Where do they get the meat?

He stood and ambled about the cavern.

Where's the way out. There must be one.

He turned back to them. " . . . Out . . . ?"

After checking with Kai, Laur gave a simple shake of her head.

Then Matt spotted something eerily familiar. Painted in crimson on the cave walls were simple paintings. They depicted a human on a lake. A man stood beneath the swirl of water, a rod in hand and its hook dug into the man's flesh. In the next picture the craft sat empty. Last, the man sat alone in a circle.

He turned to them. " . . . Is . . . this . . . me . . . ?"

Cin shook her head, which seemed to annoy Kai. He grunted at her. Her eyes deceived her, glaring Kai's way. He dropped his meat and rushed toward her.

Matt considered interfering but didn't dare. It was Ha who stepped in, trying to hold him back, but Kai was far stronger and pushed through. This interruption drew attention from Cin. Seeing this pleased Matt, not wanting to witness any part of abusing a woman. Viewing that would have made him feel dirty inside because he knew even now he wouldn't have meddled.

Kai charged Ha, knocking him onto his backside. Then he was on top of Ha, wailing on his face. Ha tried to fight back, but it appeared pointless against such a formidable adversary. Kai kept coming, too, fist after fist exploding against Ha's jaw and nose and ear. Ha's mouth opened as if to scream. A thin trail of blood raced down his chin from a gap where a tooth had once been.

Kai reached to his side and seized a large rock. Matt's eyes went to Cin, who showed no emotion. Was this the way of their people? Only the strongest survive? Had they no loyalty, no humanity? Cin watched as if accepting this fate.

The rock came down against Ha's skull. A loud *crack* resounded in the cavern, and Ha no longer moved. Kai sat on top of the corpse wailing out a shriek like some mad wolf. Then he brought down the rock again, and again for good measure. When he finished, he tossed the rock aside. Bloodied and angry, he stomped toward Joh and extended his hand in a demanding manner.

A hurried Joh retrieved the hide from his clothing and unfolded it. Found what he had been looking for and handed it over to Kai, but did not close the hide.

Kai turned to Matt, the large hook curled in his fist like a weapon.

Oh God.

Now it would come. Matt felt a lump form in his throat. It slipped out as a gurgle, followed by a few muffled words. His ears pounded, eyes widened. He felt close to fainting and tried to run, but ran face-first into a wall. It spun him around, and he tried again, only to strike another wall. He stopped, dizzied and tried to focus. His eyes cleared, and he saw the paintings, but before he could make any sense of them, he found himself being dragged down from behind.

The man straddled him, pinning Matt's hands under his knees. Kai pried Matt's mouth open with one hand and inserted the stone hook. Now Matt saw the painting quite well and understood what Kai planned to do to him. He felt the stone against his gum and screamed, but all that came out was . . .

" . . . Blue light special savings for just this weekend . . . "

Tears welled in his eyes as the pain shot up from his gums into his sinus cavity. It felt as though Kai had extracted his eyeball through the roof of his mouth. In reality, he had cut away the gum surrounding the radio emitting molar. With it exposed, Kai placed the end of the hook against the base of the tooth bringing an electric surge of pain. With his other hand, Kai lifted a rock high into the air. The rock came down fast. Struck the hook and Matt's tooth cracked. Pain rushed in like a wild river overrun with rainwater, flowing wherever it wanted with no means of stopping it. A split second later, the pain overwhelmed him and everything went dark.

* — ✦ — *

Matt awoke, blurry-eyed and dizzy. He saw the light of the fire and the forms huddled around it. The smell of meat cooking made him realize it hadn't been a dream. As his vision cleared, he felt like an outcast. Joh stood next to Kai, spreading a thick paste into his mouth.

Kai waved Matt over to the fire.

He went, not wanting to further irritate the man who had just performed rudimentary oral surgery on him despite his every protest.

There, sitting on top of a rock beside the fire, he spied pieces of his extracted tooth. Joh retrieved one of the shards and pressed it against Kai's teeth. The rudimentary adhesive held the fractured tooth in place, but Joh wound fishing line around the new addition for good measure.

Matt felt the question on his lips and tried to stop from asking, but still it came. "Ooh," escaped his lips, and he stopped himself.

Kai's eyes condemned Matt. Yet, somehow Matt thought the man understood what he had attempted to convey. He waved Joh's hands away and held up a single fist. Took up the remains of Matt's tooth and rattled them in his palm. He stared deep into Matt's eyes and smiled, his unusual mouth full of teeth now visible to Matt. Pieces of the tooth had been secured to his own, making Kai's mouth look more shark-like than human.

" . . . Only . . . I . . . speak . . . here . . . " Kai said.

That was when Matt realized he hadn't gone back in time or even to the future. He wasn't even sure this was some parallel world. Wherever he had ended up, he was trapped with people having suffered his exact fate.

One of the women held a thick wooden rod, its line extended up into a watery stone ceiling high up in the cavern. She yanked, and the blurry visage of a woman appeared in the rockwork ceiling. She came falling through the ceiling, appearing all at once, and struck the ground, where she scrambled to all fours. Staring up at them, she surely didn't notice the woman who had captured her sitting the rod aside before she returned to the fire. The new woman went to say something, but when she opened her mouth a Britney Spears song played instead.

Stunned, she closed her mouth.

Matt looked to Kai and then approached her. Touched his chest and said, "Ma."

She stared back at him, but he didn't see her. His

focus had gone beyond her to the figure on the other side of the cavern. There, in the shadows, laid a body, one he recognized as Ha.

Matt spun back toward the fire. The spit rolled over, and the juicy hand crackled.

LENNY'S NEW EYES

LIKE EVERY OTHER day, creatures had already started gathering for the most popular drink in the underworld, the octoslushie. Considered an addicting delicacy, a smart monster avoided such vices. But the cleverest of creatures found ways around denying themselves the simple pleasures of life. Lenny wasn't sure where he fit in this world just yet, but he would do near anything for a sip of his favorite thirst-quencher. And, as luck would have it, today's travels brought them close to the stand.

"I know what you're thinking, Lenny, and it's a bad idea," Thomas said, watching the crowd gather up ahead.

"What?"

As they approached the Yard of Forgotten Souls, Lenny's eyes began to itch. This was the place where they disposed of all the abducted Earthlings. Their pale, fleshy skin always got his allergies going.

"You know what I mean." Thomas squinted, looking down his beak at Lenny. "Whenever we get out this way, you always get it in your head that you're gonna get one of those octoslushies." He shook his head. "They're bad for you, you know?"

Lenny ignored him. He used his thumb to pop his left eyeball out of its socket and placed it in the palm of one of his four hands. For a moment, he observed the eye before deciding to pluck out the other, as well.

Seeing this, Thomas sighed. "Are you even listening? Remember all the trouble we got into last time, all because you *had* to have one? I never thought we'd get away that night. We're lucky we're still undead."

Lenny couldn't ignore the feeling of his eyes.

They're so sticky.

Perhaps this was the reason they bothered him so much. He rubbed his empty sockets with the back of his hand, swallowed a deep breath of stale air, and heaved. "But I'm *so* thirsty."

"You're as bad as one of those alcoholics up topside."

Lenny chuckled. "How would you know? You're not even part-human. At best, you might have run into one in the streets. Do you even know what an alcoholic is?"

Thomas was ever clever with his response. "Do you?" He glanced at Lenny's eyes. "What the— What in the hell are you doing?"

Lenny glanced up at him from the palm of his hand. "I had an itch."

"So?" Thomas said. "That doesn't mean you should go taking out your eyes. Unless . . . were you gonna—" Thomas kept shaking his head. "Lenny, put those eyes back in your head."

"What?"

A coy grin spread across Thomas' mottled face. "One of those octoslushies is gonna cost you an eye."

"Yeah, what of it?"

Thomas gestured to the plucked eyeballs resting in Lenny's palm. "You weren't going to use one of those, were you?"

Lenny shrugged. "Well, I do have two." Thinking of his eyes, another thought occurred to him. "Besides, I don't look good in brown."

Thomas sounded surprised. "What was that?"

"I don't much care for the color of my eyes."

Thomas frowned. "You better hold onto those. That is, unless you have someone other than me to lead you around this blasted place should you lose them."

Lenny let the eyes roll into a cradle of fingers and twiddled his thumbs. "Can I have one of yours?"

Thomas took a full step away. "No."

"Please." Lenny sidled up beside his old friend. Fluttered his empty sockets and smiled brightly. "I'll trade you one of mine."

"Trade eyes?" He said, sounding bewildered. "Just one?"

Lenny beamed with hope. "Yes. I'd like that very much."

After a moment's consideration, Thomas conceded. "Okay then."

Thomas plucked out one of his eyes and handed it over. In return, Lenny passed over one of his brown eyes. Thomas shoved the eye right into his empty socket, winking several times to get it right.

Lenny placed the green one in his hand beside the brown one. Feeling them side by side made Lenny giggle.

"Happy now?" Thomas said.

"Quite."

"Well, you better put those away before you lose them."

Only Lenny didn't put them away. The air had relieved the irritation some. That alone was reason enough to keep them out a while longer.

Eventually the cobblestone road gave way to a rising path. The farther they continued upward, the more the shoulder fell away into the nothingness. Pink clouds billowed in the void, thickening as they neared the underside of the planet's crust. The clouds were so dense they obscured much of the castle. The core illuminated a silhouette of what they could see of the structure with electric hues of red and orange.

After a long while, Lenny came to an abrupt halt some fifteen yards from the octoslushie vendor. The crowd around the creature had grown in magnitude, preventing Lenny from seeing all but the top of the creature's head. The creature's crown moved with squirming tentacles. Some had eyes at their tips, but most didn't. Of those that did, Lenny saw so many different colors. It made him jealous, especially when he saw the orange ones.

With one of its empty tentacles, the creature took an eye from a nearby patron. Somewhere in the crowd an eyeless human female screamed as the creature squeezed her insides into a mixing canister. Lenny knew the procedure well enough, having witnessed it up close. Several other strange-looking ingredients were thrown into the mix, and then the creature shook the rusty can between two impressive fists. Its claws became a temporary blur of motion. And what came of all that hard work . . . ?

Delicious.

A solitary eye snaked out from the creature's unnatural mop of hair. This eye, big and bright, reminded Lenny of the human's moon. It located the customer and the creature poured the resulting mixture into a wooden bowl. This time the vendor growled when the patron hesitated to take the drink.

Startled, Lenny jerked away. He had endured nightmares about the creature and its terrifying growl. As a result, he couldn't stop shivering. Not even when that customer came away from the crowd with an octoslushie mustache, slurping and smiling, wandering off in a dream-like state. Lenny continued to tremble and didn't notice when something fell out of his hand.

He turned in time to see one of his eyes rolling down the path. With only a moment's hesitation, he started after it. Less than a second later, the eye bounded along, and then it bounced right into nothingness, forever lost to him.

Thomas sighed. "Now you've done it."

In his dismay, Lenny could think of only one question. "Was it the green one?"

"Yes," Thomas said. "Of course, it was the green one. I told you not to walk around with those out of your head."

Brokenhearted, a moment of desperation seized Lenny. "Can I have yours? The green one, I mean?"

"No."

"Oh please." He grinned. "I'll give you this brown one."

"What difference does it make what color eye you have when you can't even see it?"

"I might happen upon a mirror."

Thomas moaned, turning his attention elsewhere.

Lenny tapped an impatient clawed foot, hoping his friend would change his mind. "Can I please have the green one then?"

Thomas grunted and plucked out his green eye. He handed it over to an anxious Lenny, who then surrendered the other brown eye. Thomas shoved the brown eye right into his empty socket.

"There, satisfied?" Thomas asked.

"Yes, very much so. Thank you again."

"Now, genius. Tell me how you're going to get one of those octoslushies now that you only have one eye? Mind you, take good care of that one 'cause I'll not end up being your personal caretaker."

"Okay." He popped the eye into his right socket, squinted with the other, and thought hard. "I know. I'll use a human eye."

Thomas shook his head.

Lenny knew why, too. If the most desirable beverage in all the land cost an eye, many others would've ransacked the human corpses for their eyes long ago. One could not just run up to the surface and grab any old human and take out their eye, either, because when too many humans went missing, they would grow suspicious of the things that went bump in the night. Lenny wasn't too keen on the idea of going back to that place, either.

But I want one of those octoslushies.

Optimistic, he looked up at Thomas with his singular eye. "We can try, can't we?"

Thomas sounded annoyed. "Come on. Let's head down to the Yard of Forgotten Souls and see if we can't dig up an eye for you."

"Hooray."

Lenny skipped all the way to the field of corpses, knowing many had already been used to prepare the very drink he wanted, but optimistic nonetheless.

Hours later, they had yet to make their way through most of the pile. Lenny realized he had never seen anything so dismal.

What a wondrous place, so gloomy and frightful.

The smells amazed him. He could barely contain himself, periodically letting his elation out with a squeal, followed by a sneeze, of course, because of his allergies. Now that he had his lone eye back in its socket, it itched badly.

From the side, resting on an old rotted stump, Thomas patted his hands on thin air. "This place is damn exciting and all, but if you could, hurry a little. Find an eye and let's get the heck out of here. This area gives me the willies."

"The willies?" Lenny continued to dig through the damaged corpses, taking a second to stare into to each sullen face. So far, each time two empty sockets greeted him. "How could a place like this give you the willies? It's beautiful."

"Maybe, but I don't like the vibe."

Lenny scratched his head, grabbed another drooping human body and checked its sockets. He tossed the carcass aside. "There's no vibe here. Just bodies." He exhaled dreamily. "Hundreds and hundreds of soulless human bodies, as far as my eye can see."

Thomas stood and roamed the outer rim of corpses, speaking louder now. "That's just it. You don't buy into that business about them being soulless, do you?"

A wrinkle of concern formed on Lenny's brow. "What do you mean?"

"What I mean is: Do you really think every single one of these corpses has lost its soul? I mean, sure, maybe most of them were sucked out and perhaps eaten. But surely at least one of them still has its soul intact."

Lenny had heard such stories as a young monster. He always thought them the sort of tale one told in the daytime while sitting around a hellfire. Spooked, he pointed a finger at Thomas. "Stop it. You're freaking me out."

"Well, okay then." Thomas smiled. "I'll stop. I just didn't want anything *living* to get its hands on you."

He took a few steps toward Thomas. "What?"

"You know. If one of those souls is alive." His smile glimmered. "It might touch you."

Lenny drifted closer, coming within arm's reach. "What would happen?"

"Well, if that happened . . . " Thomas seized Lenny's arm and screamed, *"BLAH!"*

Lenny raced away, all four arms waving high above his bulbous head as he maneuvered through the corpses. He tripped, fell face-first into one. Jumped up and ran several more yards. His wild eye scanned the bodies for any that might be moving.

Thomas, on the other hand, laughed so hard he almost fell over.

Lenny stopped. "Why would you do that?"

"Settle down. I was only fooling around."

It took a long time for Lenny's breathing to relax. Once it did, he still felt deflated. "This is pointless, isn't it?"

"I'm not going to lie. I think it is."

The urge to cry overwhelmed Lenny. "How am I ever going to get one of those octoslushies?"

He let his head loll to one side, identifying a squeak among the corpses. When he kicked a carcass over, a whiskered animal fled. There were others, too, scrambling around beneath this sea of bodies. Then Lenny got another idea.

The creature took the green eye into the empty socket of a tentacle. An eyeless human male screamed as the creature squeezed him into the canister and threw the carcass aside. Lenny watched with eagerness while the vendor added all the other ingredients: A batwing, liquid fire, ether from the nothingness, and much more. His head wobbled along as the creature shook it all up. When it finished, Lenny grabbed the bowl with eager hands. Licking his chops, he sipped the octoslushie as they continued on their way.

"Ahhhh," Lenny said.

Thomas stopped. "What is it?"

"I swallowed a piece of brain." He shook his head. "I got brain freeze!"

Thomas grinned. "Well? Was it worth it?"

Lenny moaned with pleasure. "Oh yes. It's yummy. I've never had one made with a man before."

Lenny looked at Thomas, angling his head so he could see him with his two tiny rodent eyes. Then, Lenny sneezed, and both eyes popped right out of his head, each bounding down the walkway. Lenny turned too fast, and because of that, he dropped his octoslushie.

His blackened heart sank, knowing he would have to find more of those rats if he meant to see again.

I wonder what it would take to convince Thomas to give up one of his eyes.

OUTCASTS: THE SICK AND DYING 3—ANNA KILPATRICK

STATIC BURST FROM the intercom and Anna despised it. Then, she heard, "432761, are you reading us?"

Finally, they had contacted her. She held her breath and prayed. When she spoke, she did so between clenched teeth. "I read you. Go on."

"This is CDC ground. Please remain patient. We're working to bring the pods back to Earth. It will take time."

She had been waiting for days since the last contact was interrupted by static. She might have been able to endure those days if it hadn't been for happening upon another pod, one occupied by the most delightful woman, cheering. Seeing that gave Anna hope again. That woman had waved to Anna. Her smile brightened upon Anna, and the woman had mouthed some unknown words.

Anna remembered shaking her head to indicate she hadn't understood. She tried to get the woman to repeat the words, but before the woman could, her pod spun away into the darkness.

The woman must have been given better news than

Anna had, and it looked like she had mouthed, 'have hope'. Or, the woman had gone mad and her hysterical words were that there was 'no hope'. If not for encountering the next pod, the one with a man who had taken his own life by ramming something into his eye socket, she might have dwelled on her initial belief longer. Instead, it was this latter thought that infected her mind over those next few days.

Of course, she wanted to believe the woman's message had been inspirational, but seeing a man who had taken his own life did nothing but drudge up negativity. She found herself worrying the woman's message had been bleak.

Stop being silly.

Yet, it was this precise absurdity that had kept her wanting to live this long, a question that had no answer. It caused her to stay awake at night, trying to rationalize with herself. Even her dreams became occupied with visions of the two pods, the man and the woman, trying to discern what she had seen.

What was it she said?

Perhaps it no longer mattered. Why should it? They were going to bring her home after all these years.

Because it does matter.

And it was just that; she didn't know what to think. Did going back now mean she had been cured? She didn't feel any better, but she would love to see the surface again, remembering the green grass, the leaves rattling in the trees due to a spring breeze, the colors of the flowers. All of it was wonderful, and she missed it, the smells, the sun warming her skin, the cool of a summer rain, the snow tingling her feet with cold, everything. She wanted to feel better, wanted to believe she had been cured, but none of it felt right.

Maybe they were just tying up loose ends? Would she get back to Earth and be worse off there? Maybe Earth wasn't worth going back to at all.

The pod jerked and she felt movement. The Earth began to grow in her window until it encompassed the entire screen. She felt pressure and heat as she breached the atmosphere.

Glancing around, it looked like a meteor shower, hundreds of pods speeding to the surface all at once. Then they were enveloped in blue, white clouds flying past faster than she could glimpse them. Blue, white, blue, white, the landscape shifting until her eyes steadied upon the ground for the first time. Only there wasn't much worth seeing.

The ground had cracked open in many places, forming deep chasms of darkness. Fire burst out from these crevices, scorching the ground, the forests, and even the bodies of water, including the lake she was about to enter.

She went underwater; blue everywhere. Her ears popped and the need to relieve them overwhelmed her, but there wasn't time. Bubbles filled her vision, millions of them all around. As they cleared, she began to see some of the other pods.

Not all of the pods were on fire, but many were, including her own. The flames engulfed the pod, unable to break through, but roasting them like fish in a frying pan. Worse yet, no one would reach them in time. No one would save them.

She screamed, men and women suffering a fate equal to hers, staring at her, and her at them, all of them burning alive.

A VERY DIFFERENT SORT OF APOCALYPSE

THEY WERE RUNNING straight for him, and Brandon Wilshire had thought them some sort of deformed monster. If they hadn't busted out with laughter right then, he might have shot them both. He had heard that merriment every damn day since. It drove him crazy. That and the fact they seemed oblivious to what had happened, which only exacerbated his frustration. Nothing mattered to the brothers except getting high, and they were always high.

I should have shot them when I had the chance.

Only that wasn't like him. Hadn't been his way since college when he went full scholarship ROTC.

The twins had been named after two prominent rock stars, a fact they spoke of often. That was nearly the only difference. Except Jagger had a scar under his left eye, and Daltrey tended to speak quite loud.

This morning, however, Brandon found himself blessed with a rare moment of silence. Suspicious of such quiet since meeting the brothers, he neglected his watch for a moment to glance their way. It didn't surprise him to see Jagger taking a hit off a rather colorful bong. Daltrey twiddled his fingers, staring dreamily at the bong.

By all rights, they should've been dead. The known world had changed, and the weak struggled to remain alive. Everything had been laid to waste by bombs and chemical warfare. Only recently were humans able to walk the streets again. The brothers didn't seem to notice any of it, and he doubted they had even gone underground when matters demanded it necessary. This disregard alone should have spelled their demise before now. Yet somehow they had survived, again and again.

And now they're my responsibility.

His own survival came from hard work and discipline. Most nights he kept watch, taking catnaps during the day to catch up on sleep. He had never needed much sleep, so he didn't mind. Though most of his reasoning for lack of sleep came from the fact he didn't trust anyone else to keep watch, present company included.

He started each day with a good cardio workout, which consisted of running in place, knees high. Afterward, he focused on endurance training, using whatever practical debris he could find lying around to aid him in this task. Although he didn't always feel up to it, he made sure to get a minimum of a good hour-long workout.

Cleaning the guns like he had back in boot camp always brought him a certain joy. When the time and setting allowed, he took target practice to keep his aim sharp. He did it all in an effort to ensure he would be ready whenever the time came to fight. Regardless of his company, he would live. If his hard work benefited them, too, that made it all the more worthwhile.

There had been other survivors, but fewer than he had hoped. He regretted losing a handful of them under his watch, though none of their deaths had been his fault. In each case, their ignorance had led to their demise, not knowing when to run and when to hide, or even when to fight.

Most people he encountered preferred being on their own anyway, and it was those individuals he understood best. Not the brothers, though. In their peculiar case, they already had one big strike against them right out of the gate. Being conjoined twins made it hard for them to get anywhere fast. Spending most of their waking hours stoned did nothing to improve their odds, either.

Sooner or later fate is gonna catch up to them.

The world had a way of doing just that. Until that day, though, he would do his best to protect them.

Daltrey extended the bong to Brandon while struggling to hold in the smoke. He wiggled it and spoke out of the corner of his mouth. "Brother man, you wanna hit this or what?"

Brandon shook his head, having never been one for drugs. He didn't care for that feeling of being out of control. Besides, a clean, healthy body and mind was the main reason he was still alive. He didn't want to jeopardize his wellbeing.

Both brothers laughed so hard that a cloud of smoke enveloped Brandon. He sidestepped, waving his hands in an effort to avoid a contact high. "Guys, you mind?"

Brandon coughed, which only made the brothers more hysterical.

He gave them both a serious look. "You guys better be careful or when the shit goes down, you will too."

They stared at him, appearing lost at first. Then the unbridled giggling returned.

"Dude, you said *shit*," Jagger said. At this, they both snickered.

This had been Brandon's life these last few weeks. They would get high and laugh at anything he said. It could be maddening at times. There were days he couldn't wait until they passed out.

They often drew attention to their shelters. He had considered leaving them behind on more than one occasion. But his nature always got the best of him. Each time they needed to run, it ended up feeling a lot like a three-legged race with them high and cackling, as if ignorant to the zombies chasing after them.

Once, an undead woman came so close to getting them. Brandon remembered being sure their time had come. He had stood frozen, watching the smiling brothers turn to face their attacker. For some reason, the woman had shambled right past them, as if she believed them already dead. Instead, she had charged after a dumbfounded Brandon, which made the brothers laugh even more.

A chortling snort shook him back to the present. Jagger had the end of a rifle shoved in his mouth. Daltrey took a hit off the bong and pressed his lips to the open chamber and literally shotgunned the smoke to his brother. Despite them being exposed in the middle of aisle #6 of this grocery store, neither looked the least bit concerned.

Meanwhile, Brandon rearranged the shelving units to form an enclosure. The structure itself didn't appear safe, but it would do. The twins loved it, regaling adventures as children when they used to create forts out of blankets and couch cushions. They treated the makeshift fortress as such, pretending like they were pirates. Brandon took advantage of their distraction to return the rifle to his stockpile.

Brandon scratched his head. *This fort likely isn't any safer than their childhood constructions.* But he was also tired.

"Listen, I need to get some sleep," Brandon said with hesitancy. "You think you guys could lay off the pipe while I catch a few winks?"

Jagger, dressed in a tie-dyed T-shirt, his blonde mop of hair draped over his reddened eyes, set the bong aside and saluted. "Yar, man." He looked over-excited by the prospect of being in charge. "Hell yar, we can. We'll keep watch all night if you want, you scallywag."

"No, that's all right," Brandon said. "Just an hour or so, okay? Wake me up."

Daltrey tugged his Batman shirt down over his exposed belly and eyed up Brandon's guns. "Hey, man, do you think we'll need one of those?"

Brandon tried to avoid letting them have guns most of the time because he didn't think either of them responsible enough. He considered how they had taken the shotgun while he wasn't looking and what they had done with it. Having worried they might shoot each other, he also considered the fact they might shoot him by accident. After some consideration, he fetched his Sig Sauer SP2022 for them.

Jagger seized the gun with anxious hands. He passed it to his brother, who did the same. Their eyes beamed on the weapon with adolescent wonder.

"All right, man," Jagger said. "Don't worry about a thing. We got this."

Brandon wasn't so sure. Already he regretted the decision. But if he managed to snap off forty winks, he would feel like a new man. He eased down in his bedroll and pulled the bag in close, hugging it to ensure they wouldn't take any of the other guns.

For a while, their whispers kept him on edge. An occasional giggle roused him. He tossed and turned. When he finally did doze off, nothing woke him for a long while.

+———+———+

A loud *bang* startled him. He shot up in a cold sweat and scanned the immediate area. Looked for the brothers, but he couldn't locate them. He stood up fast, knocking over the bong. It shattered, and, for a moment, he stood frozen.

He pawed inside his bag for a gun. Once he got his fingers around one, he hurried out of the enclosure. There, in the frozen food aisle, stood the brothers.

Brandon hurried over to them, gun raised and ready for action. When he got there, he saw nothing but a large stack of cereal boxes at the end of the aisle. Daltrey passed the gun to his brother, who then took aim and fired.

"Hell yeah, man. Did you see that?" Jagger sounded more wasted than ever. "I hit Count Chocula right in the frigging forehead." He pumped both fists in the air. "*Head shot!*"

With a rolled up joint pressed between his lips, Daltrey took a long toke and held it in. Jagger passed the gun over, and Daltrey fired. The contents of a box of Captain Crunch exploded everywhere.

"I got me the Cap," he said, laughing. The joint slanted down, and he poked it back between his lips with the end of the smoking gun.

Brandon sighed. He holstered his gun but didn't imagine it would stay there long given the ruckus. Sooner or later—likely sooner—the dead would come for them. He hurried to the brothers, but they had time to get off one last shot. Another box of cereal burst into the air.

"Cornflakes? I hate Cornflakes," Daltrey said.

"Yeah, man, but they're good on bread with a slice of Velveeta. Cornflake sandwiches *rock*." Jagger slipped into deep thought for a brief second. "And on salads, too, man."

"Guys! What the hell?" Brandon said.

The brothers laughed.

"Oh hey, Brandon." Jagger wiped tears of joy from the corners of his eyes. "We're just havin' some fun is all."

"Well, you need to stop," Brandon said. He pried the gun from Jagger's fingers.

Instant sorrow spread across their faces. Their inability to discern right from wrong had gotten them in trouble more times than Brandon cared to recall. Throw in a half-pound of weed and they were two of the biggest fuckups he had ever seen. And guess what lucky schmuck got stuck with them?

This guy.

Brandon sighed again. "You're going to attract—"

Even as the words found his lips, it was too late. He spun as the first of many zombies smacked against the front of the grocery store. An undead woman, dressed in a tattered red dress, pawed at the glass. Her gnarled gray fingers squeaked against the glass, which amused the brothers. When she couldn't get through the window, she gnawed at it instead. Her scarred face left trails of dark red across the pane.

Within seconds, an undead man joined her. He, too, tried to bite the window. When that didn't produce the effect he wanted, he pounded, lightly at first and then harder.

"Dude, they're so jonesing to get in," Daltrey said.

Brandon offered him a bothered glance. Then he stepped toward the front, unsure of what to do to reinforce the window, but it didn't matter anyway. Shards of glass tinkled against the tiled floor when it shattered. Now they would have to fight.

Or rather, I'll have to fight.

Another undead man tripped over the foundation and landed face-first on the floor. He squirmed on the floor among the glass, snarling and grasping for Brandon.

Being out of reach, Brandon ignored the man in favor of handling those who posed an immediate threat. He fired several rounds. Headshot after headshot, zombies fell. For each kill he made, a few more shambled through the opening, many drawn by his gunfire. After downing a dozen zombies, he determined they would be better off running.

He sped to the brothers and yanked them to their feet.

Several zombies floundered through the broken window. Some had found their feet already. Another wave crowded in behind them, tripping and falling over one another, clawing at each other.

Brandon considered shooting a few more while

they were down. Instead, he opted to save the ammo. Besides, he still had his failsafe, the grenades.

"Come on," he said. "Let's get the hell out of here."

The brothers stayed their ground, passing a joint back and forth while he gathered up their possessions. The only thing that concerned them was the large backpack they toted around, which of course was full of pot. If Brandon hadn't grabbed Jagger's arm, they might have stuck around too long.

He yanked them into motion, and they stumbled after him. Still, they weren't much faster than the zombies, running the way they did and laughing so hard. At least they kept out in front of the zombies, but it made everything more surreal.

"Yo, Jagger, did you see that one dude's arm?" Daltrey laughed, out of breath already. "Was all like torn up and shit." He breathed heavily, the effects of smoking too much taking its toll. "Remind you of anyone?"

"Oh yeah, man," Jagger said. "Looked just like goddamn Freddy."

Brandon had no idea who this Freddy was. Nor did he care. He waited and when they were close enough, he pulled hard on Jagger's hand. Together, they burst through the back door and out into the alley. There, a single startled face met his gaze.

She screamed, staggered back, and landed on her rear.

Brandon held up both hands, patting the air and trying to relax her.

Her eyes trained on his gun. She seemed to realize they weren't undead, but still she stumbled away. Seconds later, she got up and ran.

Brandon hurried after her. To his surprise, the brothers followed. They caught up to her in the back of a sporting goods store. There, she remained elusive, her eyes on the twins. He couldn't blame her, as he had once thought them inhuman himself.

"Who are you?" she said.

"It's okay. We're like you, man." Jagger said.

Brandon offered him a bothered look. "My name's Brandon." He pointed to the brothers, one at a time, "This is Jagger and that's Daltrey. We're survivors."

At this, she eased some, but she kept her distance.

"Yeah, dude. It's like we're destined to be the last people on Earth. Fighting the good fight and all," Daltrey said, doing his best to wax poetic.

It perturbed Brandon because she was the prettiest woman he had ever laid eyes on. For all he knew, she could be the last woman on Earth, so not all bad.

"I'm Lila," she said after a long moment.

They went into the store and shared their histories, personal stories of the apocalypse, and how they had managed. After a small dinner of marshmallows and chocolate, Brandon and Lila watched the brothers play Whiffle Ball. The store wasn't big enough for such a game, but they made up rules to accommodate the lack of space. For instance, hitting the ball off the ski equipment was a double. Off the baseball jersey display was a triple. The gun department was the prized homerun.

Brandon had to admit, he enjoyed watching them now that Lila was around. When she laughed, it made him happy, and he even found himself laughing some.

When the brothers finished, they took the Whiffle Ball bat and bored a hole in one end. They scavenged a screen from a Coleman stove and fastened it over the hole. After filling the screen with pot, they took turns toking out of the small hole in the handle. It was amazing how resourceful they could be under the right circumstances.

They offered the makeshift pipe to Brandon. Once more, he declined. Much to his disappointment, Lila accepted. It made him feel slighted. For a while, he tried to keep up with their stoner banter, as they wasted the night debating whether stars burned out or just faded away. It was all too out there for Brandon.

After everyone was asleep, he kept watch like always. However, for much of that time, he stared at Lila. He observed the way her chest heaved when she breathed. How her lips trembled when she exhaled. In that instant, he speculated as to what might become of them, and he hoped with all his heart she would end up with him.

✦━━✦━━✦

He woke to their laughter—hers included. Then it came to an abrupt end, and he knew something had gone wrong. He leaped to his feet, gun in his hand, and saw the horde of zombies swarming them. Firing several shots, he struck mouths and foreheads, but this would only keep them at bay for so long.

"Lila?" Brandon said, pointing at the brothers. "Help them."

She got the brothers to their feet and aided in gathering their equipment. Once they had everything, she joined the fight. In her semi-stoned state, she wasn't much help. Still, it was good to have someone to rely on for a change.

They backed out the way they had come in, heading

for the alley. The horde pressed through the rows of sporting goods in pursuit, knocking over mannequins, the plastic limbs rattling to the floor. Displays collapsed under the weight of the throng, the zombies plodding over the cardboard to the crunch of paper. The putrid smell of bile and rotten flesh became thick in the air. They continued to approach, persistent as ever.

When Brandon and the others reached the alley, they fled away from the main street. What Brandon hadn't anticipated was the dead end that blocked their escape. By the time they made their way back up the alley, the mob of zombies blocked any possible escape.

Surrounded. No choice now.

Lila ushered the brothers away from the scuffle but kept firing. Brandon dealt with the majority of the undead himself, which was okay. Desperate times had him digging through his pack until he found them.

Only two left.

He pulled the pin on the first grenade and launched it into the store. The explosion took out much of the wall, most of which collapsed into the street. He had no way of telling how much damage he had done inside the store, but it achieved what Brandon had planned. The rubble now blocked the path and the zombies struggled to get through the obstruction. A few managed the sizeable mound of rubble, likely by accident, but they were easy to fight off.

The other grenade, he launched into the horde beyond the rubble, hoping to reduce the numbers. Of the two-dozen or so zombies, the grenade obliterated most. Guts and coagulated blood splattered Brandon, but his focus stayed on the handful of remaining undead.

Three quick shots and two were left. Lila unloaded her clip on one. The brothers viewed the spectacle with awestruck eyes, passing a joint back and forth like they were watching an intriguing episode of Scooby Doo.

Brandon's gun jammed. He dropped everything, drew his knife and attacked the last zombie. A loud *bang* stopped him. He spun around to find Jagger holding a shotgun, smoke trailing from its barrel.

Daltrey fist-pumped the sky. "Hell yeah, bro. We killed us one of those bastards."

Seeing the two of them so proud made him grin. In watching them high-five each other, he failed to keep an eye out behind him.

"Look out," shouted Lila.

Pain surged down his arm, originating at his shoulder. He tried to shake the zombie off, but it held tight, digging its teeth deeper. When he managed to free himself, the undead man tore away flesh.

Brandon dropped to his knees. "Arrggh!"

He fell flat to the ground and rolled, looking his attacker in the eye. Two glazed orbs gazed back at him, the man's jaws chattering. He wrestled the monster, able to get his gun up. Once he had it lifted, he fired. The blast took out half the zombie's head.

＊━━◆━━＊

Lila cared for his wounds, cleaning them with a wet rag, but something about her bothered him now. Not so typical of the brothers, they stood watch over him while Lila rested. All of them, Lila included, were doing their best. But already he felt the change starting deep inside as the brothers passed a joint around, taking turns blowing the smoke into his face.

When Jagger kissed Lila, anger boiled inside of him. Mumbling a protest that went unheard, it sounded like gibberish at best. He watched as the twin held her tight and felt like . . .

Biting him.

Only he couldn't bite Jagger or anyone else, not as long as that smell persisted.

AFTERWORD

BEING SOMEONE WHO experiences chronic pain on an almost daily basis, there are days when I'm happy just to be able to make the walk down to my computer. For it's there I write each day, and that process has been mostly therapeutic to a large degree, mending my soul and mind where my body won't. But some days are darker than the rest, and sadly, most of the stories included in this collection were written and developed during a long stretch of bad days. However, as I do with all my collections, I wanted to provide some insight into where each idea came from, what I was thinking at the time, and so forth. I hope you find it enlightening (pun intended).

I've long been fond of Westerns, so I dabble in that world quite often. "A Ring for His Own" sparked in my thoughts when I saw a piece of jewelry in a Facebook ad. The ring was an octopus wrapped around the model's finger with two gemmed eyes.

For "Heirloom," the idea came from long ago, back when I used to spend a lot of time at the camera shop in a local farmer's market. I always thought those antique cameras were sort of magic, as is the one in this story.

I've been in car wrecks before, so I know that feeling of being helpless. That moment where everything goes still and time seems to flicker by like an old movie projector. You see everything at once, but it's so hard to comprehend. That's where "Rust Colored Rain" found its beginnings, in examining the fears of such an experience.

With "Prey" I wanted to examine new races on a new planet, giving a brief insight into how others might live far, far away. And what's more interesting than the big cats of our own world and reimagining them as alien creatures?

I remember sitting at the doctor's office once while my daughter was getting checked out and listening to this woman refer to her son as Porkchop. I have no idea how she came up with that nickname, but it certainly got my thoughts going. And something she said kept coming back to me, over and over again, that "It's what Mama needs."

"My Brother Bit Your Honor Roll Student" found its beginnings in a bumper sticker I created a while back on Zazzle. I thought the idea was funny, so I played with it some, trying to find the right line.

The Outcasts flash pieces were originally part of a bigger idea that never panned out. I had considered doing several of these, tying them into each other, one after another. But the project floundered, and I moved on to a few longer works.

Along with being a fan of the old Westerns, I'm also quite fond of some war movies. Hellinger was created in that imaginative space. The story picks up toward the end of "The Sanguine Wars," when Hellinger discovers himself. So, this might end up being a piece I revisit later on.

Around this time, I was writing quite a few vampire pieces, so it made sense there would end up being a flash piece here and there, floating around. "The Hunted" was one of those I felt had legs, the idea coming to me while digging in the backyard one day.

As some of you may know, I've long kept reef tanks with live coral and fish. It's a hobby I'm only recently taking a break from. Many stories like "Her Living Corals" found their roots in my time staring at my tank. It's a wondrous world we know so little about, and I much enjoyed my small slice of the ocean.

With "Puppet Strings," I examine the strained relationship of a woman who has been prepared as a politician's wife. She feels much like being a marionette, her strings always pulled, so she must figure out how to free herself.

"The Trying of Master William" is a setting I would like to revisit. Not to tell the same story or to expand upon it, but to delve into some of the lore of those days. There are some scary stories, things that horrify me and often bring me to tears. There's a lot to tell there.

"By the Crescent Moon" was clearly a play on Madoc's descendants, which I researched on the Internet for a North Carolina's themed anthology.

One of the coolest creatures I've ever encountered is a mantis shrimp. If you don't know what they are, do some quick research. They're quite interesting, and I've kept several as pets. That's where my story "Mantid" came from.

"The Underside of Time and Space" is actually a brief introduction to a much larger work I've been trying to find the right angle on. Currently the project is stalled, though I've dabbled with some ideas.

I've always been astounded by stone statues, what goes into creating them, ever since I studied them in college. I admire anyone who has the patience. But in this case, I wanted a gremlin-like story, and I figured some old rock was as good a transport as any for "The Griffon."

There's so much we don't know about our own world, so why not an underground lair filled with diamonds? And, as often is the case in stories like this, greed is not always rewarded. "Adaptable" explores my memories of an old cave, though, unfortunately there were no diamonds, at least there weren't any strange creatures either.

I've always wanted to write a Kaiju story, and with "When They Come," I'm definitely playing in that sandbox. It's a subject I'll want to revisit a few times in the future, I think.

I often play with end of the world scenarios, and "The Reassignment Project" focuses on the plight of a young woman, trying to escape the hardships of the end. This story features quite a bit of scenery from a very common place from my past, that of the sewer drain pipes.

With "Presage" I wanted to examine cloning, and how we might use that to prove or disprove. With belief being so subjective, I wanted the strict scientific process, working hard to deny what he can't deny.

"One Hopeless Night by a Clan Fire" comes from many nights sitting by a fire while camping out, grunting, farting, eating beans, and just staring at the flames. There's a lot of time to think out in the wilderness. It can be quite illuminating.

Sometimes I come up with these ideas that are just

bloody strange. "Lenny's New Eyes" was actually a dream I revisited many nights in a row. At the time, I was thinking about Abbott and Costello a lot, all those fun horror movies they made together. But the story never fully came out, so I hadn't found my line until I bought a slushie for my kids.

"A Very Different Sort of Apocalypse" was actually written for a themed anthology. I wanted to capture an unlikely survivor(s) and give them a power over the undead we don't often consider.

So, that's all I've got for you this time. I hope you enjoyed the collection. As always, my goal remains the same, to write the better story. In this, I hope you find me successful. With luck, I'll have many more stories to share with you for years to come. And so, dear readers, I hope you will continue to stick along for the ride.

Pleasant nightmares,
Kenneth W. Cain

THE END?

Not quite . . .

Be sure to check out the author's *Embers: A Collection of Dark Fiction*. Or his *A Season in Hell* novella.

Or dive into more Tales from the Darkest Depths:

Novels:
Beatrice Beecham's Ship of Shadows: A Supernatural Adventure/Mystery Novel by Dave Jeffery
The Mourner's Cradle: A Widow's Journey by Tommy B. Smith
House of Sighs (with sequel novella) by Aaron Dries
Beyond Night by Eric S. Brown and Steven L. Shrewsbury
The Third Twin: A Dark Psychological Thriller by Darren Specgle
Aletheia: A Supernatural Thriller by J.S. Breukelaar
Where the Dead Go to Die by Mark Allan Gunnells and Aaron Dries
Sarah Killian: Serial Killer (For Hire!) by Mark Sheldon
The Final Cut by Jasper Bark
Blackwater Val by William Gorman
Pretty Little Dead Girls: A Novel of Murder and Whimsy by Mercedes M. Yardley
Nameless: The Darkness Comes by Mercedes M. Yardley

Novellas:
A Season in Hell by Kenneth W. Cain
Quiet Places: A Novella of Cosmic Folk Horror by
Jasper Bark
The Final Reconciliation by Todd Keisling
Run to Ground by Jasper Bark
Devourer of Souls by Kevin Lucia
*Apocalyptic Montessa and Nuclear Lulu: A Tale of
Atomic Love* by Mercedes M. Yardley
Wind Chill by Patrick Rutigliano
Little Dead Red by Mercedes M. Yardley
Sleeper(s) by Paul Kane
Stuck On You by Jasper Bark

Anthologies:
Tales from The Lake Vol.5, edited by Kenneth W. Cain
Fantastic Tales of Terror: History's Darkest Secrets,
edited by Eugene Johnson
Welcome to The Show, edited by Doug Murano
Lost Highways: Dark Fictions From the Road,
edited by D. Alexander Ward
C.H.U.D. Lives!—A Tribute Anthology
Tales from The Lake Vol.4: The Horror Anthology,
edited by Ben Eads
*Behold! Oddities, Curiosities and Undefinable
Wonders*, edited by Doug Murano
*Twice Upon an Apocalypse: Lovecraftian Fairy
Tales*, edited by Rachel Kenley and Scott T.
Goudsward
Tales from The Lake Vol.3, edited by Monique
Snyman
Gutted: Beautiful Horror Stories, edited by Doug
Murano and D. Alexander Ward

THE END?

Not quite . . .

Be sure to check out the author's *Embers: A Collection of Dark Fiction*. Or his *A Season in Hell* novella.

Or dive into more Tales from the Darkest Depths:

Novels:
Beatrice Beecham's Ship of Shadows: A Supernatural Adventure/Mystery Novel by Dave Jeffery
The Mourner's Cradle: A Widow's Journey by Tommy B. Smith
House of Sighs (with sequel novella) by Aaron Dries
Beyond Night by Eric S. Brown and Steven L. Shrewsbury
The Third Twin: A Dark Psychological Thriller by Darren Speegle
Aletheia: A Supernatural Thriller by J.S. Breukelaar
Where the Dead Go to Die by Mark Allan Gunnells and Aaron Dries
Sarah Killian: Serial Killer (For Hire!) by Mark Sheldon
The Final Cut by Jasper Bark
Blackwater Val by William Gorman
Pretty Little Dead Girls: A Novel of Murder and Whimsy by Mercedes M. Yardley
Nameless: The Darkness Comes by Mercedes M. Yardley

Novellas:
A Season in Hell by Kenneth W. Cain
Quiet Places: A Novella of Cosmic Folk Horror by
Jasper Bark
The Final Reconciliation by Todd Keisling
Run to Ground by Jasper Bark
Devourer of Souls by Kevin Lucia
*Apocalyptic Montessa and Nuclear Lulu: A Tale of
Atomic Love* by Mercedes M. Yardley
Wind Chill by Patrick Rutigliano
Little Dead Red by Mercedes M. Yardley
Sleeper(s) by Paul Kane
Stuck On You by Jasper Bark

Anthologies:
Tales from The Lake Vol.5, edited by Kenneth W. Cain
Fantastic Tales of Terror: History's Darkest Secrets,
edited by Eugene Johnson
Welcome to The Show, edited by Doug Murano
Lost Highways: Dark Fictions From the Road,
edited by D. Alexander Ward
C.H.U.D. Lives!—A Tribute Anthology
Tales from The Lake Vol.4: The Horror Anthology,
edited by Ben Eads
*Behold! Oddities, Curiosities and Undefinable
Wonders*, edited by Doug Murano
*Twice Upon an Apocalypse: Lovecraftian Fairy
Tales*, edited by Rachel Kenley and Scott T.
Goudsward
Tales from The Lake Vol.3, edited by Monique
Snyman
Gutted: Beautiful Horror Stories, edited by Doug
Murano and D. Alexander Ward

Tales from The Lake Vol.2, edited by Joe Mynhardt, Emma Audsley, and RJ Cavender
Children of the Grave
The Outsiders
Tales from The Lake Vol.1, edited by Joe Mynhardt
Fear the Reaper, edited by Joe Mynhardt
For the Night is Dark, edited by Ross Warren

Short story collections:
Dead Reckoning and Other Stories by Dino Parenti
Things You Need by Kevin Lucia
Frozen Shadows and Other Chilling Stories by Gene O'Neill
Varying Distances by Darren Speegle
The Ghost Club: Newly Found Tales of Victorian Terror by William Meikle
Ugly Little Things: Collected Horrors by Todd Keisling
Whispered Echoes by Paul F. Olson
Embers: A Collection of Dark Fiction by Kenneth W. Cain
Visions of the Mutant Rain Forest, by Bruce Boston and Robert Frazier
Tribulations by Richard Thomas
Eidolon Avenue: The First Feast by Jonathan Winn
Flowers in a Dumpster by Mark Allan Gunnells
The Dark at the End of the Tunnel by Taylor Grant
Through a Mirror, Darkly by Kevin Lucia
Things Slip Through by Kevin Lucia
Where You Live by Gary McMahon
Tricks, Mischief and Mayhem by Daniel I. Russell
Samurai and Other Stories by William Meikle
Stuck On You and Other Prime Cuts by Jasper Bark

ABOUT THE AUTHOR

Kenneth W. Cain first got the itch for storytelling during his formative years in the suburbs of Chicago, where he got to listen to his grandfather spin tales by the glow of a barrel fire. But it was a reading of Baba Yaga that grew his desire for dark fiction. Shows like *The Twilight Zone, The Outer Limits, Alfred Hitchcock Presents*, and *One Step Beyond* furthered that sense of wonder for the unknown, and he's been writing ever since.

Cain is the author of The Saga of I trilogy, *United States of the Dead, A Season in Hell*, the short story collections *These Old Tales* and *Fresh Cut Tales*, and *Embers*. He is also the editor of *Tales from The Lake Volume 5*. Writing, reading, fine art, graphic design, and Cardinals baseball are but a few of his passions. Cain now resides in Chester County, Pennsylvania with his wife and two children.

Website: kennethwcain.com

Newsletter: http://eepurl.com/caUofP

Twitter: https://twitter.com/KennethWCain

Facebook author page:
https://www.facebook.com/AuthorKennethWCain/

Facebook: https://www.facebook.com/kennethwcain

Pinterest: https://www.pinterest.com/ozmosis7/

Instagram:
	https://www.instagram.com/kennethwcain

AUTHOR'S PLEA

Greetings, Reader. You've reached the end of my book, and I hope that means you enjoyed it. Whether or not you did, I would like to thank you for giving me your valuable time to attempt to entertain you. I am truly blessed to have such a fulfilling job, but I only have that job because of people like you; those kind enough to give my books a chance and spend their hard-earned money buying them. For that I am eternally grateful, my friend.

If you would like to find out more about my other books, then please visit my website for full details. You can find it at: kennethwcain.com. There you'll find a link to sign up for my newsletter. Or you can email me. You'll also find my social media links, which you can use to follow or contact me. I would love to hear from you.

If you enjoyed this book and would like to help, then please consider leaving a review for the book on Amazon, Goodreads, a blog, or anywhere else readers visit. The most important part of how well a book sells is how many positive reviews it has, so if you leave me one then you are directly helping me to continue on this journey as a full-time writer. Thank you in advance to anyone who does.

Hi readers,

It makes our day to know you reached the end of our book. Thank you so much. This is why we do what we do every single day.

Whether you found the book good or great, we'd love to hear what you thought. Please take a moment to leave a review on Amazon, Goodreads, or anywhere else readers visit. Reviews go a long way to helping a book sell, and will help us to continue publishing quality books. You can also share a photo of yourself holding this book with the hashtag #IGotMyCLPBook!

Thank you again for taking the time to journey with Crystal Lake Publishing.

We are also on . . .

Website:
www.crystallakepub.com

Be sure to sign up for our newsletter and receive two free eBooks: http://eepurl.com/xfuKP

Books:
http://www.crystallakepub.com/book-table/

Twitter:
https://twitter.com/crystallakepub

Facebook:
https://www.facebook.com/Crystallakepublishing/

Instagram:
https://www.instagram.com/crystal_lake_publishin
g/

Patreon:
https://www.patreon.com/CLP

Or check out other Crystal Lake Publishing books for more Tales from the Darkest Depths. You can also subscribe to Crystal Lake Classics where you'll receive fortnightly info on all our books, starting all the way back at the beginning, with personal notes on every release. Or follow us on Patreon for behind the scenes access.

With unmatched success since 2012, Crystal Lake Publishing has quickly become one of the world's leading indie publishers of Mystery, Thriller, and Suspense books with a Dark Fiction edge.

Crystal Lake Publishing puts integrity, honor, and respect at the forefront of our operations.

We strive for each book and outreach program that's launched to not only entertain and touch or comment on issues that affect our readers, but also to strengthen and support the Dark Fiction field and its authors.

Not only do we publish authors who are legends in the field and as hardworking as us, but we look for men and women who care about their readers and fellow human beings. We only publish the very best Dark Fiction, and look forward to launching many new careers.

We strive to know each and every one of our

readers while building personal relationships with our authors, reviewers, bloggers, podcasters, bookstores, and libraries.

Crystal Lake Publishing is and will always be a beacon of what passion and dedication, combined with overwhelming teamwork and respect, can accomplish: unique fiction you can't find anywhere else.

We do not just publish books, we present you worlds within your world, doors within your mind from talented authors who sacrifice so much for a moment of your time.

This is what we believe in. What we stand for. This will be our legacy.

Welcome to Crystal Lake Publishing.

THANK YOU FOR PURCHASING THIS BOOK